Peaches

Peaches

a novel by

jodi lynn anderson

HarperCollins*Publishers*

Peaches

ALLOYENTERTAINMENT   Produced by Alloy Entertainment
151 West 26th Street, New York, NY 10001

Library of Congress Cataloging-in-Publication Data

Anderson, Jodi Lynn.
    Peaches / by Jodi Lynn Anderson.— 1st ed.
        p. cm.
    Summary: Three teenaged girls from very different backgrounds, thrown together to
pick peaches in a Georgia orchard, spend a summer in pursuit of the right boy, the
truest of friends, and the perfect peach.
    ISBN-10: 0-06-073305-5 — ISBN-10: 0-06-073306-3 (lib. bdg.)
    ISBN-13: 978-0-06-073305-6 — ISBN-13: 978-0-06-073306-3 (lib. bdg.)
    [1. Interpersonal relations—Fiction. 2. Farm life—Georgia—Fiction. 3. Family
problems—Fiction. 4. Peach—Fiction. 5. Georgia—Fiction.] I. Title.
    PZ7.A53675Pe 2005
    [Fic]—dc22
                                                                        2004020846

Typography by Christopher Grassi
1 2 3 4 5 6 7 8 9 10
❖
First Edition

For the Breakspears, who taught me long
ago what friends can be

Before

That summer, at a bar on Mertie Creek, two truckers by the names of Saddle Tramp and Mad Dog emerged from a night of drinking booze and listening to Kenny Chesney on the jukebox to find girls' underwear—one thong, one Days of the Week (Sunday), and one monkey face—lying across their windshields. That same summer, rotten fish of an unidentified variety was found in the vent openings of several bathrooms at the Balmeade Country Club, and nobody suspected the connection. In late August, Lucretia Cawley-Smith was forced to admit to herself that she loved her oldest daughter best. Jodee McGowen stopped wearing seagulls on her nail polish for good. And on September 1, a migrant worker by the name of Enrico Fiol left Georgia carrying a tuft of dog fur in his shirt pocket.

Through it all, the Darlington Peach Orchard, with a past as shady as the grass under its tallest trees and a future teetering on the edge of extinction, stretched itself over the summer like it had every summer previously—softly, quietly, and shyly, like a belle walking up the stairs of her first ball.

That spring, Murphy McGowen, sixteen, of Bridgewater's Anthill Acres Trailer Park (whose mom, Jodee, had dated, in chronological order, the WRUZ Praise DJ, Horatio Balmeade, and one of the Bridgewater High School Statesmen football players), did not notice anything that might be interesting about the orchard, her town, or existence in general. Murphy was missing from her own life and she didn't even know it.

Walking by Hidden Creek Primitive House of Worship one Sunday, Murphy didn't know that Birdie Darlington, of Darlington Orchard, was inside, stuck between her parents like the peanut butter in a sandwich that was falling apart, wishing she was anywhere else, although she wasn't sure where. Nor did Murphy know that Leeda Cawley-Smith was four miles away getting a maple sugar massage at her family's B & B, wondering how she could look like a million dollars but feel like twenty cents simply because her sister, Danay, was lying next to her, looking even better.

So, that spring morning, Murphy just kept walking, staring at the sign out in front of the church with the weekly message scrawled in black block letters. This week's message was Let It Be.

It was funny. That was probably her least favorite Beatles song— and Murphy had a tiny tattoo of Ringo Starr beside her left-lower-back dimple. Murphy wasn't about to buy into the message. But then, if she had, the summer would never have come to be what it was.

Birdie and Leeda might never have found their answers. Two truckers would have been less three undies. And Murphy would have never realized she was missing from her life at all.

One

Every spring since she had turned thirteen had started the same way for Murphy McGowen. She started feeling restless at the very same time as the crocuses began busting out of their buds every year. She'd start to want to bust out of her skin too, into a skin that lived, say, in New York, or Paris, or Buenos Aires, anyplace that wasn't Bridgewater, Georgia. Outside the historic downtown district—which was basically unlived in and which barely any tourists came to—the town was mostly a strip of motels, fast-food joints, and traffic lights.

From then on, each spring had started with

A.   The restlessness

B.   The ache in her chest for the thing she didn't know was missing

C.   The guy with the hand up her shirt

At fifteen, there was also the addition of the other hand, down the pants—usually cords, sometimes army surplus, all three dollars or less at Village Thrift. The boys she hadn't bargained for; they had just sort of come. Because like many girls in Georgia, Murphy was as girl as a girl could be. Green eyed and smooth skinned with beauty marks here and there on her cheeks, with brown wavy hair and high apple breasts. Like most young girls at the Piggly Wiggly on any given day, she was more juicy than fine, more sexy than delicately beautiful. In a word, Murphy McGowen was yummy. A few more words that had been used to describe her were *brilliant, bold,* and *rotten.*

Her favorite spot for *C.* was the edge of the Darlington Peach Orchard, just two miles out of the center of town, but what felt like a million miles from anything resembling the Piggly Wiggly. Most of Bridgewater felt like a collision of old southern big-porched homes and a giant strip mall. The orchard, with its endless acreage and overgrown greenery, felt like the Garden of Eden.

Murphy, who wasn't much into nature, didn't know why she liked it. In lots of ways it was a mess. The white fence that ran along the property line was chipped and rotting. An old tractor had been abandoned by the train tracks and was grown over with weeds. The farm itself was obscured by layers of over-growth along this edge so thick that even now, when there were no leaves, Murphy could see only tiny glimpses of the peach trees themselves and the white farmhouse through the brush.

The cold metal of the tracks dug into her butt as she took a sip of warm Mello Yello. She kicked off her sticky old Dr. Scholl's sandals from Village Thrift, letting her bare soles bask in the warmest night they'd had since the fall. Across the grass behind them, Gavin's car was choking out staticky Coldplay, a band Gavin said was brilliant, though Murphy claimed all their songs sounded exactly the same.

Murphy watched lazily as Gavin, whose last name she didn't

remember, ran his fingers lightly up and down the back of her calves like they were made of gold. His eyes trailed up and down her legs.

"What do you wanna do?" she asked, pushing her toes into the grass. She mentally urged Gavin to say something original. *Impress me*, she thought. Already she was wishing she'd come alone. Gavin was oblivious to their surroundings, which was depressing.

The truth was, there was *nothing* she wanted to do. She wanted to float out of her body, out of Bridgewater, up to the moon. Coming to the orchard always made her restless. Energized with nowhere to put it. Stuffed up.

When her mom had used to take her here on picnics, before the onslaught of boyfriends paraded into their lives, Jodee had said, "It makes me feel young, baby." And maybe that was it. Sneaking onto the orchard grounds made Murphy feel the way she figured a girl her age was supposed to feel—awake. Though Gavin was making a valiant effort at bringing that down a notch.

He squeezed her calf and then moved onto his knees like he was praying to her, putting his hands on her tight coil of a waist. Murphy held her can of soda aside to accept the touch of his lips. He was ridiculously cute, she had to admit. But a lot of guys were. Somewhere along the line that had stopped being exciting. While he moved his mouth to the soft skin on the side of her neck, she watched the moon above them, which was three-quarters full and surrounded by a white haze. It made her think about how she couldn't believe how big the universe was, but how small it was for her. Maybe she'd be sitting in Bridgewater when she was eighty, making out with somebody with just gums.

"I'm bored." It came out matter-of-factly. She extracted herself from him.

Gavin pulled back and frowned at her from under his eyebrows, hurt. "Thanks." He ran a hand through his messy brown hair and then scratched at his stomach through his thin White Stripes T-shirt. He pulled a pack of cigarettes out of his pocket and held one to his lips, lighting it. He looked irritated.

Murphy wasn't surprised. It was typical. Boys came in one flavor. The flavor that couldn't stand it when you didn't let them play with your toys.

"Anyway, your tongue's all slimy," she said, bouncing up onto her feet. "Don't you swallow, ever?"

"You're rough, Murph."

"Murphy. I hate it when people try to give me nicknames."

"Right, Murphy. Well, nobody else I've dated has complained."

"We're not dating," she said evenly.

Gavin shook his head at her the way boys sometimes did, like he'd touched a hot plate and had to put it down. "Well, if you're bored, what do you want to do?" His eyes squinted as he took a puff of his cigarette.

Murphy jumped from one side of the track to the other, then back, then gazed into the trees that, she knew, led to the real heart of the orchard and up to the house. She knew this because she'd seen the house down the long dirt driveway on Orchard Drive, although she'd never explored beyond this area around the tracks.

"Who cares? I just want to go somewhere."

"Done. We'll hit Bob's Big Boy. I'm starving," Gavin said, substituting love of sex for love of food in the grand tradition of all guys everywhere. He sat up.

"I'm not allowed in there."

Last year Murphy and a couple of friends had dismantled Bob's Big Boy and left his giant punctured body parts scattered across downtown. When she'd finally gotten caught, the Bob's Big Boy people had taken her picture and put it up in the manager's office. Now she had to eat at Kuntry Kitchen.

But when she'd suggested going somewhere, she hadn't meant anything like that, anyway. She'd just turned in a report this week on a tribe of lesbian monkeys in Zambia, a topic she'd chosen to spite her ultra-homophobic AP Bio teacher, Mr. Jackson. She'd like to go to Zambia and see the lesbian monkeys. But despite the fact that she'd nailed the gay primate report, which she'd titled "We're Here, Ooh Ee Ah Ah, Get Used to It," Google was probably the closest Murphy would ever get to anyplace halfway exotic.

"If we don't do something vaguely interesting, I'm going to kill myself," she said, hooking her index and middle fingers into the heels of her sandals and starting to walk.

She stared at the droopy layer of branches up ahead. She and her mom had never breached them when they were both younger. It had been an unspoken thing between them: that the McGowens didn't belong beyond the growth, that it was nice to have boundaries, and that some things were best when they were secret. Things were different now, though. Even with Google, lesbian monkeys had lost their mystery.

Murphy's pulse had picked up slightly, like it always did, at the thought of doing something with a high risk-to-reward ratio.

She felt Gavin's eyes traveling over her body behind her. Murphy took it as a matter of course. She knew what she was; she never looked in the mirror and wondered whether she was pretty or not, sexy or not. Gavin followed, not because he wanted to touch the mystery, but because he was a guy, and he couldn't help it.

Murphy dropped her sandals at the edge of the cool grass and tiptoed up onto the porch of Birdie Darlington's house, where Birdie's mother, Cynthia, the other half of the sandwich, had lived until just that morning. Murphy squinted at a plaque beside the door that proclaimed the house had been built in 1861.

The door was locked. Murphy tiptoed over to the window to the left and tried it, sliding it open without a problem. She had shimmied through many windows—of boys' rooms, of camp cafeterias, of the school gym. She shimmied through this one with ease, leaving Gavin standing on the grass in front of the porch, where he was without a doubt watching her butt.

The house *smelled* like it had been around since 1861. Murphy let her eyes adjust to the dark and then took a few creaking steps, listening for any sound. Nothing. She was in the dining room—a good place to start. She looked through the mahogany cabinet on the far side of the room, then the sideboard cupboard. Nothing.

She wandered out of the dining room into a hallway and then down the hallway to where it dead-ended at a small kitchen.

There was a little round table here and some framed photographs on the walls of a woman—Mrs. Darlington, Murphy assumed—standing in a black low-rimmed hat, holding a stirrup cup, and smiling in a Botox-like way that didn't affect anything on her face but her lips. There was one of Mrs. Darlington and a gawky young girl, tennish, standing in front of the World's Largest Peanut. Murphy remembered seeing the two before—in Bridgewater you saw everyone eventually—the girl trailing behind her mom like a puppy. In the picture, neither of them looked too thrilled about the peanut. But they wore twin smiles, and like in the other picture, the smile looked out of place on the faces.

A bowl lay on the floor just to the right of the table, decorated with flowers and butterflies and personalized with the words *Property of Toonsis*. On the table, a piece of paper lay unfolded. Murphy had spotted a pair of curtains in the far corner. Walking over and parting them, she revealed what she'd thought she would, a stacked pantry—full of cracker boxes and cereal boxes and jelly jars filled with preserves and bags of bread. On the top shelf, tucked between a package of napkins and a bag of marshmallows, was a bottle. *Crème de menthe.*

Well, it beat nothing.

Biting her full bottom lip, Murphy stepped onto the bottom shelf to reach it, frowning as she pulled it down and swilled around the liquid inside. It was only about a quarter full. As she stepped down, she lost her balance slightly and landed on the linoleum with a little thud.

Damn. She froze and listened.

Tap tap tap. Tap tap tap. From directly above her head came the sound of paws on hardwood, tentative, thoughtful. Tiny dogs' paws.

Murphy sucked in her breath and stayed still for a few seconds, listening to the silence. A few seconds later she tried to move soundlessly, stepping toward the archway into the hall. The floor creaked beneath her.

"Yip yip yip!" *Tap tap tap tap.* Now she could hear the dogs—more than one—moving across the floor above in a dead-straight line, their little footsteps slipping and sliding as they tripped over what sounded like the beginning of stairs, yipping in unison. A sound of heavy feet hitting the hardwood overhead followed.

Murphy dashed down the hall as quietly as she could and hung a hard right into the dining room, hearing the dogs slip and slide down the stairs, frantic now. She clasped the crème de menthe to her breasts with one arm while holding her balance on the sill with the other, flinging one leg out the window.

The dogs hit the ground floor with more yips.

Murphy dove through the window, scraping her side against the molding, and yanked herself out with her free hand, planting it on the deck and pulling her other leg out.

"Hey!" a male voice thundered from deep inside the house. Murphy didn't look back. She jumped onto her feet. Gavin stood on the grass in front of her, his eyes wide.

"Not a problem," Murphy hissed, leaping over the three stairs that led from the deck to the grass. She broke into a run as soon as her bare feet touched down. Gavin raced after her. She could hear his breath behind her as he tried to keep up and the sound of the front door of the house opening.

"Get back here!" the voice called from behind them. After that there was silence for a second, then the unmistakable sound of a shotgun being cocked. *Oh God.*

They started really running now, Murphy's heels practically kicking her butt as they sprinted between the trees. She looked back once, her heart pounding, and saw a tall, broad man behind them, lumbering after her. Out ahead of him on the ground, yipping away and moving across the grass as fast as their skinny little legs could carry them, were two of the tiniest dogs Murphy had ever seen, their huge ears flapping.

But three-inch legs could only move so far, so fast. She and Gavin were pulling way out in front. Up ahead, through the gap in the trees, she could see Gavin's beat-up old Honda parked on the grass. She looked back again to reassure herself they were going to make it.

Umph!

Murphy's foot hooked into the bridge of a protruding root. She landed with her upper body sprawling across the train tracks. Underneath her, the crème de menthe shattered and stabbed at her through her short overalls. At the same time, her ankle exploded with unbelievable pain.

"Help!" Murphy called. Gavin had landed on the other side of the tracks and turned to look at her, then beyond her.

"Yip yip yip!"

"Help me up!"

Gavin seemed to be considering.

Murphy stared at him, helpless and disbelieving. "Come on!"

"Sorry," Gavin said, then turned and sprinted. Murphy watched him hop into his car, the engine of the Honda roaring to life. Without lights, he peeled out, sending gravel flying up behind him. In another second the sound of the engine faded into the distance.

" 'Ooser," she slurred into the bit of metal that was up against her mouth, trying to roll over. But her foot was still stuck in the root, and it just made another arrow of pain shoot up her leg. "Shtupid shree." She let her body relax into the tracks again, only stirring when she felt something wet on her cheek. Two something wets.

"Uck," Murphy mumbled, trying to wave her arms to swat away the tiny dogs. She managed to flip onto her back and sit up just in time to see the two big bare feet of Walter Darlington as they arrived next to her own.

Walter, gray at the temples and big boned, held his rifle over his shoulder like a fishing pole, looking both extremely pissed off and extremely satisfied, and took in the shattered glass surrounding Murphy's butt, the cuts on her hands, the last of the crème de menthe seeping into the rocks. Behind him, just arriving and panting from the run, was the Darlingtons' fleshy, puppy-like teenage daughter. She swooped down beside Murphy immediately and snatched up the dogs, one in each arm, her big brown eyes wide and staring.

"Your tree tripped me," Murphy murmured, ready to make the case that she could sue. It was the tree that was at fault, not her.

Walter glared, shaking his head. "Sweetie, you picked the wrong day," he wheezed, his shoulders heaving as if he'd run a hundred miles instead of a couple hundred yards. "You couldn't have picked a worse one if you tried."

On June 11, 1988, Jodee McGowen and her boyfriend snuck onto the Darlington Peach Orchard to pick peaches, and got distracted in the pecan grove. A boy named Miller Abbott had carved a jagged heart into a nearby tree with Jodee's name inside, but Jodee had no idea. Three weeks later she found out she was carrying her first and only child.

Date: April 10
Subject: Murphy McGowen/Trespassing/Theft
From: MAbbott@GAjudicial.gov
To: DarlingtonPeaches@yahoo.com

Walter,

I've reviewed Miss McGowen's record and feel that if both parties are willing, the punishment I've suggested is more than fair. Why don't you call her mother first and see if she'll agree to give her up to you for the spring break? Make it clear to her that she'll be working long hours on the trees, that it would be for the entire two weeks, and that of course there would be no pay—I don't want any misunderstandings here.

I'd give her community service either way, so it would be in her best interest to do it through the back door, without the courts and another spot on her record. I'll impress that upon Miss McGowen if you need me to. Let me know if you need me to talk to Jodee as well—I'd be happy to.

I don't foresee any problems, but let me know if you need me to intervene at any point. The girl is a firecracker.

Golf Sunday?

MA
Judge Miller Abbott
Kings County District Court

Two

Leeda Cawley-Smith stuck a spoon into the hole of her lobster claw pastry and dug out a giant dollop of amaretto crème. She stuck the spoon in her mouth and sucked on it, watching to see if her mom would say something. Nothing. Leeda dug two fingers in this time, sticking them between her lips and letting them linger there like the mandibles of an insect—a praying mantis. Her mom didn't flinch. Leeda sighed, removed her fingers from her lips, and dipped them into the lilac finger bowl by her plate, swirling them around irritably.

Every time Leeda's sister, Danay, came home for the weekend, which was just about every other weekend, their mom spent most of her time gazing at her in awe, like the eldest Cawley-Smith daughter was the second coming of Jesus. Only instead of having risen from the tomb, Danay had driven from Atlanta in the Mercedes their parents had bought her for her high school graduation gift. And instead of bringing absolution for all of the Cawley-Smiths' sins, she brought black-and-white cookies from Henri's bakery in Buckhead and her fiancé, Brighton, whose family had a fabulous rock-lined pool that nobody swam in and threw parties where nobody smiled.

Right now, Leeda's mom and the messiah were talking about wedding invitations.

"What color and black did you say they were, pumpkin?" Mrs. Cawley-Smith cooed. In reply Danay flashed her brilliant Emory University smile, the one she'd been giving her parents ever since she'd left Bridgewater. Despite the Cawley-Smiths' money, their huge antebellum mansion, and the three hotels the family owned—posh by Bridgewater standards—they were still small-time in the eyes of the rest of the world, a notion Danay apparently bought into wholeheartedly. She looked at their mom like she thought she was cute. Cute in all of her unsophisticated glory.

"Lehr & Black, Mom. It's not a color, it's a brand."

"Oh." Mrs. Cawley-Smith nodded. "Well, you sure are on top of things, sweetie. And with classes and all to keep you occupied, I don't know how you do it."

Danay smiled graciously. "It's not that bad."

Leeda watched both women dig delicately into their matching endive-and-Stilton salads. Danay leaned her elbows on the table, lounging over her food like she might be at a picnic on the beach instead of in a stuffy dining room. Occasionally she reached over and placed her hand on their mother's wrist, patting it affectionately as she talked.

"I couldn't believe it when I saw the lights in the rearview," she said, referring to a story she'd started earlier about how she'd been pulled over last week for going eighty-five in a fifty-five. "Two hundred fifty dollars, can you believe it? He wouldn't even knock it down to eighty."

Leeda watched the faces surrounding the table. Everyone, including her parents, shook their heads softly, agreeing with her, wearing amused expressions. It was this—Danay's demeanor while telling the story, that lazy perfection—that always managed to take Leeda by surprise. Somehow Leeda always forgot it, and when she witnessed it all over again, it sank into her stomach like a lead weight. Danay could screw up (not that she did very often) and absorb it into her perfection, like it was another jewel on her sparkling aura.

Leeda took another bite of her pastry. She'd managed to charm the waiter into bringing her the lobster claw instead of the prix fixe appetizer, pulling out her best eyelash-fluttering southern debutante look. She occasionally glanced at her mother to see if she'd say anything. She didn't.

Instead the entire Cawley-Smith family sitting at the table moved on to the wedding that would take place in mid-August, talking about the cake (red velvet, boring), the honeymoon (the West Indies, typical), the signature drinks (the Danayrita and the You Brighton My Life Banana Daquiri, no comment), and the wedding song ("From This Moment On," by Shania Twain, vomit). Chewing loudly, Leeda let her attention drift across the table to Brighton, who smiled at her with his usual kiss-up-to-the-family expression. She frowned back, letting her pink puffy lips droop in disdain, then looked at the space just beyond his head. A giant acrylic painting of a miniature Shetland pony watched them eat, its big brown eyes frank and pleading. Beneath it a white banner read: *Mitzie Needs Your Help*.

As usual, Leeda's grandmom's annual Shetland Rescue dinner was a rousing success. The Primrose Cottage Inn, a sprawling

Cawley-Smith–owned B & B with enormous white porches and rooms decorated in the style of different states, was packed, despite the hefty price tag of $250 a head. Leeda surveyed the crowd, looking for one cute guy or at least one guy below fifty. One man across the room, Horatio Balmeade of the Balmeade Country Club, locked eyes with her and gave her the old triangle stare: left eye, right eye, chest. Leeda curled over herself protectively.

"Don't slouch, Leeda. It's unattractive." Her dad had temporarily looked up from his papers, which he took any opportunity to shuffle through. Leeda suspected he did it even when he didn't have to in order to shield himself from the women he was always surrounded by. She straightened up and sighed loudly, hooking a finger into one of her blond starlet curls.

"And honey," her mom added stiffly, "smile."

Leeda smiled huge and fakely and rolled her eyes almost undetectably. It was one of her mother's pet theories that if you smiled, even when you were pissed off or depressed, it made you actually feel happy—which Leeda thought was a load of crap. But she acted like she believed it. With her mother, Leeda acted a lot.

Ever since she'd been little, Leeda had sensed the way her mother's eyes lit up when Danay entered the room and how when Leeda entered, they glazed over. Leeda had pushed herself into the top of her class while Danay had landed there with ease. Leeda'd tried to develop the same style of jokes, the same fine-line walk between casual and flawless. She had never been able to wear it as well. And maybe that was why her mom never filled her end of the bargain Leeda had secretly struck between them. Lucretia never lit her eyes up any brighter for her youngest daughter. After telling Leeda to smile, Lucretia let her eyes drift to Danay like metal to a magnet.

Leeda scanned the room, noticing that the waiter who'd brought the lobster claw was glancing at her every so often. Leeda was generally loved by waiters. In fact, she was pretty sure she was loved by just about everyone except her mom. At school, people courted her friendship like they were paying homage to a queen. When she went out, people's eyes lingered on her. Last summer, when the Cawley-Smiths had visited Tokyo, she'd been so loved by all the guys at the clubs, they kept asking if she was Charlize Theron.

Leeda was like David Hasselhoff. She was loved in Japan.

"Hey," Danay said, tapping Leeda's toe under the table and meeting her with a sparkling, perfect gaze of sisterly love. "What're you doing for spring break?"

"Camping at Tybee Beach. With Rex."

Danay looked at their mom. "Y'all are letting her go camping with a guy? You wouldn't even let me go with my girlfriends!"

Lucretia fiddled with the rings on three of her fingers, then scanned the wall for the clock. Leeda's parents liked to forget that Rex existed since he lived in a crappy brick duplex on the edge of Pearly Gates Cemetery across town, among other things.

He'd been Leeda's boyfriend since October. He was the hottest guy in Bridgewater, without a doubt. And he adored her. When he'd asked her out, her knee-jerk reaction had been to say no. Her second knee-jerk reaction had been to say yes because it had suddenly occurred to her that dating someone like Rex might make her mom sit up and take notice for once. Only Rex had turned out to be an okay guy. A great escape. And maybe the one place in her life where she felt maybe she was showing her parents who she truly was after all. She wished he had come; she always felt more solid with her family when he was around.

"Actually, Leeda, your father and I were talking. . . ."

Leeda felt her stomach clench instinctively.

"We think it'd be nice for you to stay with your uncle Walter for the break, help him out with the orchard a little, and spend some time with Birdie."

"Birdie?" Leeda never saw her second cousin Birdie except at weddings and funerals on the Smith side of the Cawley-Smith family, which her mom mostly wanted to forget.

"Sweetie, you know they're having a tough time with Cynthia gone," Leeda's mom whispered, almost gleefully. She loved being the bearer of personal info, even when it involved her own cousin running out on Birdie and Uncle Walter.

"But I already promised Rex. . . ." Leeda frowned, her perfectly arched blond eyebrows descending rapidly. Though she hated camping, she'd imagined she'd end up begging Rex to stay in some resort overlooking the ocean, somewhere where she could wash the sand out from between her toes. Where she could shop in the lobby and lounge at the waterfall pool bar, a safe distance from the creepy things that lurked under the ocean's surface—hermit crabs, blowfish, seaweed. Rex liked to catch things like that and stick them on her legs. "You guys can't."

"Walter was saying what a nice young lady you are and how he'd like his Birdie to be more like you."

Leeda rolled her eyes. "Birdie makes me uncomfortable. C'mon. You can't."

Leeda felt a familiar helpless lump in her throat. This was the way her parents worked. Requests were never requests; they were just orders all dressed up. Naked orders would be too tacky for the Cawley-Smiths.

"You just don't want me to spend time with Rex." Leeda crossed her arms tightly, lilac water from her fingertips dripping down her palms and the pale side of her wrists.

Mrs. Cawley-Smith sighed, a derisive grin spreading itself on her face. "Really, honey, don't you think that's a little dramatic?"

"You guys are such snobs!" Leeda said, tossing what was left of her lobster claw onto her plate. A few people at the surrounding tables stared. Horatio Balmeade leered.

Danay stared around, wide-eyed and scandalized, a perfect replica of their mom. "Leeda, you're being a brat."

"I'll leave, then." Leeda shot out of her chair and stalked out of the room and into the back garden of the Primrose Cottage Inn. She flopped onto one of the wrought-iron chairs, crossed her legs, and whipped out her cell. She was going to call Rex immediately.

He'd rev up his dirty pickup and be here in five minutes flat. That was the kind of guy he was. At times like this, she wanted him more than ever.

People like the Cawley-Smiths, by the way, got buried on *this* side of town, at Divine Grace of the Redeemer—miles from both Pearly Gates Cemetery and Anthill Acres Trailer Park.

Three

*B*irdie's window was wide and broad, with a window seat for sitting in and a view of the garden her mom had planted years ago. Cynthia Darlington had spent tons of money on fancy latticework, gazebos, and exotic breeds of roses—and then left her creation to the kudzu. She had fostered Birdie into the world in much the same way she had fostered the garden. She'd insisted on homeschooling her "because you never know what kind of trash they're teaching in the Georgia public schools." She'd insisted on art lessons, French language, and cello, though Birdie wasn't interested in any of the above.

The only thing Birdie was ever interested in was home. There was nothing Birdie loved more than to curl up in her window seat and watch the orchard. She knew what animals burrowed where, and what flowers bloomed when, and what trees produced the best fruit. She listened to the farm's rhythms through the screen like the beat of the heart of someone she loved.

Cynthia Darlington had installed the fancy latticework in her daughter's life and then driven away with her dog. Near dawn, Cynthia'd been spotted by the Darlingtons' neighbor, Horatio Balmeade, driving their 1988 green Jaguar onto the on-ramp to Route 75 north. According to Horatio, Cynthia wore a scarf in her hair and Toonsis, a Burberry collar that had seen better days. According to Horatio, they had both been smiling.

She'd left a letter on the table. Birdie had it beside her now.

Walter,

The dog is coming with me.

I debated taking him from you, sweetie, but you know Toonsis and I have a special bond. Crazy as it may seem, I took him to a pet psychic in Perry three weeks ago, when you were away selling the camper. As I suspected, he shares my sentiment about your blessed peaches. Toonsis and I are both tired of the smell, we're tired of the fuzz sticking under our fingernails, and we're tired of playing second fiddle to fruit.

Tell Birdie I'll call her. I'll be sending for her at the end of the summer, when I'm back from New York. I don't want to unsettle her quite yet, but of course it'll have to happen before school starts in the fall.

Don't fight me on this, dear. We both know Birdie needs a woman's guidance at this, her most delicate and impression-able age. High school can be hell.

Yours,
Cynthia

The first thing Walter had done when he'd realized they were gone was to go out and buy Birdie two papillon pups, the breed her mother had always said she wanted, as an invisible "screw you" to Cynthia. At least, that was what her mom was saying now.

Birdie had the cordless up to her ear, pinning herself against the molding of her window as if it was connected to a long curling cord. Conversations with her mom made her feel like that. Trapped.

"He's just rubbing them in my face."

Birdie had thought of it another way. She'd thought Walter had given *her* the dogs to cheer her up. But Cynthia was already on to another topic.

"Hell on earth. That's what that place is." Cynthia was talking about the orchard now. "I started hating it the year we moved in."

"But you moved in the year I was born, Mom," Birdie pointed out.

"That's right. I remember the dirt in that place, scrubbing those floors; that was before Poopie, you know," Cynthia said, referring to the Darlingtons' longtime housekeeper. "And then the peach work was endless. You know we only had fourteen hands that year. I thought my fingers were going to fall off from all the work."

"I didn't know it was so hard for you," Birdie offered, feeling guilty somehow. As if the fetus of Birdie could have slacked off just a little less.

"My friend Nancy always said you were my little bad luck charm," her mom went on. "Of course that's not true, honey. It's just the timing was so bad with you and the orchard, and I really stopped loving your father that year. Fell completely out of love. Poof."

"Wow." That was all Birdie could think to say. Her ear had started to itch. Really bad. "Mom, I gotta go."

Cynthia got quiet on the other end. "I'm sorry, honey. I know it's not fair for me to tell you these things. I just . . . ugh. Your dad is such a jerk."

"That's okay, Mom. Poopie's calling me."

"Okay. Bye, sweetie."

"Bye."

"Sweetie?"

Silence.

"I love you."

Birdie held the phone between tight fingers. "Love you too."

Birdie laid the phone down and leaned her head back against the molding. She sighed, then reached out and stroked her dog Honey Babe behind her butterfly-wing ears. Majestic stuck her nose in for a pet too and licked Birdie's fingers. She smiled weakly.

Birdie looked at her bookshelf. Most of it was filled with things other than books—three porcelain clown dolls that Poopie said gave her the giggly wigglies (which meant heebie-jeebies in Poopie-speak), a collection of fairy figurines, a plush Tinkerbell from Disney World, a trillion manifestations of birds (stickers, ornaments, stuffed animals), and a couple of books people had given her.

Last year at Christmas, Birdie's aunt Gladys had given her a book she'd bought at Wal-Mart titled *Angels Have Feelings Too*. Birdie had flipped through it stoically, looking for something she could comment on to make her aunt feel like she'd read it. She'd finally marked a section about finding an outlet for your emotions, like a musical instrument. Just look at the angels and their harps, it said. She'd managed to convince much of her extended family that she did, in fact, find solace in her cello.

Right now, it was leaned on the wall beside her closet, a thin layer of dust asleep on its surface.

She stood up, the pups leaping off the window seat and following at her heels. She looked at the cello, then looked in the mirror on her closet door. How had she gotten so fat? Oh yeah. She opened her closet and pulled a box of solace off the top shelf.

She gave Honey Babe and Majestic, each named after a breed of peach, a caramel-drenched Girl Scout Samoa, then polished off the rest of the box herself.

"What're you doing lazing around in here all day?"

Birdie was lying in her bed in a cookiefied stupor watching VH1. There was a fascinating show about eighties Hair Bands.

"Nothing," Birdie said, sitting up and wincing at Poopie in a pathetic attempt at a smile. Poopie had started working at the house as a cleaning woman some fifteen years ago when she'd come from Mexico to pack peaches, shortly after Birdie was born, but now she mostly cooked and had Birdie clean instead. If Birdie's mom was the neglectful gardener in Birdie's life, Poopie was the kudzu. She was hearty and she had staying power.

"You know we don't have nearly enough help and you're in here feeling sorry for yourself," Poopie said, thrusting out a bucket. "Get down there to the cider house and start cleaning up the press. You'll feel better."

Birdie slid off the bed and took the bucket obediently from Poopie's hands. Poopie smacked her on the butt on the way out. Birdie had more cushioning there than she used to.

•　　•　　•

On the porch, Birdie bumped into Horatio Balmeade, who took off his hat and smiled with straight white teeth.

"Hi, Birdie."

"Hi, Mr. Balmeade."

Horatio Balmeade was the Darlingtons' only neighbor. He owned the country club next door, and he was always looking to expand. Birdie knew a visit from him inevitably meant an offer on the orchard. He'd made offers every year for the past five years, though her dad always made it clear he'd rather throw himself under the wheels of Horatio's Mercedes than sell his family's orchard to a golf course developer.

He was like a mosquito that hovered just out of reach as you tried to smack at him, only to sail back the moment you had forgotten him. He wasn't big enough to do much harm, but he was big enough to itch. He was probably the only person Birdie had ever met that she actually hated. She glanced around the porch, feeling self-conscious about the peeling paint and the wood rot on the banister, the dirtiness of the rag rug at the top of the stairs.

"Can I help you?"

"Oh, just calling on your dad," Horatio said through his teeth.

Birdie knew Walter's patented responses to Mr. Balmeade—he wasn't home, he was busy. "He's over checking the—"

"Hi there, Horace." Walter stepped onto the porch behind Birdie. He thrust out his hand and shook Mr. Balmeade's, a joyless smile on his face. "I've been meaning to get over there for that game of golf."

Birdie looked at her dad, then at Mr. Balmeade. *Horace?* "C'mon inside, Poopie's just made a fresh batch of sweet tea."

Mr. Balmeade turned back to Birdie. "Thanks, honey."

Birdie watched them, boggled, as both men disappeared into the darkness of the house. She stared at the closed door for a minute. And then she walked down the porch stairs.

Birdie lit out across the clearing and over the hill toward the cider house, trying to shake Horatio Balmeade out of her head, the bucket knocking against the side of her ample right thigh, her auburn hair bouncing in its ponytail. Maybe her dad was desperate for friends since her mom had left. The thought that he might actually sell the orchard was too ridiculous for Birdie to even consider.

After a few minutes the movement and the air lifted her mood. She loved the smell of spring. She could predict how and when everything would start blooming. The magnolia by the cider house always unrolled its prehistoric petals later than the ones on top of the hill. Piles and piles of blackberry bushes would flower at the far back of the property near the bridge and ripen around the third week of June, when Birdie would trek across the acreage and go pick them for Poopie to make pie.

Birdie could see a few of the newly arrived workers criss-crossing the grounds, and this made her smile too and give them little waves. Spring meant the return of all of the workers, who were old friends to Birdie and her dad. She looked forward to seeing them all roll in the way other people might look forward to visits from relatives. They were so much family that Birdie couldn't imagine life without them.

Every year the orchard produced batches of cider to distribute to farm stands in the area and batches to distribute to wineries that would turn the juice into wine. Birdie had been handed the job of supervising the press two years ago as her first major responsibility. Now it was just one of her many duties.

When she got to the cider house, tugging at the leaves of the nearby magnolia as she passed it, she could hear clanking inside, and she slowed down, wondering if a possum had gotten in. She held the bucket back over her shoulder like a weapon, prepared to throw it if she needed to.

She peered around the corner of the door. But there was no possum in sight. Instead a boy leaned over the press with his profile to her. He had a nice, straight-bridged nose, brown hair, and almond-colored arms, which were stretched over the press, scraping a scrub brush back and forth. Crap. Birdie would have preferred the possum.

Birdie's hands immediately flew to her sloppy ponytail. She hated talking to strangers. Especially guys her age. Especially good-looking ones. Living on an orchard and being homeschooled, she had the social prowess of the Hunchback of Notre Dame.

"Um," Birdie began, preparing to say hi, and introduce herself, and ask him if he was the new cider guy. But instead she took one step forward and *squish*. Birdie went flying, her feet sliding forward and up into the air and her butt landing with a thud, followed by her head. A splurt of goo came flying out of nowhere into her face. Another soaked its way through her shorts and onto her butt cheeks.

Birdie had a straight view of the ceiling for a moment before the guy's face appeared above her, his eyebrows knit in concern and his mouth pursed in an "ouch" expression. He had perfect eyebrows. Damn. He looked good.

Birdie remained lying with her eyes on the ceiling, too

mortified to stand up and a surge of heat racing through her stomach. "I'm okay. I'm okay." She wanted to wait till the red ran out of her cheeks. But she felt his hands on her shoulders and he was pulling her up, and she felt herself go redder.

Birdie looked around her. She was sitting in a pile of old moldy peach sludge.

"*Lo siento,*" he said.

"It's okay. Not my fault. I mean, not your fault, totally my fault," she said, trying to climb onto her feet. She was halfway up when she realized that her butt was sticking out and that her boobs were probably looking all lopsided and big.

"I'm Birdie," she said, reaching out a hand.

"Enrico," he said with a heavy accent. "Nice to meeting you."

He took her floppy, halfhearted hand in his strong one and shook once, the rough of his palms scratching against the rough of hers.

"Okay, well, I just brought a bucket down," Birdie said, wiping the slime off her right butt cheek. "If you need one. Um, if you need anything else . . ."

Enrico was looking at Birdie with a strange smile. She lost her train of thought. Her voice stuck in her throat and she swallowed. He wiped at his forehead.

"*Come se dice . . . tienes la cara sucia.*" He rubbed harder at his forehead.

Birdie tried to remember what little Spanish she knew. Why had her mom made her take French when they were surrounded every summer by a ton of Spanish speakers?

"You want something for your itchy forehead?" Birdie ventured. Maybe the guy had poison ivy.

Enrico shrugged. "P-pardon me," he stammered, grinning, "but you have peaches on your forehead."

Birdie rubbed at her forehead with the back of her wrist and looked at the spot it left on her arm.

"Oh. Thanks. That's, um, very polite of you."

Enrico broke into a smile, then started laughing softly. He rolled his pretty brown eyes. "Pardon me, but you have peaches on your forehead," he repeated, laughing at himself.

The laughter was contagious, especially with Birdie's nervousness. She giggled.

"Pardon me, but there are peaches on my butt," she replied, brushing off her rear end with both hands. Enrico laughed a little harder. Then he looked down at her butt. Birdie felt her face flame up again.

"Well," she said, backing away. "If you need anything, just let us know."

She actually couldn't believe her luck. She had handled the whole thing so gracefully. She stepped onto the threshold, wanting to quit while she was ahead. "See ya."

Birdie turned to walk out the door, then turned back to give Enrico a little wave. As she turned, her feet caught each other wrong, and she fell backward into the grass. So much for luck.

Four

"**M**om, you can't do this to me."

Jodee McGowen looked in the rearview mirror of her maroon 1990 Pontiac and smoothed her Wet 'n' Wild Passionflower-lipsticked lips together. "Honey, you did this to yourself. You know I'll miss you."

Murphy rolled her eyes at the hypocrisy of it all. If someone was always "doing it to herself," it was her mother.

"Judge Abbott made it pretty clear—" Jodee added before Murphy interrupted her.

"You're ruining my life," she said, and opened the door quickly to get out. She walked around to the back of the Pontiac and rapped on the trunk with her knuckles. The lock popped open.

Murphy hoisted her green army-issue bag onto her shoulder and then slammed the trunk. She walked back to the open window. "This is worse than jail. Can't I just go to juvie instead?"

"How do I look?" Jodee asked, moving a wisp of her copper hair away with one fingernail. All of her fingernails were long and had tiny little seagulls painted on them above tiny little oceans. Murphy and her mother looked nearly alike, but Jodee dressed to accentuate her femininity—low-cut tank tops from Wal-Mart, short skirts to show off her admittedly perfect legs, long nails that her boyfriends seemed to go for.

"You look like a floozy," Murphy muttered.

Jodee frowned at her. "Watch your mouth."

But Murphy only shrugged. Her mother was the least intimidating person she'd ever met.

Jodee looked in the mirror again, unsure now. "I happen to think I look very nice. He works at Pep Boys. His name's Richard. He's taking me out to dinner. Not bad, huh, baby?"

"Are you going to Burger King or Arby's?"

Jodee lifted one plucked eyebrow. "I might just never come to pick you up."

"Tragedy," Murphy said darkly.

"I'm gonna run off to Mexico and drink margaritas every day," Jodee threatened.

"That would be fine."

Murphy backed up and gave a half wave. Jodee blew a kiss to her.

"I love you, honey. See you in two weeks."

"Not if I die of boredom first," Murphy said.

The Pontiac pulled away, its wheels crunching in the white dirt of the long drive out of the orchard. Murphy sent up a silent prayer that Richard wouldn't be that interested in her mother. She didn't know if she could take another of her mom's boyfriends. Then she looked around.

Damn.

Murphy dropped her bag and stuck her hands in the pockets

of her cords, surveying the orchard. The house stood directly behind her. In front, stretching back toward the road and to either side as far as the eye could see, were the peach trees, their tops low and dipped in the middle like cereal bowls, rows of white sandy dirt striping straight paths between them. The branches were dotted in tiny spots of fluorescent green where the leaves were sprouting. To her right were two other houses, about twenty-five yards apart, strange looking because they were both sort of sunk into the ground and more run-down than the main house. To her left was a barn, also worn and sunken, its red paint closer to an ambitious brown.

It was different than at night. Murphy felt like the one thing that did not belong in the picture.

"Well, hi," she heard, and turned. There was Chickie Darlington, cuddling one of her dogs against her chest. The other stood by her heels.

Murphy just stared at her. Chickie seemed to falter, her hands freezing on the enormous ears of her dog. "I'm Birdie," she said, trying to sound bright in that fake way Murphy hated. Birdie. Chickie. Whatever. "This is Honey Babe." Birdie held one dog forward, then nodded down to the other. "And Majestic. Welcome to the farm."

Murphy stared coldly at the dogs, then looked up at Birdie— a picture of innocence with huge brown eyes and softly wavy auburn hair. "What kind of name is Birdie?"

Birdie's cheeks flushed. "When I was little, I had, uh . . . these little chicken legs." She seemed on the verge of saying more but stopped.

"Uh-huh." Murphy looked her up and down. Birdie was sort of

plump, definitely not chicken-y. Still Birdie but without the legs.

"Dad asked me to come and show you where to sleep."

Murphy lifted her bag back over her shoulder. "Lead the way."

Murphy walked behind Birdie, watching the way she walked, self-consciously, like each step was carefully thought out. Yuck.

They made their way across the grass up to the smaller of the two houses. Birdie veered toward the one with the sign at the top of the stairs that said Camp A.

"This is the women's dorm," Birdie said, opening the door and leading Murphy into a tiny yellow-walled hallway bordered with a kitchen and then a common room. The whole place smelled delicious and looked like something from an old movie.

"Everyone just had lunch," Birdie said, hovering in the archway into the common room, which was filled with three old La-Z-Boys, a table with three legs, a worn plaid couch, and the dark-haired, dark-skinned women who occupied these seats.

"This is Emma, Alita, Isabel, and Raeka," Birdie said, smiling shyly at the women and then back at Murphy. "*Hola,*" she said softly.

"*Hola,*" everyone said back absently. Birdie continued down the hallway to the bottom of a set of stairs. "They'll be picking and packing too. They're all nice."

At the top of the stairs Birdie stood back to let Murphy walk into the first bedroom on the right.

"This is your room," she said, standing back so Murphy could go inside. The room was bare, with an old beat-up desk and bed with a blue mattress beside a window that looked out at a row of trees. By the door was a list of rules: No smoking, no loud music, curfew 10 p.m. Murphy immediately knelt on the bed and tried to open the window. It was jammed shut.

"This is a fire hazard," she said, flashing her green slitted eyes at Birdie, who hovered by the doorway looking like a deer trapped in headlights. Birdie held her cheek out to be licked by one of the dogs in her arms. Her pink worm of a tongue darted along her skin twice. "I have rights. I want a window that opens. I could sue you guys."

"Um. But I don't know. . . ." Birdie trailed off, looking nervous. "It's an old house."

Murphy rolled her eyes. "Whatever." She tossed her bag onto the bed and started unpacking. She'd figure out how to un-jam the window.

"If you need anything . . ."

Murphy could think of many things she needed. She needed to be getting stoned outside the Ryman auditorium. She needed a real spring break, one of the few joys of life. Now, thanks to Birdie and her dogs, she had neither.

"Don't you think that's hypocritical?"

Birdie shifted her weight. "What do you mean?"

"Well, you're asking me what I need, but I already told you I need a window that opens, and you can't do that. And what I really need is to go on break like every other normal person in America, and I can't do that either. And I have you to thank for that and you, Honey Butt." Murphy nodded at the one dog. "And you, Ambrosia Salad." Murphy nodded at the other.

"It's Honey Babe and Majestic. They're named after peaches. . . ."

"I don't know if that's how you spend all your time, sitting around waiting to bust people's balls because you don't have anything else to do. Guarding your dad's crème de menthe."

"Bust balls ... but we weren't ... ?"

"Yeah, bust balls. You and your fascist dogs."

Birdie's bottom lip quivered. "But I didn't . . . I . . ." Birdie blinked a few times, unsurely. Then, to Murphy's amazement, she simply pivoted on her heel and took off down the stairs.

Murphy came to the doorway and watched her disappear. Maybe she had hit a sore spot and Birdie really was afraid that her dogs were fascists. She imagined them giving each other little Nazi salutes with their paws.

"Chickie," she called with a giggle in her voice, wanting to apologize. But the sound of the screen door hissing closed announced that Birdie had already gone. Murphy walked to the end of the hall, which was marked with a big square window, and peered out to see her and her dogs rushing across the grass toward the house, still walking self-consciously with no one behind to watch her.

"Damn."

Murphy's eyes drifted over the landscape. It was a far cry from Anthill Acres, where the foliage consisted of the kudzu that lined the telephone poles and the moss that stuck up through the cracks in the concrete patios.

Just emerging from one of the rows—on a path to intersect Birdie if she'd been walking instead of run-hobbling—was a figure. Murphy watched it closely, making out a man, well, a guy, in an orange T-shirt and jeans. He was nice to look at, definitely, though he had very little style—his jeans weren't any kind of hipster blue and his T-shirt looked like Hanes standard variety. Murphy was into style.

Still, she could tell just by the way he walked that he had to be good looking. Guys who knew it had a certain walk that didn't show off—their looks could do it for them.

Murphy made a mental note of him. And then she slunk back down the hall and forgot about him altogether.

Up on the porch, several people—mostly young Mexican men— were milling around speaking Spanish—sitting on the porch rockers and standing on the stairs, their skin brown and warm looking. Leeda parked her Beemer as close to the house as possible and primly made her way through the crowd. *"Pardone, pardone."* She wasn't sure if that was right, though she'd taken two years of Spanish so far. Of course, she'd spent most of that time snapping the split ends out of her hair and being courted via note by ninety percent of the boys in the class and half the girls.

Inside, the house smelled like mothballs and boxwood— the signature scent of Uncle Walter's. Uncle Walter himself carried the smell with him wherever he went, much like Leeda's mom carried the smell of Givenchy Very Irresistible, claiming that every woman should have a scent others could remember her by.

Leeda let out a long, nervous sigh. She hadn't been to the house in over a year. Looking around now, she could see the signs of Aunt Cynthia's sudden disappearance. Bare spaces where pieces of furniture had been. The dining room table covered in papers, the chairs pulled out and in disarray. Cynthia had always been in Walter's office, on the phone with some client, solving some issue for the workers, or handling the bills. It felt quiet without her high southern voice lilting through the rooms. Leeda wished she had Rex with her. Or one of her friends from school.

Poopie came out of the kitchen, wiping her hands on a dishcloth. "Hiya, honey," she drawled in her weird mixture of Spanish and southern accents.

"Hi, Miss Poopie." Leeda kissed her on her warm, dewy cheek. Poopie didn't smell like mothballs. She always smelled like warm cookies.

"You look more and more like a movie star every day. How many boyfriends you have?"

Leeda smiled. "Just one for now."

Poopie shook her head. "A waste. I hope he's sweet to you."

"He is."

Poopie smiled too, showing three gold teeth. "Well, it's good to have you, sweetie. We need every hand we can get this year. I'm about to drive the van into town to take the workers shopping. This young man is helping me get everything organized." She nodded to a cute, dark-skinned guy standing in the archway of the kitchen. He smiled at Leeda. Leeda smiled tightly back, polite. People who didn't speak her language always gave her the giggly wigglies. "Go on up and see our Birdie. She's hiding from me."

Leeda plodded her way up the droopy, lopsided stairs, miserable. She wondered if her parents would have ever sentenced Danay to two weeks with the Darlingtons. She tried to picture it. Instead the picture leapt into her head of the day Danay had left for Emory (the Harvard of the South, as her mom liked to say)—her mom and dad with their arms genteelly looped behind each other's backs watching her drive away, tears in their eyes. It made a lump rise to Leeda's throat.

In the upstairs hall, the same dresser held the same knick-knacks that had been there since Leeda could remember. The same piece of cinnamon candy had been sitting there for at least sixteen years. Leeda wrinkled her nose. She liked things new and shiny, not old and dusty.

Birdie was sitting in her giant window, flipping through a *Cosmo* and nibbling the chocolate off a Goo Goo Cluster. Aside from the Goo Goo Cluster, she reminded Leeda of a Renoir she'd seen in Paris last summer—soft and full and pretty. Two papillons lay sleeping on each other's necks at her feet.

"Hi, Birdie."

Birdie jolted and tucked the magazine behind her, her cheeks turning pink. Leeda scanned the room to the TV, which was playing some Nelly video.

"What are you doing, Birdie?"

"Nothing. Um, hiding from Poopie."

"She knows you're up here."

"She wants me to go into town with the workers and take them shopping."

"Well, why don't you?"

"I don't know."

"There's some cutie downstairs, looks like a worker. Maybe you should go anyway."

Birdie blushed harder, clasping her hands like an old lady. Birdie was more like an old lady than any old lady Leeda knew, and she knew a lot because old ladies loved the Primrose Cottage Inn, their fluffy white hairdos poking over the backs of the rockers on the verandah all summer long.

"What are you reading?"

"Nothing."

"Well." Leeda cleared her throat, remembering her posture and throwing her shoulders back. "Where should I put my suitcases?" she asked brightly.

"Dad wants you to sleep in here with me. He said we should pull out the trundle bed."

Leeda sank deeply into one hip. "Are you serious?"

Birdie nodded solemnly.

"No way. I need my privacy."

"I told him. I need my privacy too. I said we're not ten anymore. He didn't listen."

Leeda surveyed the room and wondered. It hadn't changed much since they were ten. The same four-post bed, the same stuffed animals on the shelves.

"Well, it's just not happening," Leeda said, stiffening in the way she did when she was resolved. "I'm going to talk to Uncle Walter. I think you should come with me."

Birdie let out a breath and stood up.

Leeda frowned. Her cousin made her uncomfortable for a couple of different reasons. One was that she didn't chitchat. She would let long silences drift into a conversation and make no attempt to get out of them or to help Leeda when she tried to fill up the empty space. The second reason was something a little filmier and harder to grasp. There wasn't any artifice to Birdie—her big brown eyes were always earnest and truthful. Being around her made Leeda feel like she herself was a little bit artificial.

Leeda glanced behind her. Birdie's magazine was opened to "Three Things Every Guy Craves in Bed."

·　　·　　·

Two minutes later, they were both standing in the entry to Uncle Walter's office, which was a tragedy—with piles of paper leaning like towers, and unwashed plates stuffed into crevices of shelves, and bills spread out with big red stamps at the tops of each one.

"Hey, Uncle Walter?"

Uncle Walter looked up from his desk and gave Leeda a heartbreaking smile, because she was Leeda and people treated her like velvet, and smiled at her when there was no reason to be smiling. He looked ten years older than he had the last time she'd seen him.

Birdie brushed past her and began trying to organize some of the papers, looking self-conscious. The whole scene, with Birdie included, made Leeda's question freeze in her throat. The bold-type notices on the papers were things like *Past Due* and *Account Frozen*. Leeda pretended like she didn't notice. Walter was still looking at her expectantly. "Uh, do you mind if I sleep at the dorms?"

It was easier than she expected. Walter didn't even consider it; he looked back down at his desk. "Sure, honey, that's fine."

It had taken a few seconds for Leeda to take it all in and realize something that for all her thoughtful slowness, Birdie didn't seem to recognize at all.

The Darlingtons and their orchard were perched on the edge of disaster, and Birdie didn't even know it.

When Poopie Pedraza arrived at Darlington Orchard in her late twenties in search of work, she looked to the sky and saw the shape of the Virgin Mary in the clouds. Poopie took a picture that appeared in the paper the next day. People flocked to the orchard hoping for more holy cloud sightings, until, on closer inspection, it was determined that the cloud in Poopie's photo actually looked more like a potato. After that, the miracle cloud was completely forgotten by everyone but Poopie, who wasn't sure she believed in miracles, but who waited for another sign.

Five

$\mathcal{M}$urphy woke up to the sound of a bird chirping.

She pulled her pillow over her head and then pulled it away for a moment. "Shut up," she yelled, and pulled it back.

The bird went on chirping, its shrill song drilling right through the glass and the fabric of her pillow. He was doing it on purpose. She knew he was.

Murphy shot up to a sitting position and looked outside. It was just after dawn. There he was, a blue jay, right next to her window, looking at her insolently from a drooping branch. A chickadee two branches above appeared to be ignoring him.

"See, nobody likes your stupid song." Murphy slapped her pillow and staggered out into the hallway, pulling on a thin navy blue sweatshirt. She'd heard people moving about a while ago and had stayed in bed, praying no one would wake her up. Blessedly, they hadn't. One of the women, Emma, she thought, rushed by her with a baseball cap. Then slid to a halt, backed up, and gathered Murphy into the crook of her arm. "*Es tarde.* You are late."

Murphy shrugged. "I'll catch up." Whether she understood or not, Emma hurried on down the hall.

Murphy returned to her room, smell-tested the armpits of her Craig Nicholls T-shirt, and changed into that and a pair of shorts. A few minutes later she straggled into the bright spring sunshine. The air felt warm and cool in patches, like it hadn't yet evened out, and it was full of the sounds of different critters buzzing, chirping, legs rubbing together in the trees. Murphy could see that a group of people had gathered up at the house.

Pulling a Doral out of the pack in her pocket, she walked around behind the dorm to smoke, promising herself that if the blue jay was there, they'd have a good talk and she'd threaten him with cigarette burns. Instead she saw a guy crouched about fifty yards away, doing something in the dirt where the orchard began.

Curious, Murphy walked a little closer, admiring his butt. She knew you always had to be careful about checking out guys from behind. Then they'd turn around and be ugly and you'd feel all grossed out.

Murphy walked closer so that he'd hear her and turn around. He did. It was the guy from the lawn the day before.

She could see now it was a fledgling tree he was working on. He was tying a white band around its tiny trunk, which was skinny as a baby's wrist. His hands worked deftly at the twisting. Murphy had the impulse to look away, as if she'd walked in on something intimate and private. Instead she took a long drag of her cigarette and stared at the guy's knuckles. He was older than her, maybe by a year or two.

"Are you our tree nurse?"

He turned back toward her. "Aren't you supposed to be working?" he said, nodding up to the farmhouse.

Murphy nodded. "I guess so." She thrust out her breasts

slightly, because he didn't appear to have seen them. "What's that white stuff for?"

The guy looked at her for a moment, as if she were Dennis the Menace, still not taking in the breasts. "It protects the baby tree from the animals. And it shelters the trunk from the insecticides we spray for the bigger trees. It takes them three years to grow big enough to bear fruit."

Murphy shrugged. "I'm against insecticides."

The guy smiled at her, as if he was in on some joke she wasn't. "Right."

Murphy frowned. She intentionally took forever to finish her cigarette, letting the silence work its way out and kicking the toes of her sneakers, which were damp, into the dirt. The guy didn't seem to notice.

"Well, I'm Murphy. I'll see you." She reached out a hand toward him, just to show him she wasn't intimidated.

He reached out and shook it, the dirt from his fingers rubbing off on hers.

"Rex," he said. "See you."

Murphy rubbed the dirt between her fingers and walked, putting a little more swing in her hips in case Rex was watching.

Up on the porch, Walter Darlington was speaking in a hopeless monotone, with Birdie on one side and a dark-skinned woman on the other, talking in unison with him in Spanish.

"We want to thin ten percent of the trees. That's one in ten peaches we want to knock off. We have about a hundred acres and about eighty-five trees per acre, so that's a lot of peaches to knock down. Those of you who don't know how, watch the ones who do."

Murphy raised her hand and interrupted. "Don't we *want* peaches to grow?"

Everyone looked at her and muttered. Walter frowned. "You missed that part, Murphy. You'll need to ask someone later." Walter cleared his throat. "Birdie oversees the dorms, so if you have any problems with the living space or if you need something like charcoal for the grill, cooking supplies, or toilet paper, let her know. She'll be by to check on everyone every day."

Birdie fidgeted where she stood beside Walter. Murphy grinned. It was hard to imagine Chickie overseeing much of anything.

"You won't get cell reception. There is one phone, over in the supply barn. It takes quarters. This"—Walter gestured toward the Latin American woman standing next to him—"is Poopie Pedraza. She's in charge when I'm not around. And she . . ."

Murphy tuned him out and looked around her at all the brown faces. How did these people do it? All spring and summer, working in the sun. Her eye caught a movement back toward the dorm and then a sight a lot like a leprechaun. Leeda Cawley-Smith emerged from Camp A, her blond ringlets a-frazzle, dark circles under her eyes. She wore silky pajama pants and a pair of slippers and walked carefully across the grass, watching the ground as if something might jump out and grab her. Leeda came closer and closer, finally hovering on the edge of the crowd to listen to Walter with everybody else.

When Walter was finished, the workers—about twenty in all—fanned out among the trees. Murphy straggled after them into the outskirts of the orchard. Now that Murphy really looked, she could see that in addition to the budding leaves, the trees were covered with small green buds, about the size of Super Balls, clustered out along the lengths of the limbs.

Murphy watched the other workers begin to yank at them and drop them onto the ground, letting out tiny *thud thuds* as they landed. Then she looked back over her shoulder. There was Leeda, right behind her.

"Hola," she said when she saw Murphy looking at her.

"Oh God."

Leeda squinted at her, the circles under her deep-set, fluffy-lash-rimmed gray eyes crinkling. "You speak English?"

"I'm in your bio class."

"Oh, you're right," Leeda said, tossing back her hair with one hand. "Do you work here during the summers?"

"No."

Leeda nodded. "Oh. Well, I don't work here either." She looked around at the other workers, as if she were slightly embarrassed. "Walter's my uncle."

Murphy stuck her hands into her pockets, fingering her empty cigarette pack. "Wow," she said flatly.

Leeda faltered, seeming unsure of whether Murphy was teasing her or not.

"You're staying in the dorms?" Murphy hadn't seen her last night.

Leeda nodded. And yawned, covering her mouth. Her fingernails were bubble-gum pink. "What're you doing here?"

"Got caught on the premises. Having wild sex. It was so good I didn't hear anyone coming."

Leeda stiffened before Murphy turned and walked several yards down the row.

The trees were set up like checkers—in every direction you looked, they made a straight line. They were just Murphy's size—short and full, each ending at the same height. But within that uniformity, the trees themselves were as unique as snowflakes—their small trunks and limbs zigzagging, messy, awkward knots of wood marking the unexpected turns of growth, as if the trees themselves hadn't known which way they were going to grow and had started one way and changed their minds.

To Murphy, they appeared miniature and delicate, and when she looked up and around, the collective impression was so vast that it made Murphy feel far away from everything—from the dorms, definitely from home. Like she'd stepped onto the checkerboard and out of real life.

She tackled a tree, swatting at the raw peaches. The branches bent like rubber bands, bouncing back at her after every swat. Murphy shrank back, startled.

Someone giggled behind her. Murphy turned to see Emma, the woman from this morning, laughing at her.

"What?" Murphy asked, defensive.

"You angry at trees?"

Murphy huffed. "Nooo."

"Here, you pick gentle." Emma tugged at a cluster of peaches and set them falling to the ground—*thud thud thud thud thud.*

Murphy watched her, then glanced at Leeda, who was down the row picking one peach at a time and then ducking to lay them down on the grass, agonizingly slowly.

"Maybe you should go help her instead."

Emma looked at Leeda. "She do okay. You . . ." She nodded to the tree. It had knobs in several places and branched out at strange, crooked angles.

Murphy picked a few the way Emma had. Finally Emma stood back and smiled.

"Okay, thanks."

Emma walked back to her own tree. Murphy watched her for a moment, then swatted at hers again a few times. All she knew was that it seemed backward that you had to thin a tree to get it to make fruit right. Still, the next hour or so passed without Murphy noticing the time. What she did notice was the way the air cooled and heated up depending on where she was standing. The trees didn't offer much shade, but the tiny dips in the land did. Murphy had the kind of hungry brain that noticed these things, and surprisingly, it didn't find itself bored all morning, until she remembered why she was here and that she didn't want to be. She swatted at another branch, and it bounced back and stuck a twig into her thick hair, clinging to it.

When Murphy had extracted herself, her mood was worse than when the day had started, and she suddenly felt tired. The expanse of trees felt endless. All she really owed Walter was a quarter bottle of crème de menthe.

She looked around to make sure nobody was watching, then she walked the two hundred yards to Camp A, climbed the two sets of stairs, and crawled into her bed.

When Emma knocked on her door to invite her to eat lunch, the smells of Mexican cooking wafting in through the cracks in the door, she pretended she was sleeping and held the pillow tighter over her head.

•   •   •

The Darlingtons had always invited the workers to dinner on the first night of thinning to celebrate the start of the season. This year, though, Walter had opted for a quiet family dinner instead, and now he, Poopie, Birdie, and Leeda sat around the kitchen table alone.

On the chalkboard beside the refrigerator Poopie had written down the phone messages for Walter. It used to be that Walter or Cynthia would see them, take care of them, and erase them. In the weeks since Cynthia had been gone, they had collected and stayed there, glaring at everyone all day long. Now the neglected board listed calls from Horatio Balmeade, Bridgewater Savings and Loan, and Wachovia.

Next to Birdie, Honey Babe had his short little legs on her cousin Leeda's calf and was trying to jump up to sniff her crotch. Birdie tugged him gently by the tail.

"Get in your place, Honey. Go on, get in your place." Honey stared up at her mournfully for a second, then pranced over to the corner by the olive green stove and lay down, tapping his paws in a gesture of contained restlessness that Murphy would have been able to empathize with had she been invited to dinner.

Leeda, though, wore a wrinkled nose and a frown and held her hands tight over her skirt. Why she'd brought skirts to wear to the farm was anyone's guess. Birdie shot glances at her over Poopie's signature rib eye steak, feeling resentful. She hadn't asked Leeda to come in the first place. But here Leeda was, wrinkling her nose and obviously judging. Judging Birdie's room, her dogs, her house's out-of-date kitchen. Birdie tucked a forkful of sweet corn in her mouth, wondering why she still cared so badly what Leeda thought. It had been this way since they'd hit puberty and drifted apart. Birdie had always wanted Leeda to be her friend, and she still had no idea why.

"Birdie, why don't you keep your elbows off the table? Look at Leeda." Walter nodded in Leeda's direction.

Birdie looked at her dad, who hadn't said so much as a word through dinner so far. Then at Leeda, who sat with her legs crossed and her wrists resting at the edge of the table like a china doll, occupying Cynthia's old chair and yawning occasionally. Birdie pulled her elbows to her side. From the corner, Honey Babe let out a tiny squeaky sympathetic howl. Everyone chewed loudly.

Exhausted from the day, which was always one of the most challenging of the year, Birdie snaked a hand shyly across the table and patted her dad's fingers. Since her mom had gone, Birdie had noticed the ways it mattered that her mom wasn't around, and today—with all that Cynthia would have been doing to help get the season moving—had been a major day for that. The big ways Birdie missed her mother were expected. The little ways were hard for their own reasons, because they took her by surprise. Birdie knew her dad felt it too.

"That software I got is great, Dad," she said, referring to the program she'd bought a couple of weeks ago at Wal-Mart to help organize payroll.

Walter merely sawed on his steak, so halfheartedly that he barely made a slash through it. "Did you bring the old bottles down to the cider house?"

Birdie shook her head. "Not yet." Actually, she'd done extra chores in other areas to *avoid* the cider house. So far, she'd managed to avoid Enrico completely. Which, on a small farm, was actually quite a feat.

"I've renewed all the insurance stuff except for natural disaster." She changed the subject. "That just came today." She stared at Walter. No response. "But I'll do that first thing tomorrow."

"Don't bother. We won't renew this year."

"Really?"

Walter didn't reply. Nobody spoke for several seconds, and in that time Birdie wolfed down several pieces of steak.

Poopie looked from Birdie to him and back again and rolled her eyes. Poopie was a better communicator than either Birdie or her dad and had said many times that the two of them together were like two mimes talking, except she called them "mines."

This look encouraged Birdie to be bolder. "Daddy, I think you should renew the insurance. You can't be too careful."

"It'll be a miracle if we can afford to keep up what we have this summer."

Birdie swallowed. The farm's financial situation had been bad for the last few years, but usually her dad tried to keep it quiet, as though neither of them noticed. Last year, to pay their taxes, Walter had sold two of their tractors and a vacant plot of land he'd bought several years ago, hoping to plant it. They'd hardly exchanged more than two words about it.

"But if something happened to—"

"Birdie, you're just like your mother. If we had the money, I'd insure everything. Christ, we could insure the dogs. The porch. The rocking chairs."

Birdie stared down at her fork.

"If this frost comes, they'll be tearing up the floorboards from right under us. I wouldn't worry about tornados."

Birdie's stomach rolled over. "There's a frost coming?"

Walter didn't bother to reply. He just kept chewing in silence. Which nearly drove Birdie over the edge. Peach trees were most vulnerable when they had their buds out, and watching over them those weeks was almost like watching the delicate, early stages of a pregnancy. But she also knew her dad thought that he had some innate sense of the weather and that he often spoke about weather patterns before anything was predicted. He kept track of cold fronts in Canada like some people kept track of the stock market.

Birdie looked at Poopie. "When are they saying it might hit?"

"They're not," Poopie said. "Your *father* is saying the end of next week."

Birdie calculated. Thinning would be wrapping up then.

"No sense worrying over something that may not happen," Poopie said.

"You're right," Birdie muttered back. But her dad was good at what he did. He never spoke idly. The Darlingtons had field heaters they had bought years ago for the threat of late frost, but most of them were broken or too decrepit to do much good. Birdie had read about farmers setting fires to keep their trees warm, fighting a losing battle against Mother Nature. The universe wouldn't be that cruel, would it?

"Um, this steak's really good," Leeda offered. Birdie had always noticed the Cawley-Smiths liked to pretend nothing was wrong, ever.

Poopie looked at her and sighed. "But you haven't touched hardly a bite."

"Oh, you know, I'm not into A1 sauce," Leeda said. "And I'm becoming vegetarian. Well, I'm trying to stop eating meat when it's rare." Birdie looked down at her own bloody steak. She too had lost her appetite.

"What are you up to for the summer, Leeda?" Poopie asked.

"Well, hanging out with my friends. We'll go on some trips, probably." Leeda tucked a tiny forkful of green beans between her lips.

"Birdie, why don't you make friends like Leeda does?" Walter asked.

Birdie looked at Leeda again, mortified. "Dad, I have friends." She didn't add they were Honey Babe and Majestic and Poopie.

"Five calls to your mother a day doesn't count as socializing."

Birdie put her fork down. "We don't talk five times a day."

Walter eyed her. "I know she complains about me."

Birdie swallowed. She didn't have the heart to tell him that complaints from her mother were nothing new. Cynthia had been complaining to her for years.

"Walter, a girl as pretty as Leeda has got friends beating down her door," Poopie interjected, as though this was a better direction to steer the conversation.

Birdie scowled. Was that supposed to be defending her? Birdie stood up from the table and began clearing plates.

"Poopie, I'll help you wash up."

"You go for a nice walk with your cousin," Poopie said, rubbing Birdie's back and squeezing her shoulder. "I need you to pick some early bloomers for me to put in the vases." With little movements Poopie could usually tell Birdie all sorts of things, but Birdie wasn't quite sure what this one was supposed to mean. Was it, "I'm sorry you're so unattractive"? or, "I agree that your dad is a grumpy aloof shell of his former self"?

Birdie gave Poopie one of her famous grimace smiles and trailed after Leeda onto the porch, then down to the grass and along the driveway. The fields were empty since most of the workers had quit for dinner. The dogs tapped out after them. Birdie eyed her cousin sideways from time to time. It was true. Leeda was pretty enough to knock down doors. And it kind of made it hard not to want to be friends with her. But she was also kind of cold and uptight. Birdie couldn't imagine living her life all buttoned up the way Leeda's was. But for the moment she looked at Leeda with envy. Birdie felt the weight of the orchard's problems like a pile of stones on her chest sometimes, and now was one of those times. Leeda didn't have to worry about anything like that.

Birdie fiddled with the braid in her hair, taking comfort in the cool cotton of her filmy white shirt and the hemp capris her mom had bought her at Squash Blossom in Atlanta. The orchard spread out beyond the porch, looking as bright green and healthy as it ever had. But with its trees so small and so exposed, it was hard to ignore that it was also delicate. And that was what scared Birdie the most.

"Whadda you want to do?" Leeda asked, peering at the scenery beyond the porch with a crinkle at the bridge of her nose.

"We could go to Smoaky Lake," Birdie suggested.

"Um." Leeda's nose crinkle deepened. "How about sitting in the AC and watching a movie?"

The rare sound of a car pulling up the drive made the dogs perk up their huge butterfly ears. A few moments later a rusted-out white El Camino came chugging around the bend, blaring twangy, peppy Latin music and leaving a stream of gray exhaust in its wake. Several people came to the front of the dorms to see what all the noise was about. The engine cut out, and then Enrico emerged from the driver's side, running his hands along the top of the door and then shutting it.

Several workers converged on the car. A couple of the women climbed in. Enrico looked slightly embarrassed. He tucked his hands into the pockets of his gray shorts and started talking to a couple of his friends. He stood a full head taller than all the guys around him.

In the crowd one of the women noticed Birdie up on the porch and walked over, grabbing her hand.

"Come on, Pajarita." *Small bird.*

"Oh nooooo." Birdie pulled back, planting her feet, but Raeka overcame her, and Birdie went trailing along behind her, followed by Leeda.

Raeka pulled her right up to the car, and when she pulled away, Raeka let her go at the same instant, and she went stumbling back into one of Enrico's friends.

"Sorry," she said, looking at him, then meeting eyes with Enrico. "Um." She looked over her shoulder. "Nice car."

"Oh." Enrico laughed under his breath. He looked from her to Leeda, and Birdie waited for him to take Leeda in the way guys did, like she was something the heavens had just spat out like a miracle. But his eyes drifted back to Birdie's immediately. "Thanks, Birdie. It is . . . not that nice. But . . . uh." He tapped his head, looking embarrassed. "Cheap. My English." He shrugged.

Birdie's lips and fingers and toes tingled. She was pleased and horrified that Enrico even remembered her name, though being the boss's daughter, she was hard to miss.

"How much did you pay for it?" Murphy McGowen emerged

from the crowd, sidling up beside Birdie and sizing up the car with her sharp green eyes.

"Seven hundred fifty." Enrico smiled.

"Way too much," Murphy said.

Enrico's smile dropped slightly; now he was unsure. "Really?"

Murphy ducked into the driver's side, looked at the dash, and ducked out again. "It's got over 200,000 miles on it. I wouldn't have paid over three. And by the sound of it it's not going to last you very long."

Enrico stared at her earnestly and thoughtfully. He clearly hadn't followed all that Murphy had said, but he seemed to have gotten the gist. Instead of acting defensive, though, he nodded good-naturedly, taking the information in. Then he looked at Birdie.

"You think I have bought a piece of lemon?"

"No, I . . . I think it's great." Birdie shot a look at Murphy. Despite how mean she'd been to Birdie yesterday in the dorm, Birdie disliked her much more at this moment.

Murphy gave her a "what did I do?" look back and then rolled her eyes to show that if she *had* done something, she really didn't care. Then she looked at Enrico, then back at Birdie, then at Enrico, and something in her green eyes clicked.

Enrico gazed at his car, then nodded at Murphy. "I pay too much. You are right."

"Why don't you two go for a ride?" Murphy suggested, looking from Enrico to Birdie and back.

Enrico shrugged, swiveling his hips toward Birdie and pulling his hands out of his pockets. "You want to go?"

"Um—well," Birdie stammered. Immediately the picture of

her and Enrico riding down Orchard Drive together played like a movie in her head, with Birdie leaning against the window in the breeze and Enrico laying a hand gently on her leg. It sent shock waves up her actual, real leg. Birdie felt her body go ramrod straight.

"Can't. I've gotta get back to the house. Work . . ."

"Oh." Enrico frowned.

Birdie gave him a hard, fake smile and turned back toward the house, walking at a clip. Behind her the car engine coughed to life again. Once it had pulled away, no doubt to be parked behind the dorms, she turned to watch the workers trailing back inside. Only Murphy McGowen stood with her hands on her hips and stared after her.

Once Birdie got inside the house, the phone rang. She could see on the caller ID that it was her mom, calling for the fifth time that day. Birdie chose to screen the call.

Six

Over the next couple of days Murphy steered clear of as much work as possible.

Each morning she listened to the other workers rise at dawn and hid her head under her pillow, waiting for them to go away so she could fall back asleep, trying her best to ignore the blue jay that started chirping as soon as everybody else went out. At night she was too exhausted by the little work she did do to break curfew, which was at ten. She wondered if the fresh air had too much oxygen in it.

Between the time work ended and lights-out, Murphy was free to do what she liked. But unlike the others, she wasn't allowed to do it outside of the circle delineated by the dorms, the supply barn, and the house. She walked this circle endlessly like a caged tiger until she knew every inch of grass on the way from Camp A to Camp B to the Darlingtons' front porch. She'd noticed the way Walter checked up on her from time to time, coming by the dorms a couple of times each evening. She looked for Rex and spotted him once or twice, but he didn't come around the dorms, and their interactions were limited to

Murphy glimpsing him here and there and not getting glimpsed back.

On Wednesday afternoon she was meandering along her usual evening route when she noticed Poopie Pedraza placing a small statue on the railing of the porch. She knew Poopie had just been to the dump, but she didn't make the effort to ask Poopie what it was or if that's where she'd gotten it. The statue looked like some kind of tiny saint—it wore a red cape and had its hands pressed together in prayer. Murphy was staring at the statue and walking, and so she didn't notice Walter Darlington until she was right in front of him.

"I was just coming to find you." Walter was wearing a frayed straw hat with a leather loop around the front, which he tugged slowly as he spoke. "Judge Abbott called to check on your progress." Murphy squinted up at him, her hands over her eyes, not replying. "I told him you have a couple of choices. You can start getting up on time with everyone else, or you can work the hours you miss at midday." Walter paused, making sure his words were sinking in. "He offered to remove you to a road-cleaning crew instead." Murphy continued to squint at him, but Walter didn't seem bothered. "It's your choice," he said, and brushed on past her, his broad farmer's back listing slightly left to right as he walked.

On Thursday morning Murphy crawled out of bed at dawn.

Through Thursday and Friday she spent most of each morning trying to look as busy as possible while doing very little. She stood in front of the farthest trees with her Walkman blaring, tugging occasionally at the peach nubs and then resting her arms. She liked to go back to the farthest trees of the row they'd been told to do that day, where she rarely saw another worker and could turn in a 360 and feel like there was nothing but peach trees leading off the edge of the earth.

Already she felt like the edge of the earth was exactly where she'd landed. Even in the dorms, but especially in the fields, Bridgewater felt like it had to be a thousand miles away. The orchard smelled thick: Scents of mud, buds, insects, and early-blooming flowers overlapped one another. Murphy had spent all her life breathing the aroma of fry grease and parking lot weeds. Squirrels darted up and down the trees, and rabbits and the occasional groundhog watched Murphy work, reminding her that the orchard was the world to them, that they'd never seen Taco Bell and would never be roadkill. It was actually comforting. It was still earth, but without the crap.

Occasionally she'd get a glimpse of one of the other workers down a row, peeping out and disappearing. She paid special attention to glimpses of Leeda, who did her own brand of shirking by picking one hard peach at a time, rolling it around in her fingers gingerly as if it were an exotic jewel, and then gently dropping it to the ground. Murphy watched her curiously, wondering why she looked so tired every day, a little bitter that Leeda was able to do her shirking so openly. Under their feet the piles of hard, raw peaches grew so that you could hardly step without your foot rolling on one. By Friday, Murphy felt her feet rolling in her sleep.

That night, like every night so far, the workers gathered in a group around the barbecue, talking and laughing. Getting up from her third nap of the day, Murphy tugged a pair of cords over her hips and went down to join them.

The air was slightly chilly, and Murphy walked up to the grill, placing her hands palm out. Everyone was still sitting around staring at the fire, talking. Emma and the other women made a place for her, albeit a little less enthusiastically than they had the first couple of days. Murphy could glean a little bit of Spanish since she was taking Advanced French and some of the words were similar. But she was mostly lost. She sat for a while, listening to the buzz of the radio drifting from the windows of the men's dorm and the buzz of voices. Every few minutes someone made an effort to include her, explaining the current topic in a few words of broken English.

"We are talking about the frost," one woman said, leaning in to her. Murphy couldn't remember if she was Raeka or Isabel. "They say we might to get next week. Very bad for the trees."

Murphy nodded, feeling like this might be one of the most boring conversation topics of all time. While the workers continued talking, she swiveled to look over her shoulder and saw Leeda Cawley-Smith picking her way down from the main house, where, presumably, she'd been eating dinner each night. It made no sense to Murphy that she slept down in the dorms. She did everything she could to avoid the people who lived there. Without looking at anyone, Leeda edged to the side of the dorm and disappeared inside.

After a while Murphy stood up and walked to where the light coming from Camp A met the dusk. She lit a cigarette and zipped up her hooded sweatshirt. It was just getting dark, and the crickets had started to chirp. The breeze gave Murphy a tingly feeling in her stomach. For a second it reminded her why she had liked the orchard and how she'd ended up here in the first place. The shadows made it look inviting and cool and restful. She decided to stroll over to the supply barn.

Once she reached the barn, she picked up the phone and stared at the dial pad. She thought about calling her mom, but she couldn't stand hearing more about Richard. They'd been on three dates in the few days Murphy had been gone. If Murphy called next week, it was more than likely he'd be out of the picture by then. So instead, she dialed Max, a hip neo-bluegrass musician she'd met at C.W.'s Smoking Lounge in Macon who was way too old for her. He was an amazing kisser.

"Max, it's Murphy. Feel like spending some time on a farm?"

Two hours later, when everyone in the dorm had fallen asleep, Murphy was sliding out the screen door and trucking through the trees.

She could feel her heart throbbing in different spots—her wrists, her throat, her thumbs. Murphy always liked to weigh the risks of anything she was doing, but in this case she couldn't gauge what they were. She didn't know how vigilant the Nazi dogs were. Or what Walter would do if he caught her a second time. But that was, of course, part of the appeal. Also, zigzagging down the rows of small trees, with her feet sliding on the discarded buds, was different at night. She felt like she might run into Hansel and Gretel. Or Snow White.

"Yow." Murphy slapped at her leg just as she reached the overgrowth that separated the farm from the tracks. A fat, juicy black fire ant clung to her ankle. She slapped it again, smushing it. "Damn."

Murphy had a particular bitterness, and also an admiration,

for fire ants. They were like stealth fighters. They climbed up your legs on tiptoes, knowing you wouldn't notice them, and then when one bit you, it released a pheromone that signaled them all to bite you all at once. Vindictive little suckers.

Murphy jumped back and forth on the ties of the track while she waited, challenging herself to do different tricks—jumping on tiptoe, jumping backward, jumping backward on tiptoe. She smoked another cigarette and waited another hour. It had started to drizzle in a fine mist, and still no Max. He'd probably found some party and bailed. She began the long walk back to the dorms.

As Murphy came along the front of the men's dorm, her body relaxing, she froze. A figure backed out of the door, closing it softly, sneakily. Murphy watched it for a moment, her pulse spiking again, making sure it was who she thought it was. When she was sure, she padded forward and tapped the figure on the back. Leeda shot straight up and squealed, snapping around.

"Oh God, you scared me."

"Shhh. What're you doing?"

Leeda eyed her suspiciously. "What are *you* doing?"

Murphy shrugged with studied carelessness. It drove her crazy to think Leeda Cawley-Smith—of all people—had somewhere to sneak out to while she didn't. "Just stuff," she whispered.

Leeda nibbled her lip. "Oh." They both stood there for a second, awkwardly. "Well, do you want to come with me? I hate walking by myself."

Murphy thought for a moment, mentally weighing a night of being unconscious against a night hanging out with Leeda, which would probably be almost as boring. But she was wide awake and full of energy. The thought of shutting out the night and the sounds of the orchard was depressing. "I guess."

With their heads bowed, the girls started back across the wide, exposed area of grass, looking toward the house for any movement. Once they reached the trees, Leeda grabbed Murphy's wrist. Murphy looked at her quizzically.

"Do you think there are rattlers?" Leeda whispered. From the purplish light still coming in through the edge of the trees, her face was shadowy but mostly visible. Her eyelashes were wide and fluttering. Murphy was pretty sure that her own eyelashes had never fluttered. Not once.

"Oh Jesus," Murphy whispered back. The moon had popped out from behind the clouds for a moment and the bare branches of the trees cast shadows across the footpaths.

"Where are we going?"

Leeda blinked some more and started forward. "I'll show you." They disappeared into the view.

The rows went on much farther than Murphy had ever gone or ever expected to go. It was several minutes before they emerged from the last stand of peach trees onto a sloped grassy hill. The grass became a wide, dark blotch at the foot of the hill, barely distinguishable from the dark lake in front of it, except that tiny plunks of water were bursting all over its surface. Murphy thought she could easily have walked by the lake and never noticed it was there. The girls stood and gazed at it. Murphy wanted to say that it was gorgeous, but she didn't want to say it to Leeda. She had the immediate thought that nobody had ever seen this lake but the two of them.

Murphy sank down onto the grass. Leeda sat down beside her, primly pulling in her knees and tugging the hem of her robe down around her ankles. She peered beyond Murphy's shoulder, then scanned the trees. Murphy leaned back on her elbows and sighed, pulling her hood over her already-wet head, and decided she would have to put this evening in her book of things she never thought would happen, right below being incarcerated at a peach orchard and meeting a person whose first name was Poopie.

A pounding noise behind them made them start and turn around.

"What the . . ."

A large dark figure came bursting out of the bushes before Murphy could get the words out. She and Leeda jumped to their feet. But before Murphy's body could coil enough to run, the figure was across the grass and in front of them, shooting an arm around Leeda's waist and lifting her into the air, her legs flinging up behind her at right angles.

Leeda was squealing and then laughing as her feet hit the ground. Murphy watched Leeda turn around in the guy's hands and push him away. And then Murphy made out that it was the face of Rex looking over Leeda's shoulder at her, or not quite at Murphy but toward her.

"What's she doing here?"

"I asked her to come," Leeda said, breathing hard, looking back at Murphy but also, it felt like, through her.

"Murphy, right?" Rex asked.

"Yeah. Tree nurse, right?"

He turned to Leeda, seeming not to hear Murphy. "Let's go swimming."

"No way, it's not even May yet."

"Ah." Rex turned toward the lake, looking frustrated and restless, then back to her. "But you won't be here in May, and you're here now."

Leeda had pulled her robe tight over her chest and was shaking her head. "I don't have a bathing suit."

"You don't need a bathing suit, Lee." He stripped down to his boxers. "Anyway, you're already wet."

Murphy felt like an idiot. A huge third-wheel idiot. She shouldn't have come. She sank back down under a nearby tree that hung its droopy limbs out over the water and picked at the grass between her legs. She looked up at Rex under her eyelids.

He had a bad boy's kind of body. Finely muscled, with one tattoo Murphy couldn't quite make out just below and to the left of his collarbone. He had a body that would let him get away with things with girls.

Rex and Leeda were talking low and giggling, and Murphy could see that Rex was trying to sweet-talk Leeda into getting in the water. After a moment's deliberation Murphy stood calmly and pulled off her T-shirt. "I'll go swimming." Anyone at Kuntry Kitchen, Bob's Big Boy, or Bridgewater High School could have told them that Murphy wasn't going to take being odd girl out lying down.

She had only a second to see Leeda's look of surprise, her mouth curved in a perfect O, before Murphy dropped her shorts. She stood in her skivvies for a moment, grinning at them, waiting for Rex to do the inevitable breast gaze. But his heavy-lidded eyes moved to Leeda. Murphy waited for them to wander, but they didn't, gleaming as if there was some kind of joke going on that only Rex got. It made her cross her arms over her chest.

"Fine," Leeda said, yanking off her robe or, rather, letting it waterfall off of her to reveal a perfect set of pale green satin panties and a bra. She walked up to the water, held her arms up in the air, and executed a stunningly beautiful shallow dive.

Murphy watched in astonishment, then looked at Rex, who shrugged at her. He still hadn't seemed to notice she had breasts. "That's my girl." When Leeda surfaced, he barreled in after her.

Murphy stared for another moment, then looked at the tree she'd been sitting under. She reached up to the long limb and wrapped her arms around it, pulling her feet to it like a monkey and yanking herself up. She stood on the limb, holding her hands back behind her against the trunk.

"Oh, Murphy, please don't. The lake's shallow. There're rocks in here."

Murphy smiled at Leeda, then took a running leap off the tree, squeezing herself into a cannonball and sailing far, far out. She landed and went under. The water was as cool and refreshing as a gin and tonic in August. She let out her breath and let herself sink to the bottom.

When she came back up, Leeda was on top of her, tugging at her by the shoulders to pull her out farther.

"Oh my God, are you okay? Are you okay?"

Murphy spit water in a big fat stream onto Leeda's face. Leeda's eyes widened for a second, and then she splashed her back, getting Murphy right up the nostrils. Murphy let out a loud "Ha!"

"You scared the hell out of me!" Leeda squealed.

"Ha ha ha." Murphy looked over Leeda's shoulder at Rex.

He had lounged back in the water, fanning his arms out slowly. "We're very impressed," he said, sounding the opposite of impressed.

Murphy scowled at him. But she felt the words anyway and the way he looked at her, like she was small. She turned to Leeda with a forced grin. "I think Dad's mad at me," she stage-whispered.

Leeda looked behind her at Rex, then down at the water. "There's probably all sorts of snakes in here and lizards and stuff. I think I'm gonna get out." As she turned to head to shore, Murphy tackled her waist.

They both went tumbling down, laughing, sending glossy rings rippling across the lake.

Seven

Leeda stretched out on the bank, her wet hair slapping the backs of her shoulders, her chest heaving with her breath. Goose bumps crawled on her skin in the cool spring air. She hadn't been swimming in ages. Lain by the pool, yes. The Cawley-Smiths had summer whenever they wanted, and she'd spent several winter weekends by pools in L.A., Miami, and the Keys. But she didn't really like to get wet, and she rarely swam.

Beside her, Rex had splayed out on his back, holding her hand gently in his, the way he always did, like a big brother letting her know he was there. Murphy splashed around in the cold water, occasionally calling to them. "Hey, guys, there's an alligator, help!" "I've got a cramp and I can't make it to shore." "Oh my God, what's that?!" Duck diving. Back diving in little flips in the water.

Her energy was infectious. Leeda remembered Murphy from school clearly now. She was the kind of girl who had always intimidated Leeda—sharp, strong, acid. There was a small percentage of people at Bridgewater High who weren't interested in Leeda Cawley-Smith in some way. She figured Murphy was probably one of them.

Leeda went to tons of parties. Her friends threw ones where just about everybody invited was nice to look at, there were vodka ice blocks instead of kegs, and everyone fooled around in the bedrooms and passed out. But Murphy was never at those parties.

"Aren't you freezing?" Leeda called.

In response Murphy leapt into the air and sank beneath the water like a pin, then splashed onto her back and stroked to the other edge.

Leeda glanced at Rex from time to time to see if he was watching.

"I think she has more fun doing nothing than I ever do," Leeda said.

Rex was looking at the sky. "I think it's mostly show."

Leeda watched Murphy a while longer, wondering.

"I guess we should go soon," she said, yawning. "Hey, Murphy, are you ready to go back?"

Murphy emerged from the water dripping, looking like a fertility goddess with all her curves. "Sure. Whatever."

They stood up and Leeda shivered, letting Rex put his arm around her and rub her shoulders to warm her up. She led them back through the pecan grove, where the dwarfy, droopy acres of peach trees were replaced by huge stately trunks with crackled, sheathy skins. When they reached it, Murphy let out a breath. "Wow."

"It's pretty, huh?"

"Sure," Murphy said, regaining her edge.

The pecan trees were lined up in two perfect rows. Leeda knew from Uncle Walter that they were at least a hundred and fifty years old and still produced nuts. The Darlingtons had neglected the pecans for years, but in the summers Poopie sent Birdie to gather them and made a mean pecan pie. Leeda knew it was time-consuming to harvest pecans, and for the first time it occurred to her that maybe they didn't harvest them because they couldn't afford to.

"It looks like the land of the giants," Murphy said.

Leeda had never looked at it that way, but it was true. There was something creepy about the trees standing in rows, holding their branches out above them like the marines had held out their swords at her uncle Gabriel's military wedding.

"I've always hated the woods," Leeda whispered. "But I like this."

"This isn't exactly the woods."

"I *know* that. I'm just saying, I don't really like trees."

Murphy squinted at her, her green eyes narrowed. "How can you not like trees? That's like not liking water, or the sun, or breathing."

"She just doesn't," Rex said irritably, squeezing Leeda's arm protectively.

But Murphy didn't acknowledge him. "You have a childhood tree trauma?"

Leeda nodded. Rex knew all her humiliating childhood stories, but Murphy looked dubious. It made Leeda want to defend herself.

"I used to really like climbing trees when I was little." She paused, waiting for Murphy to ask her to go on, which Murphy didn't. "Daddy said it wasn't ladylike and I shouldn't do it, but *you* know."

"Did you have a little pony?" Murphy asked teasingly.

Leeda ignored her. "Anyway, one day I got stuck way up in

one of the trees in the backyard. I called for help, but nobody would come get me down. So I'm traumatized." She finished quickly because Murphy looked bored, and Leeda prickled with annoyance and embarrassment, shutting her mouth in a tight line.

"Well, how long were you up there?" Murphy asked. Leeda could tell by the tone of her voice that she thought the whole thing was silly.

"Forget it." She leaned closer to Rex.

"It was about six hours," Rex answered for her. He always remembered everything.

"Six hours, really," Murphy said, disbelieving.

Leeda sighed, frustrated, seeing very clearly how Murphy saw her and not liking it. "My mom came out on the deck with a drink in her hand and sat for about an hour and watched, but she didn't lift a finger. I was crying and crying and she just watched me and drank." Leeda paused again, remembering the day with the lump in her throat she often got when she thought of things her mom had done to show her how she didn't measure up. "To teach me a lesson, I guess. I was out there way past dark. My sister thought it was hilarious."

Murphy's feet slowed down despite herself.

"I was crying hysterically and then I just stopped and kind of went numb. They sent a maid to get me." Leeda shrugged, trying to downplay it now.

"That sucks," Murphy finally said, sounding contrite.

"It really did," Leeda agreed, and after meditating on it for a few seconds, she added, "I hate trees."

A few minutes later they emerged along the property line,

where there was a rusted, wildly crooked fence lined with bushes marking the end of the property.

The girls sidled up to the bushes and peered over.

On the other side, it was a different world. A huge, rolling lawn, neatly and tightly trimmed, was punctuated with sand traps, bottlebrush, and imported Italian pines. In the distance was a huge clubhouse, lined on either side with enormous, identical stucco houses.

"Where did that come from?" Murphy asked, sounding shocked.

"It's the Balmeade Country Club," Leeda answered. "The owner's a friend of my dad's. Well, business friend. Rex works there, busing tables," she said proudly, wanting badly to prove to Murphy that she wasn't a snob.

Up until a few years ago she had spent much of each summer at the country club pool with Danay, drinking chocolate malts out of huge frosty glasses. The houses were exclusive, overlooking the eighteenth hole of the club's golf course, and Leeda's parents owned one. But she'd stopped going when Danay had left home. And now, with her feet planted in the thick grass of the orchard and the lake water still dripping from the ends of her hair, looking over the fence at the country club was enough to drain something right out of Leeda.

"The owner's such a creep. He tried to feel me up at Steeplechase last year." Leeda thought back to how Horatio had woven up to her last spring, a stirrup cup full of Jack Daniel's in his hand, and stood so close to her that his knuckles kept grazing her chest. He was one of those guys who tried to touch you without you finding out he was touching you. It was also common family knowledge that he had long had his eye on the

Darlingtons' property, though Walter and Birdie skirted the name Balmeade like the plague at dinner every night. Around the Cawley-Smith dinner table the opinion was that Uncle Walter was selling himself short by holding on to a relic like the orchard, and Leeda had always believed it must be true.

"Horatio Balmeade?" Murphy murmured.

"You know him?" Leeda asked, surprised. She didn't think somebody like Murphy would.

Murphy was staring across the bushes like she was looking at a snake. She crossed her arms over herself protectively. "I hate him."

Leeda was about to press further when Rex gave her a meaningful look and interrupted. He pulled Leeda tight to his body and spoke to Murphy over her shoulder.

"I think the Darlingtons hate him too. He wants the farm."

"Uncle Walter would rather die," Leeda said, not sure if she was criticizing him or not. She stared out from the shelter of Rex's chest at the carefully controlled, carefully maintained grounds of the club and tried to imagine that same landscape being where the shaggy pecan trees and the budding peaches and the lake now stood. "But I don't know if he'll have much choice."

Murphy laughed. "So Horatio Balmeade's gonna take up farming?"

Rex shook his head. "He wants to put in townhouses. And extend the golf course."

"You don't know that," Murphy said, frowning at Rex. Rex eyed her, equally annoyed, even though Rex was rarely annoyed with anyone.

"Well, that's what Horatio Balmeade says. Over drinks. To people," he sputtered.

Looking around, it was hard for Leeda to imagine the orchard in financial trouble. It was practically brimming with life. But dinner conversations at the Darlingtons' told a different story. So did the sinking floors of the house and the outdated machinery. "Things are pretty bad," she murmured, agreeing. It was sad, really. Leeda had lived in the same town her whole life, but she realized that having the orchard there had always made her feel like she had some kind of root planted in the ground.

"This place has been here forever." Leeda knew the orchard was one of the oldest in Georgia. While most had either died completely or survived by tacking onto bigger, consolidated orchards (there were four major ones in the state), the Darlington peach orchard had somehow managed to survive. "Maybe they should just declare it a historic landmark or something."

"You think everything's so easy, Lee," Rex said doubtfully.

"It's toast," Murphy said, actually agreeing with him.

Leeda looked at her, thinking about Danay in Atlanta. She would never be tromping around with Murphy McGowen in an orchard. She wondered if the orchard gave Danay that rooted feeling too and figured probably not.

"This is where I leave you," Rex said, tugging Leeda toward him with one hand and giving her a chaste peck on the lips. Murphy watched the kiss curiously and gave Rex a halfhearted wave when he nodded at her before he turned and walked off.

They were standing at the north side of the pecan grove, the dividing line between the orchard and the country club about thirty yards behind them. As they watched Rex disappear into the darkness, Murphy toyed with the idea of asking Leeda what the kiss had been all about. She'd never seen two extremely attractive people kiss with such lackluster abandon. Maybe they weren't into PDA. Maybe Leeda didn't have anything else in her. Murphy was pretty sure that Rex must, but she made her imagination stop at that.

The girls walked toward the dorms in silence, the glow of their dip in the lake fading behind them. The talk about the Balmeade Country Club had been a buzz kill. Murphy had always had a deep distrust for things that were perfect and sterile, like the view over the fence had been, and the fact that that view was connected with Horatio Balmeade was an added down note. The thought that it could spread and envelope the orchard was almost sadistic.

They came at the dorms from the far side of the Darlington house, and Murphy's heartbeat picked up again as they made their way across the front of the house, skirting the circle of the porch lights. Murphy looked at the cloud-dipped moon. It was probably two. Maybe three.

"What's that statue?" Murphy whispered as they passed the stairs of the porch and the railing where Poopie had left her little figurine.

Leeda smiled. "That's one of Poopie's saints. She has one for everything. If you want to sell a house or if you want to get pregnant or if you're in trouble for evading your taxes. Everything."

"Is that a . . . Mexican thing?" Murphy whispered, surprised she'd be asking Leeda a question about a foreign culture.

Leeda shrugged. "I don't think so. Poopie's into everything. New Age. Meditation. Saints."

"Well, which saint is that?" Murphy asked.

Leeda squinted at it. "Actually, that's Saint Jude," she said, obviously proud she knew the answer. Murphy had heard of Saint Jude. Her mom had dated a deacon once. The meaning of Saint Jude was just on the tip of her tongue.

"What's it the saint of?" she finally asked, caving.

They looked at each other, then Leeda bent to brush at her leg. Murphy's eyes followed her hand to the crawling black blotches all over her legs. She gasped at the same time Leeda let out her first piercing scream.

"Oh, damn." Murphy watched Leeda jump up and down on the lawn, slapping at her legs, flabbergasted, then chased after her, trying to slap at the fire ants too.

The lights in the house flared up.

"Yip! Yip yip!"

The door flew open, and the first one out to see what was wrong was Honey Babe, followed shortly by Majestic. And then there was Poopie Pedraza hurrying across the grass in a pink nightdress.

Murphy considered running. She scanned the porch as she looked for the best route. The house lights flicked on and created a wide circle around the statue of Saint Jude, and suddenly Murphy found her answer.

Saint Jude was the patron saint of lost causes.

When Cynthia Darlington was renovating the Darlington house in 1989, she accidentally plastered her birth control compact behind a wall. It was five and a half weeks before Cynthia squeezed out the time to visit the gynecologist, and then it was only to find out that her prescription wouldn't do her much good for the next eight months.

Eight

*B*irdie hoisted her suitcase down the stairs, and the papillons followed her to Camp A, where all three moved onto the couch in the common room.

Birdie had a little thrill running through her as she unpacked her stuff into the bureau that held the TV, though she hadn't felt this when Walter first announced that he wanted her to stay down at the dorm so that she, Majestic, and Honey Babe could keep an eye on Leeda and Murphy McGowen.

The other night, when she'd come downstairs to see what all the noise was about and found Poopie irritably rubbing Leeda's legs with alcohol, the first thing she'd felt was hurt. Birdie had ducked out of sight, feeling embarrassed and left out. It was embarrassing that Leeda—her cousin, whom she'd known her entire life—had snuck out with Murphy, while she, Birdie, had gone to bed at ten o'clock after watching a rerun of *Dawson's Creek*. It made her feel like a freak of nature, an eighty-year-old trapped in a fifteen-year-old's body.

And then Walter had made it worse by sentencing her to the dorms, tearing her out of her comfort space. And here she was.

Only between then and now Birdie had realized that sleeping in the dorms also meant sleeping approximately fifty feet away from Enrico, and that was what made her a little breathless. She looked out the window toward the men's dorm, wondering which was Enrico's window and if he kept his blinds open.

She was leaning onto the windowsill, still looking, when Murphy came in from the field, covered in white dirt, with dry leaves in her hair as if she'd been taking a nap in the grass. Murphy came to a dead stop in front of the couch.

"Hey," Birdie said quietly, forgetting Enrico and blushing slightly.

"What're you doing here?" Murphy asked, her full lips parted as she waited for Birdie to stammer out an answer.

"Um—uh, my dad wants me to stay down here to, um, stay for a while."

Murphy sank onto one hip. "To spy on us, right?"

Birdie swallowed, avoiding Murphy's eyes. Her gut sank. "Um, not spy on you, just to . . ." Birdie searched her head for a euphemism for spying. She looked at Honey Babe, then Majestic, as if they could supply one. Her excitement of a moment before had completely vanished. "I'm going to help. . . ."

Murphy held up her hand in a stop motion, smiling sardonically. "Yeah, okay. Whatever." She scowled at the dogs, at Birdie, then trudged up the stairs.

Murphy had just vanished onto the upstairs landing when Leeda walked in and closed the front door behind her, looking puzzled when she saw Birdie and the blanket-strewn couch. Her trepidation was thinly veiled—very thinly.

"Are you sleeping over?" she asked.

"Dad wants me to stay down here for the rest of spring break."

Leeda's shoulders actually *heaved* in disappointment. She looked around the room, apparently trying to think of something to say, and then finally realized she had nothing. Leeda walked up the stairs too. Birdie could see the backs of her legs covered in brutal red bumps.

Birdie went back to unpacking. Deflated, she shoved her things irritably into the little bit of space left in the bureau and then put her toiletries into the cabinet under the sink.

Birdie felt humiliated. Did Leeda think "keeping an eye on them" was her idea of a good time? But the most humiliating part was that Birdie had *never* snuck down to the lake with anyone, and she lived here. Life was chugging along, and Birdie had never even gotten on the track. She was stranded at the station while people like Murphy and Leeda were actually *living,* moving forward, looking back at her like she was some kind of alien spy.

The thing was, she didn't know how to get out of herself. She just didn't know.

"I don't know," she said to the dogs, who obviously thought she was fabulous either way. It was in their eyes.

She went into the bathroom and saw they were out of cotton balls. Birdie sighed. She made a mental note to get some for Leeda the next time she and Poopie drove the workers to town.

Once she ran out of unpacking to do, Birdie cleaned the kitchen. A few minutes later the women started trickling in, fiddling with the radio and clucking over Birdie's new living arrangements. Birdie sat with her legs together, unnerved by the commotion that she was supposed to live in for the next five days. When Leeda floated down the stairs to grab a snack from the kitchen, they all gave one another meaningful looks until Leeda'd gone back up. Then they started in on Birdie and what a good girl she was, and on how lazy other people could be. Emma raised her eyebrows in the direction of upstairs and squeezed Birdie's knee affectionately as if they—the women and Birdie—were older and wiser and Murphy and Leeda belonged to some other generation entirely. Someone switched the radio to weatherband, which they were all addicted to, though it was all in English.

The radio buzzed with static as they chatted and waited for the Southeast forecast. When Florida was mentioned, everyone quieted down.

Farmers in Florida, Georgia, and Alabama are gearing up for a late frost, scheduled to descend on the Southeast later this week. Temperatures are expected to drop to twenty-eight degrees, a level that for the season's early crops could mean . . .

Birdie pulled her knees up to her chest and rubbed her opal necklace between her fingers. When she looked up, the women were all staring at her. She let out a ragged breath, smiled her grimace smile, and walked out onto the screen porch. There she sank onto the decrepit wicker rocker and rocked back and forth, sweating from the heat of the indoors and trying to quell the rising panic in her belly.

"*Por qué tan triste*, Birdie?"

Birdie looked up. Enrico had his face pressed against the screen so that his nose was flattened back against his face. Birdie could imagine, with his nose smushed up like that, that he wasn't so cute after all and that she didn't want him.

She wiped at the sweat on her upper lip and smiled. "Heugh."

Enrico stared at her. Birdie had meant to say "hi" but then at the last second had decided "hey" was more casual, and it had come out "heugh." She blushed. "Um. *Estoy muy bueno.*"

"*Muy bien,*" Enrico corrected.

"*Muy bien.*" Birdie beamed at him.

Enrico smiled back, not warmly but only politely. He seemed to be staring at something near her mouth. She wiped at her upper lip again.

"I try to find your dad. Do you know where the label maker is? I thought I start that early, for bottles." He was very earnest and all business, his brown eyes steady and not at all sparkly like they'd been last week.

"Oh." Birdie patted her ponytail. After a long day of work she was covered in a gritty layer of sweat and dust. "I think we still need to order them," she said.

"Okay. You let me know when they come?" Enrico smiled tightly. He could have been smiling at her dad.

"Yep. Will do."

As soon as Enrico walked away, Birdie trudged to the bathroom to peer in the mirror and get a glimpse of the Birdie Enrico had seen. She let out a groan.

Where she had wiped at her upper lip, she had wiped a swath of dirt over her mouth so that she had a thick dirt mustache. The only thing missing was a sombrero.

She turned to peer through the rectangular window that looked out from the bathroom onto the path toward the house, where Enrico was still visible for a moment before he veered toward the cider house.

Who could blame him for not wanting to flirt with a chubby girl with a mustache?

She watched him walk away, holding her hand up to her neck, letting her pulse thrum against her fingers.

Over the next few days Leeda's wounds, inflicted by the thirty-seven fire ants that had swarmed on her legs, formed zit-like pus bumps that she tried to fastidiously dry with the rubbing alcohol Poopie gave her. She hid from Rex whenever he was around, ducking back into the trees whenever she saw him walking across the property, which made him laugh while he pretended not to see her. It was just too gross for a guy to see his girlfriend's pus bumps. Leeda knew her mother would agree.

Birdie was like an angel, checking on Leeda constantly in her quiet way, turning the fan on above the couch when Leeda was crashed out watching TV, taping little bags of cotton balls to her door. But whenever Leeda thanked her, she couldn't get her voice to sound sincere. The cotton balls didn't make up for not being able to sneak out anymore, since after dark had been the only time when Leeda had gotten to spend any real time with Rex anyway, and now it was the only time she was willing to let him get close to her at all.

Out in the field that Friday, Murphy and Leeda drifted by each other like they had every morning since the lake—awkwardly, muttering hellos but nothing more. Today they moved down the row in the same slow unison.

Leeda kept glancing at Murphy sideways as she took up her station a few trees away. Whatever strange mood had stolen over Leeda at the lake had vanished the moment she'd seen Poopie in her nightdress and hadn't come back since. She cringed thinking that Murphy had seen her swimming in her skivvies and then cringed harder thinking about the way she'd told Murphy about her weird thing with trees. It was the same feeling she'd had a few times after getting drunk at one of her friends' parties, when she'd wrapped her arms around people, planting sloppy kisses on their faces, begging them to tell her if they really liked her or not. Only at the lake she'd been completely sober.

Murphy, who'd gotten too lazy to hide her laziness, let Leeda catch up with her.

"How're the bites?" she asked.

"Ugly," Leeda said, pointing down to her legs, which had started on a new phase yesterday of itching like crazy.

"Too bad."

Leeda nodded. "Yep." She looked at Murphy's slouch and the way she swatted at the peaches. She tried slouching a little bit too. And then she saw Rex.

"Oh, crap." Leeda ducked behind Murphy as Rex cut a diagonal across the row. He looked their way, rolled his eyes and shook his head, and kept walking.

When Leeda stood up to her full height again, Murphy looked at her quizzically.

Leeda shrugged. "I don't want him to see my pus bumps."

Murphy's lips twisted into an amused grin. "You're not letting your boyfriend see you until your pus bumps go away?"

"No." Leeda knew it sounded stupid, but suddenly it sounded really stupid with Murphy looking at her like she was. "I'm just particular," she offered airily.

Murphy was shaking her head and swatted at the peaches, though Leeda knew she knew they weren't supposed to swat.

"Nah. That's anal," Murphy said matter-of-factly.

Leeda was too tongue-tied to retort. Murphy blinked at her frankly, twirling the bottom of her T-shirt around her fists until two workers walked by and they both turned to watch them. Some of the men and women came to the farm in couples, and these two were holding hands as they walked and talked. They snuck a kiss before separating to their different trees.

"They were talking about the frost," Murphy said. "Sounds like it's definitely coming."

"I know."

"Are they talking about it?" Murphy asked, nodding back toward the main house.

"Kind of." Leeda considered telling Murphy about the long silent dinners. She wished she could explain to someone how Uncle Walter had looked smiling up at her from his desk with his office falling apart all around him. The orchard had broken up his marriage, it had turned him gray, and now it was making him broke. "Maybe it's better for him to get out of farming," Leeda added finally.

Murphy eyed her critically. "It's never better to be forced out of something that's your whole life," she said in a superior, knowing tone that got under Leeda's skin.

"Well, people get what they deserve," she retorted. "If Uncle Walter wasn't so stubborn about selling . . ."

Murphy laughed. "Of course you can say that when your family's loaded."

Leeda opened and closed her mouth, feeling stupid. Then she sucked her bottom lip into her mouth and bit it irritably. Murphy shook her head, annoyed, and walked down the row, leaving Leeda standing there feeling like an idiot.

Leeda scanned the rows for Rex and then walked out onto the grass. She found him kneeling beside one of the tractors with a rag spread out, his old tools laid out on top of it.

She crouched beside him. His skin smelled like tractor grease, which made her scrunch up her nose, but she put his hands on her bumpy calves, and, when he turned his face toward her, she kissed him on the corner of his lips. She was well aware it wasn't like the other couple's kiss at all. Their kiss had been secret, stolen, special. The kiss she gave to Rex was sweet but flat—like a Coke without the bubbles.

Murphy usually knew why she was miserable. She could enumerate the reasons proudly, like a kid counting out birthdays on his fingers, and she liked to enumerate them often. But Friday afternoon she had to search herself for why she felt so dark, and it didn't come easy. With two nights left on the orchard, she blamed it on the fact that her spring break had just about ended and she could never redeem it. Coming to the closing point was a fresh reminder that two weeks had been stolen from her. That was what she told herself, but it didn't ring quite true. It kept nagging at her that since the weeks of hard labor were over, she should feel like a jailbird spreading its wings. And she didn't. She felt like she was about to fly into a window.

She thinned trees that afternoon, hardly noticing she was doing it at all. After her run-in with Leeda she steered clear of everyone altogether, feeling like a menace to society. Before she knew it, the workers were straggling in ahead of her instead of behind her like they usually did. She lingered in her row, watching them disappear, and continued to thin the trees here and there, feeling the emptiness of the rows around her. She finally walked out to the edge of the trees and stood there, looking toward the dorms. She couldn't deal with the sad, worried faces of the workers as they listened to the radio, like they had at breakfast and lunch. They shook their heads at the radio as if they were trying to will the frost away, and it just made Murphy darker. So instead of walking up the stairs of Camp A, she turned right and walked alongside it. There was low brush behind here, Murphy knew, but now that she got close, she noticed a tiny overgrown footpath. She followed it.

The air smelled like invisible flowers. Murphy breathed it in as the trail lost itself a few times, becoming tall grass and brambles, and then sorted itself out again into a little dirt line that wound toward the side of the Darlingtons' farmhouse, ending at an odd little open patch with a trellis in the middle.

Murphy peered around, then touched a few of the bushes, letting her fingers run along the ridges of the leaves while she looked at the different shapes and structures of them and the plants they belonged to. There were rosebushes, azaleas, peonies— none of them blooming yet, all being strangled by kudzu and grapevines. It was like a nightmare garden—the kind a creepy old lady with a bunch of cats would have, Murphy decided. A creepy old lady in an old wedding dress she'd been wearing since being jilted at the altar fifty years ago.

Murphy pulled a cigarette out of the pack in her pocket and lit up, taking a deep inhale and looking at the disrepair of the garden. It only blackened her mood. She was thinking it was typical. People didn't know how to finish what they started.

A rustle came from behind her, and Birdie emerged from the

trail that went toward the house. Birdie stopped, startled, and blushed.

"Oh. Hey, Murphy."

"Hey." Murphy was at a loss for words with Birdie. She looked stricken. Murphy shoved her left hand in her pocket. "This your garden?"

Birdie looked around as if trying to orient herself. "Oh. My mom's." Silence. "I tried to revive it a couple of years ago. But there's too much other work."

Murphy nodded, as if she knew what Birdie was talking about. But she'd never had too much work. She'd almost made a full-time job out of avoiding work of any kind.

"Poopie planted that nectarine tree, but the fruit is always filled with bugs." Birdie looked up at the tree. "She said it'd be a miracle if it ever made a healthy fruit," Birdie added quietly. Again, silence.

"I bet it gets boring."

Birdie looked confused. "Farm work?"

"I mean, living on an orchard in general." Murphy only half believed this. She said it more out of trying to be helpful about the frost thing. Like, *Look on the bright side—your life really sucks anyway.*

"Oh God, it's not boring." Birdie smiled gently and sadly. That was all.

Murphy took a long drag on her cigarette. "So your mom ditched the garden, huh?"

Birdie lost her smile. "She ditched . . . it, yeah." She looked worried, shy, nervous, lost—each expression passing over her face like a cloud. Murphy tried to imagine the layers of crap she'd have to peel away to let people see *her* feelings cross her face that way. It was too many to count.

"Well . . ." Birdie said. "I'm going to get the field heaters ready. We have a few that work." She gave a little half wave. "I'll see you."

"See you." Murphy watched her disappear down the trail.

When Birdie was out of sight, Murphy turned and eyed the garden, focusing on a tiny rosebush that was being devoured by a gang of grapevine weeds. It suddenly offended her deeply. Murphy crouched and started yanking out the weeds one by one.

She lost track of time. When she looked up, it was dusk, and her skin was cloaked in a slight chill. She sank back onto her haunches, her hands covered in dirt and stained in green stripes of chlorophyll. The lights of the Darlington house had come on, spotlighting the inside for the outside. In one of the upstairs windows Murphy could see Birdie's figure clearly. She was on the telephone, sitting in her window. She hadn't noticed Murphy. She was turned toward the fields beyond the dorms, her body looking curved and defeated.

Murphy looked around the garden, feeling like she'd been in a trance, noticing that she'd cleared a large circle of weeds. She let the handful of weeds her fingers were clutching fall to the ground, stood up, and headed back down the trail.

Nine

All the next day the orchard felt like a ghost town inhabited by predominantly Mexican ghosts. The workers drifted from tree to tree, frowning, talking to one another in whispers, and rubbing their hands together. The air was noticeably cooling as the day went on. It sent a chill into even Murphy's heart, which was usually cold enough.

Ghostiest of all was Walter, who lingered on the porch, watching over the orchard with slumped shoulders, looking still and solitary. He stood out as a gray figure, much like the lord of the underworld probably would.

By dinner the static flying through the workers' talk was matched only by the energy with which the thermometer beside the Camp A door dropped, and by nightfall the static had become a steady buzz.

Murphy was thinking about tomorrow, and whether her mom and Richard would still be an item, and how much he'd be around if they were, but she could also feel the frost buzz through her closed door, and it was hard to ignore. Late in the afternoon Walter had had them drag out the few field heaters to the farthest trees, which were the lowest, and where the frost was most likely to settle. They had started their way in the back and worked their way up, so now when Murphy looked out her window, she could see the place where the heaters had run out and there were only solitary trees for the last stretch toward the dorms.

Tap tap tap. *Sniff sniff sniff.* Murphy stood up and opened her door. One of the dogs, Honey Butt or Majestic, she didn't know which, stared up at her pitifully.

"Where's Mama?" Murphy asked. The papillon tilted its head at her.

"You are an ugly dog. But come in."

Murphy plopped back down on the bed and let the dog hop up beside her. Birdie had been running around like a madwoman all day, which was probably why Honey Butt felt deserted.

Murphy stared at her toes. Maybe she had foot fungus. She'd had that once, back at Camp Bright Horizon, which was a camp outside Macon for supersmart broke kids. She'd been able to pick her toenails off then; they'd just painlessly shed in her fingertips. She tried that now, but the toenails stayed. She was interrupted by a knock at the open door. Leeda stood there, her gray eyes unsure and her slate gray silk pajamas shining silkily.

"C'min."

She plopped down on Murphy's bed, making Murphy move her feet.

"What're you doing?"

"Trying to figure out if I have toenail fungus."

She thrust her feet out toward Leeda, who surveyed them casually, trying to impress Murphy with how unsqueamish she could be. Murphy stretched farther to touch her toe against Leeda's thigh. At the last minute Leeda bailed, shoving at her calf. "Ew."

"It's too nerve-racking being in my room. Everybody's so tense."

Murphy nodded. "Yeah."

Leeda reached out and stroked Honey Butt's back, which made Honey Butt let out a whimper for sympathy.

"The dogs are obsessed with Birdie, aren't they?"

Murphy shrugged. There was a long silence while Leeda seemed to try to think of some other topic of conversation. Murphy, in a rare act of generosity, provided one.

"I can't wait to get back to my life."

Leeda blinked a few times. "Me too."

Murphy tried not to feel jealous of anyone, but sometimes she still did. She was jealous, right now, that Leeda had a mom who neither dated high schoolers nor very married men. That Leeda could go home and not have to wonder if Richard from Pep Boys was going to be parked on her couch. That Leeda had friends to go home to, where Murphy only had guys who would leave her lying on train tracks for Walter Darlington. And that Leeda actually *did* look forward to going home, while Murphy was only lying.

"Poor Birdie," Leeda offered.

"Yeah." Leeda looked so thoughtful, her eyelashes doing the fluttery thing again, and it made Murphy regret how snotty she'd acted the day before. She shifted on her bed awkwardly.

"Well, I wonder if they'll make us do much work tomorrow," Leeda said, standing up.

"Probably not if all the trees are dead," Murphy joked.

Leeda half-laughed obligingly. "Rex says it'll be a while before they know if the frost has done any damage."

"I guess he knows everything."

Leeda's mouth tightened. "He's a great guy."

"I'm sure he is," Murphy said. She didn't know why she'd said what she'd said. She couldn't stop herself sometimes.

Leeda stretched her long, pale arms over her head. "I'm gonna try to get some sleep. See you."

"See you."

The whole thing had the air of a final good-bye to it, though they would see each other Monday in AP Bio. Leeda disappeared through the doorway.

Murphy listened to her radio for another hour, doodling in a book she'd brought by Nietzsche. When she moved across the room to turn off the light, she froze. Her breath drifted out in front of her in a tiny white cloud.

Murphy's heart sank. She turned out the light and crawled under the covers thinking of poor Birdie and how life just kicked people when they were down.

A few minutes later she was staring at the ceiling that she couldn't see in the dark when an orange flicker sped its way across the wall. Murphy thought she was imagining it until it happened two more times. The third time she sat up and looked out the window, and her heart stood still.

There was Birdie Darlington, dragging something huge and heavy out of the supply barn and down between the trees, where she heaved her whole body forward, plunging whatever it was on top of an enormous fire. Lit by the firelight, Murphy could see that Birdie's face was tear streaked and red. Murphy watched, entranced. Birdie had lost it and she was burning down all the trees.

Birdie stared at the flames for a minute, then launched into a run again toward the barn, emerging a few seconds later with a broken wooden chair. She dragged it to the next row of trees, looking back and forth, trying to gauge the distance.

Murphy realized she was wrong. Birdie wasn't trying to burn the trees down. She was trying to keep them warm.

Murphy was paralyzed. It was perhaps the saddest thing she'd ever seen in her life. Birdie's body was graceless as she hauled and dragged whatever she could carry into the rows of trees. It was pure survival and clearly a losing battle. From Murphy's high window Birdie looked small and foolish and awkward, and Murphy knew there was no use searching herself for the cynicism that would make it seem distant and dark instead of raw and terrible. Birdie was trying to save her home single-handedly, and there was no way she could.

Murphy sank against the window, her forehead pressing against the glass, and tried to let it go, the way she let it go when she drove past an abandoned dog or saw a news spot about something she couldn't do anything about. She imagined every-one else in the dorms was doing the same thing.

And then a figure appeared beside Birdie—taller, leaner, and more muscular. When he got close to one of the fires, Murphy saw that he was one of the guys from the men's camp. He said some-thing to Birdie and then raced into the barn, and then Murphy could hear feet pounding down the hall outside her door.

Murphy opened the door and watched the women rush past and disappear down the stairs. The screen door below slammed. Leeda stood in the doorway opposite her, looking confused.

"They're trying to save the orchard," Murphy said, at a loss. Leeda didn't say anything back.

Murphy walked into her room and to her window. The workers had poured out into the trees, and several small fires had popped up now, all randomly spaced apart, like stars on the ground. It was beautiful. It was like fireflies.

Murphy stood for several minutes, having a heated argument with herself, her heart in her throat. She wanted to help. And she wanted to keep driving. She wanted to belong with people who helped one another. But it was so foreign that she needed to convince herself that she could.

Finally she decided it would hinge on Leeda. If Leeda had the nerve to go down there with all those people, who had worked through the two weeks while she and Murphy had slacked, then Murphy would too. Murphy's ears perked, listening for her to come out of her room.

After a few more minutes Leeda's door creaked open, and Murphy heard her walk down to the bathroom. A minute later she came back down the hall, and her door creaked again behind her, closed. There was the faint sound of bedsprings creaking as she crawled into bed.

Maybe Leeda couldn't see herself down there either.

Murphy closed her door. In her bed, she watched the fire lights dancing across the ceiling until she fell asleep.

Ten

$\mathcal{B}$irdie tugged up the waist of her jeans, which were threatening to slide off her sweat-slicked hips, and landed on her knees on the grass. She shifted around onto her butt, slumping back against the nearest tree, and peered around at the damage they'd done.

It was almost morning. It wasn't a shade lighter than night, but the animals had started moving around, the birds had started chirping, and it smelled like day.

A few of the workers were still shadows straggling up and down the rows of trees, tossing this and that dead limb, or piece of farm debris, onto the fires scattered at intervals down the white sand trails. A few branches were smoldering. And the fires themselves were beginning to burn out. But the night was over. And they were out of fuel. There wasn't much more they could do.

Birdie's dad had come out to supervise only briefly, looking so depressed that Birdie thought they should set a fire at his feet so he wouldn't freeze too. And then he had gone back inside. The workers, on the other hand, who had no ownership in the orchard and had a million other places they could work, had stayed all night. Over the past half hour the majority of them had begun to straggle inside to bed, many stopping to hug Birdie and kiss her on the cheek before disappearing across the grass. Birdie just couldn't believe how good people could be.

And also how disappointing.

Neither Leeda nor Murphy had emerged from the dorms, and this befuddled Birdie. She hadn't noticed their absence until the past half hour, when the work was calming down. But now that she had, she couldn't help but feel let down. "Whatever," she muttered. They'd be gone by tomorrow, and Birdie didn't care anymore.

A few minutes passed, and soon the last figure left was the first that had come out to help Birdie. She watched Enrico from her spot by the tree, sure that she was hidden, and admired the way his arms worked over the fires and how his shirt was soaked in sweat. That sweat had all been for her orchard, and that made it that much more mesmerizing. She stared at him, willing him to see her.

And then he turned and started walking toward her, and she realized he'd known she was there the whole time.

Enrico sank down beside her, onto his knees like she had, then into a cross-legged position.

"Birdie, I think you must be Supergirl," he said, giving her an exhausted smile. He swiped at a smudge of ash beside his eye. "You are very strong."

Birdie shook her head and stammered. "Oh—oh no. I don't have a choice, you know. But you guys . . ." Birdie felt choked up. She was too tired to be embarrassed, though, and she simply let her voice trail off.

Enrico, who appeared equally incapable of being awkward at

the moment, let out a long, serious breath, his smile fading. "You have choice. Your dad choose to go to bed, no? You choose to try." He shook his head. "You are crazy."

"Oh." Birdie shifted uncomfortably at the thought that Enrico might be criticizing her dad and her, but he quickly set her at ease by moving on.

"Not everyone is as, um, strong . . . not everyone cares like you. That is it."

"Well, everyone else cared enough to help. You cared enough . . ." Birdie offered, not seeing what kind of strength he was talking about. She knew she was a big girl. She had brute force—but she wasn't sure she wanted Enrico pointing this out.

But Enrico looked at her very seriously. "Birdie, they do it because of you. I do it because of you. Maybe you don't see this." Birdie was speechless, so he continued. "My mom say things like this. She say I am a thoughtful guy, smart, good guy. I don't see it. I just think, I am . . ." He searched for the English words he needed. "Normal. But maybe it's better to believe good things when you hear them."

Birdie smiled. "Take a compliment."

"Yeah." Enrico nodded solemnly.

"Maybe." Birdie swiped the sweat off her face and then stopped.

Enrico looked concerned. "What?"

"Um." Birdie stared at him. "Um. Do I have a dirt mustache?" Enrico looked at her for a second and then started laughing. Like the time in the cider house, she felt like he wasn't laughing at her, just with her. So she started laughing too.

"See. What girl would ask this? Crazy."

Birdie had always thought of herself as the opposite of crazy. She thought she liked being crazy, the way Enrico said it.

When he stopped laughing, Enrico looked at her for another moment and then stood up.

"Temperatures go up today, no?"

Birdie nodded. "Yeah. I think so."

"When do we find if peaches are okay?" Enrico asked, dusting the grass off his butt. The way his body twisted while he did this, making the muscles of his shoulders stand out, made Birdie achy. But then his question settled in, and she was filled with fear.

"Not till they ripen," she said. "And we start to pick. In June."

Enrico nodded. "I leave for Texas tomorrow."

"Are you coming back?" Birdie asked, trying not to sound too agonized.

"Yes. I will see you then." He reached out his hand and Birdie took it, letting him pull her up. Then he shook it. It was a quick, hard shake, and Birdie suddenly felt he was distant again, even though he hadn't gone anywhere yet. "Bye, Birdie."

She squeezed his hand back. "Bye."

As she watched him walk away, Birdie considered going after him, in a way that they did in the movies. She pictured calling him and running up to him and just planting a kiss on him. She envisioned him turning and walking back and planting one on her. She imagined sneaking into his room in a few minutes and kissing him then.

But the farther away he got across the grass, the more glaring it was to Birdie that a lot could change between April and June. He could come back with a girlfriend. Or not come back at all.

She trailed far behind him and paced outside the dorms for

several minutes, meditating on the third movie option. She even walked up the stairs of the men's dorm. But really, she was kidding herself. She didn't even come close to going inside.

She decided to take a walk through the orchard to clear her mind. She ended up at the pecan grove and then beyond it, at the edge of the country club.

The sun had just laid the first orange slices on the horizon. It lit up the manicured grounds of the clubhouse on the rise, the rooftops of the condos in the distance, making the country club look a bit like Disney World. Birdie had been to Disney World, but she'd never liked it. It didn't feel like real life.

The view was enough to make a person think that God was smiling on Horatio Balmeade. He would never have to worry about frost, unless it might kill his imported pine trees, which had no business being in Georgia in the first place. A person could assume that his club would never have any problems, that it would always be perfect, and that at some point it was inevitable it would swallow up the mess of the orchard.

But Birdie saw it differently.

She took it as a good omen that the sun, though it was shining on Horatio Balmeade and all of his glittering property, was the exact same color every morning. That is, it was the exact same color as peaches.

In 1976, two teenagers were making out to the sounds of Sonny and Cher in an unplanted orchard field when they were struck by lightning. Both survived, but from that time on, the boy, Richard, who went on to work at Pep Boys, claimed to have a mental connection to the airwaves that enabled him to predict whenever "I've Got You Babe" was being played on the radio.

Eleven

Though April wandered on into May with heavy showers and scattered thunder and the rain in Bridgewater continued relentlessly for almost fifteen days straight, it was bright and perfect on Danay's graduation day. Which, Leeda figured, was the only way God would have it, since apparently He too loved Danay best.

The Cawley-Smiths and Brighton's family, the Wests, ate at Nikolai's Roof after the ceremony—which had a 360-degree view of Atlanta and a bunch of hot Russian waiters. Leeda sat in a strapless, flowy GSUS dress she'd bought in Buckhead the day before. Her legs had returned to their usual creamy white milk-and-honey complexion, with nary a fire ant scar in sight. Her hair was perfect, and the few freckles she'd picked up working at the orchard a month ago had faded. She looked perfect, but of course nobody, aside from her friend Alicia who she'd brought from Bridgewater, noticed.

While the adults talked with one another, Leeda and Alicia gossiped.

"How's Rex?" Alicia said, raising her eyebrows suggestively.

Alicia always wanted to talk about him, as if Rex were the most fascinating subject of all time. It made Leeda feel possessive, proud, and bored all at the same time.

Leeda shrugged. "He's good. Working at the country club and the orchard. I hardly see him."

"Too bad. He's worth seeing."

Leeda smiled halfheartedly. The first few weeks she and Rex had dated, she'd definitely been infatuated with his looks, his body. But she'd sort of stopped seeing that after a while. It was like it had faded into the background. Which was probably what had happened for Rex too. She wondered how he saw her now.

"Alicia, do you think I'm anal?"

Alicia shook her head. "No way. You're just particular."

Leeda eyed her friend. Yesterday at Lenox she'd chosen almost the exact same dress as Leeda had after she'd seen Leeda try it on.

Leeda sighed. She was leaning toward mostly bored.

The conversation had turned to the weekend, when the Cawley-Smiths were having a graduation dinner for Danay at their most upscale hotel, the Bridgewater Plantation View. The name Horatio Balmeade drifted across the table.

"You guys aren't inviting him, are you?" Leeda asked.

Her dad was dipping into a platter of beluga caviar. "Of course we are. Horace is a good friend of mine."

"Daddy, I can't stand him."

"All the more reason to learn to like him. He's been a good business partner to me."

Danay was rolling her eyes as if this was the same old crap, different day. Leeda's mom was nibbling on the caviar with a glazed-over expression.

"Dad, he hits on me. I hate it."

Mr. Cawley-Smith glanced at the Wests with embarrassment. "Leeda, that's enough. You're exaggerating. He thinks you're a nice young girl."

Leeda's blood began to simmer. She rearranged the silverware in front of her. Next to her Alicia shifted uncomfortably, then excused herself to the bathroom. Danay took the opportunity to sidle up beside her sister.

"So have you started your speech yet?"

Leeda wiggled farther into her seat. As maid of honor, she was supposed to plan a speech for the wedding reception. But she couldn't imagine having to get up in front of all those people and ooze over her sister, on top of all the people who were already going to be oozing all over Danay.

"It's coming along," she muttered.

Danay's lips parted in an excited smile. "What about the bachelorette party?"

"Um." Leeda hadn't even thought about it. In fact, she'd kind of forgotten that was her job as maid of honor.

Danay grinned, squeezing her wrist. "Well, I know it's supposed to be a surprise and everything, but I think it would be fabulous if we did it here in Atlanta. I'd like to get that Fur Bus around the city." Leeda winced. The Fur Bus was, as the name suggested, a bus covered in fur, lined inside with strobe lights and disco balls, that tooled around the city while its riders got drunk and rowdy. Leeda hated drinking and motion at the same time. "And I love the desserts at the Ritz;

I love Xavier Salomon. Dancing would be good. I hear Compound is great."

"But I won't be able to get in."

"Oh." Danay frowned. "That's right. Damn."

"And no strippers, Leeda, please," Mrs. Cawley-Smith added from across the table wryly.

"Mom, don't be gross," Leeda growled.

But Danay and her mom were giggling, like they were suddenly women together.

"I don't even know why you're having me plan the party if you already have it all planned out yourself."

"Leeda, really," Mrs. Cawley-Smith said. "It's Danay's night. It should be perfect. Don't be such a baby."

"You know." Leeda put down the spoon she was playing with and pushed her chair back from the table. "Maybe it would be better if I got out of your hair. You're so *in sync*. I could just spend the whole summer in New York. Or with Uncle Walter and Birdie. I could plan the party on my laptop."

Lucretia blinked at her a few times. And then she smiled. "I think that's a nice idea." Before Leeda could say more, her mom leaned behind Danay's back to look at their dad. "Leeda wants to spend the summer at Walter's. What do you think?"

"Leeda, that's great."

Leeda was a bug paralyzed by a spider. She wanted to say she hadn't meant it, but her pride wouldn't let her. Her chest ached.

She whipped out her cell phone. "Do you have their number?"

•   •   •

That night, Leeda lay in bed thinking about Murphy McGowen. She hadn't thought of her much since the orchard, outside of the first few awkward days in Bio, when they'd both tentatively established that although they had known each other for a while, they didn't know each other now.

Leeda wondered what Murphy would have done in the same situation with her family. Not keep her mouth shut. Not lock herself into something she didn't want to do. But Murphy was this full person. Leeda was mostly empty.

She rolled over and stared at the clock. It was 2:13 A.M. Leeda wanted to go swimming in the lake. She wanted to do something daring, something that made her feel like she wasn't this perfectly controlled mess, but a real, messy mess.

A few minutes later, not wanting to wake her parents with her car, she hopped on Danay's old Trek to ride over to Rex's.

She'd never ridden a bike through town in the dark, much less through Rex's side of town, which was empty at this time of night except for the rows of fast-food joints and the lines of traffic lights, blinking aimlessly, red yellow green.

She parked the bike on the edge of Pearly Gates Cemetery and then lifted his basement window open and slid in silently. He didn't wake up. At home, Leeda had just pulled jeans on under her silky tank top, so now she just slipped out of them and slid silkily into his bed.

Rex started, shrinking back against the wall.

"It's me," Leeda whispered, planting a kiss on his warm, soft mouth.

"God, Lee, you scared me."

"Sorry." Rex's body was toasty and relaxed, his hair was

messy, and his body felt more fragile than it usually did—a little defenseless with sleepiness. Leeda snuggled into it like an old T-shirt. "I just wanted to see you."

She nuzzled up against his neck and kissed him just beneath his jaw. He began kissing her back, first on the top of her head, then on the lips.

Leeda let him pull her tank top off and run his hands lightly over her body. This was all they had ever done. Rex had always been the perfect gentleman.

"Rex," she whispered, stopping his hands. "You're working in the orchard for the rest of the summer, right?"

"Yeah, why?"

"Well, I kinda told Daddy I was going to spend the summer there."

Rex sat up, incredulous. "Why'd you do that?"

Leeda sat up too. "I just don't want to be around them this summer. And they don't care if I'm around or not. So I might as well be at the orchard."

"Oh, Lee." Rex put his palm to his forehead, laughing softly.

"What?" Leeda frowned.

"Lee, you're so spoiled sometimes."

Leeda scowled. "What does that have to do with anything?"

"When did you pull this diva maneuver?"

Leeda frowned. "At Danay's graduation."

"I see."

"Rex, you're supposed to support me." Leeda pulled her tank top on. "You don't understand. They don't love me like they love her." Leeda stood up to leave, but Rex touched her back.

"Come 'ere." He took Leeda's wrist and pulled her gently

back onto the bed. He kissed her on the corner of her lips and then on the cheek. "Just tell your parents tomorrow that you didn't mean it."

"I can't. I already called Uncle Walter. I can't take it back."

"Good one."

"Rex."

"Lee, look at your spaghetti arms." He waggled her wrist, making her skinny arm wiggle. "You weren't made for picking peaches."

"I'm leaving."

"Okay. Bye."

This was something Leeda hated and loved about their relationship. Other guys who liked Leeda would do anything to keep Leeda from freezing them out, but Rex was never intimidated by her ice-queen routine. He slid back down on his back.

"C'mon. Lie down with me awhile. It doesn't matter. What were you going to do with your summer anyway?"

"I don't know. Go to France. Get pedicures." This was the problem: Leeda didn't have things she loved doing. Rex loved working with his hands; Danay loved school. Her cousin Birdie loved small dogs and peaches.

"See? Maybe it's a good thing."

Leeda relented and lay down. Rex always made her feel better and worse about things. Usually because he told her the truth. She let him pull the covers around her and wrap his muscular arms around her shoulders.

"So will you keep working there?"

"Sure. Whatever."

"Thanks, Rex."

She lay beside him for another hour or more until she was in that dreamy trance state where cartoon-like scenes played themselves out in her mind—Danay riding the Fur Bus, Rex sitting with her on Tybee Beach, and the endless motion of Murphy and Birdie thinning the peach trees, plucking the buds and dropping them on the ground.

Birdie laid down her fork and took a sip of sweet tea, smiling at her mom. Cynthia looked fabulous, dressed in a bright red summer set, her hair freshly trimmed in a freshly tinted bob. On the orchard she'd always looked unkempt.

Cynthia made the sign toward the waiter for the check.

Liddie's Tea Room was one of the most old-school and most popular restaurants in Bridgewater, with tiny round tables that were always full of loud women who sat practically on top of each other. Cynthia had to lean toward Birdie to be heard.

"Don't worry about it, honey. That orchard's been dying for years. It'll be nice for it to have a fresh start. Have you lost weight?" Cynthia fiddled with her red beaded necklace.

Birdie took a bite of the salad plate her mom had ordered for her before she'd arrived and tried to talk herself out of the stomachache that was gathering below her ribs. Hearing her mom talk so casually about the orchard made her feel like it was already lost. And it also made her feel melodramatic for feeling that the whole thing was ripping her in half. Her mom made it sound so ordinary.

"I've heard Mr. Balmeade is going to have the man who did Howl Mill do the condos. They're beautiful. Who knows, in a couple of years maybe we could move into one on the very same spot as the house!"

Howl Mill was the gated community Cynthia had just announced she was moving into, which had obviously started the lunch off on a low point for Birdie. When she'd told Birdie she was coming into town and asked her to pedal out to Liddie's to meet for lunch, Birdie had thought maybe she was reconsidering the divorce. Now it seemed it was just becoming more concrete. Cynthia couldn't stop talking about it.

"No grass to take care of. No anything. The management does it all."

"That's great, Mom." Birdie took another sip of sweet tea, biting lightly on the straw. She was trying to imagine this was the same woman who'd trucked in the mud getting the tractors— which were older, more run-down, and more ornery every year—ready for spraying. When she was a kid, they'd had a huge picnic and a tug-of-war, and Cynthia and Birdie had been on the same side and the last to let go on their team. And then Cynthia had given up, plopping into the mud, and it had just been Birdie, who was no match for the other side. They'd dragged her clear across the middle line.

"And you can move in as soon as I do. It'll be perfect. I'm planning on August fifteenth, which gives you a couple of weeks to get situated before school."

"But, uh . . ."

"You'll love your room. It's lofty. And there's a place for the piano and your cello—like a *conservatory*," Cynthia drawled.

"I think that's when Danay's getting married, Mom." It was the only protest she felt like she could voice.

"We'll send a nice gift."

Birdie sighed quietly. She had no desire to move out of her house. She couldn't even imagine what her dad would do without her. She just didn't know how to tell her mom that.

"I'll bet the place is a mess, isn't it? I know you've got Poopie, but one woman isn't enough to take care of that man. . . ."

Birdie listened and nodded as her mom went on and on about Walter, then about how she loved having her own place, how she'd gotten into yoga, and how if Birdie could avoid it, she should never get married. She asked her about her schoolwork and the summer and how she planned to spend her time.

On her way over, Birdie had pictured spilling to her mom about Enrico, the way the girls on *7th Heaven* and Tampax commercials seemed like they might do. Several times she started to mention him and then stopped.

After the check came and went, Cynthia swept up and smoothed back her hair. Birdie stood up beside her. "Tell your dad he needs to get those papers back to me, okay, hon?"

Birdie held her hand to her stomach protectively, touching the soft fabric of her nicest shirt. They walked out into the parking lot. "I'll call you soon, sweetie."

"Yep."

When she got home, Birdie went straight to the study, Honey Babe and Majestic trailing behind her and taking up their post by the door. She looked at the piles of papers on the desk, squinting at them as if there were some solution her dad just wasn't seeing. She shuffled through bills, then looked over the profit-and-loss statements, getting confused by all the columns and numbers. She wasn't very good with figures anyway. She wasn't into things she couldn't touch with her hands.

Birdie knelt on the floor, trying to organize what was there. The old natural disaster insurance form was buried underneath a stack of papers beside the trash can. She wondered if she should renew it, just in case, behind Walter's back. She held it up, then dropped her forehead into her hands. She stuffed the corner of the paper into her mouth and bit it without having any idea why.

"What'd your mom say?"

Birdie looked up and yanked the paper out of her mouth. She swallowed. "She said you should send her the papers."

Walter looked at the carpet, studying it, his shoulders sagging.

"Right."

Birdie stayed on the floor a long time. If her dad had given up and her mom had given up, then how could she hold things together on her own?

She crumpled up the insurance form and lobbed it at the trash. It went in, nothing but net.

As usual, Murphy was late for school. She rattled through the pantry for a box of Froot Loops, eyeing her mom's bedroom door, which contained her mom and Richard. She sank onto one of the kitchen chairs to eat a few handfuls straight out of the box, staring at herself in the bathroom mirror, which she could see from where she was sitting.

The door cracked behind her. *Damn.*

"Hey, Richard."

"Hey, Murph."

"It's Murphy."

Her mom appeared behind him, stroked his back, and smiled blissfully. "Well, next time I want to hear Sonny and Cher, I'll check with you," she said low, and giggled. She looked at Murphy, noticing for the first time that she was there, then looked at the clock. "Murphy, you better get going, baby—look at the time."

"I know. I know."

Murphy hopped down the front steps and into her car. "Bring on death," she said out loud as she turned the car on. It gave its signature rattle, loud enough to announce to the classes in session at Bridgewater High School that she was arriving at 9:10.

To make itself look like a big modern facility instead of the podunk dump that it was, Bridgewater High School had installed a huge tiered fountain at one corner of the building, engraved with some words in Greek. Everyone had long since forgotten what they meant. Murphy tossed the last of her handful of Froot Loops into the water as she passed by it and pushed through the double doors into the hall, making her way down to Brit Lit.

Mr. Meehan taught the class, and he had a major crush on her. He only nodded quietly at her as she slipped into the room and into her desk.

Her textbook was full of little drawings she'd done—of food (when she was hungry), of band logos, of herself, and more recently, of peach trees, which she couldn't get out of her head.

She was a subpar artist, but she practiced a lot. She searched for an empty, relatively large space and started sketching a baby tree, with the white stuff wrapped around it and a pair of hands making it secure.

Mr. Meehan droned on about the Wife of Bath and Murphy sank onto her hands. She never listened in class since she much preferred reading on her own. She used class time as a kind of brain vacation. Behind her, Allan Brewer, who she'd let touch her boobs in tenth grade, pushed on her bun from behind and whispered, "Beep beep." She lifted her hand behind her back and gave him the finger.

On their way out of class, Allan caught up with her. "Hey, Murphy, why'd you flick me off?"

"That's what I do to people who annoy me."

"Listen, I'm having people over tonight...."

"And you're wondering if I can come over so you can give me whiskey and Gatorade and try to feel me up. At which point I'll smack you."

"You're right about everything but the slapping part." Allan grinned.

Murphy came to a stop. Down the hall Leeda was walking with the usual flank of three or four girls who dressed like her, ate like her, and talked like her. Murphy leaned against a locker, casually, and decided to talk to Allan until Leeda'd passed. She always felt weird seeing Leeda and usually liked to pretend she didn't see her at all, even in the class they shared.

"So listen, since I'm friends with you, do you think I can get a free oil change?"

Murphy frowned. "What are you talking about?"

Allan frowned back and gave her the old nudge. "Since your mom's hooking up with that guy from Pep Boys."

Murphy felt all cramped up inside. How did everybody find out about everything?

"Shut up."

Allan made a sex face and started slapping an imaginary butt. "Oh, Jodee. Oh God."

Murphy smiled hard at him. "Can I look at your binder for a sec?"

"Sure." Allan handed it to her, grinning too.

Murphy opened the binder, then started ripping out the pages, one by one.

"Hey, what the hell?"

Rip rip rip.

Murphy backed away as he grabbed for his stuff and continued to rip and rip until every page had come out, cascading down around Allan's shoulders and through the hall. When she was done, she shoved the binder against him. Around them everyone in the hall had come to a standstill, including Leeda, whose gray eyes were huge and shocked.

The only movement was Mr. Meehan plowing toward her.

"I don't need an escort," Murphy said, and pivoted in the direction of the administration office at the end of the hall.

"Murphy, do you know what your grade point average is?"

"Yep. It's when they add up all your grades and divide them by the number of classes. Sure do."

"Four point oh. That's perfect. That's the highest anybody can hope for. There's no four point one."

Murphy rolled her eyes. If Mr. Lafitte, the principal, had to speak to everyone this slowly, it was no wonder she had a four point oh.

"Do you know how hard some people in this school work to get grades as good as yours?"

"Nope." Murphy didn't care to know. She nibbled at a hangnail on her thumb. She picked at the run in her stockings and fiddled with the zipper on her short skirt.

"Look, Murphy, I know you have some problems at home. I just want you to know if there's anything you want to talk about, that's why we have a counselor here."

Murphy stared ahead blankly.

"I'm not going to suspend you. I could." Mr. Lafitte looked at her meaningfully. "I'd be the first to admit that nobody's perfect. But it seems to me a lot of people have cut you a lot of slack. We have a lot of faith in you. I think it's time you paid us back by readjusting your attitude. Senior year could be your time to shine."

Murphy eyeballed him blankly, in the manner of a dead fish.

"You'll need to re-create Allan Brewer's binder from scratch. You guys will meet every day after school to go over it until it's done. Got it?"

"Yep."

"And if I see you back here again in the minuscule amount of time that's left before school's out, things will get a lot more serious."

"You bet."

Murphy walked back down the hall, her arms crossed over her chest, feeling like a powder keg. All the class doors were closed, and she could hear the drone of her AP Bio teacher talking about the lab today, which he'd explained yesterday would involve trucking down to the freezer by the cafeteria to retrieve the dry ice being stored there.

Murphy kept going. She ducked into the empty darkness of the A/V room and leaned against the wall inside the door, throwing her head back. She let out a deep breath and stared at the row of TVs and movie equipment. On the wall were posters for *Star Wars, American Beauty, Casablanca.* Standing directly across from her was a knee-high replica of Yoda, a full-size Darth Vader mask propped on the table beside it.

Murphy stuck her thumbnail in her mouth and smiled.

Date: May 18

Subject: Murphy McGowen/Darth Vader

From: MAbbott@GAjudicial.gov

To: DarlingtonPeaches@yahoo.com

Walter,

If you read Sunday's paper, you've seen the picture of the Bridgewater High School fountain. It's hard to get a sense from a photo, Walter, but Miss McGowen really outdid herself this time. My wife was actually the first person to see it—you know she does part-time work at the administration office. She said she nearly jumped out of her bloomers when she saw Darth Vader's head up there on the top tier of the fountain, looking like it was just hovering, surrounded by clouds of white smoke.

They figured out pretty quickly that it was dry ice making the smoke and Darth Vader's head had been taken from the A/V room. I hear Veda Wilkes Teeter actually thought it was an alien. You have to admit, the girl is sharp. Not Veda. Murphy, I mean.

Anyway, I'm writing to discuss Murphy. The school office has contacted me, and I've taken the liberty of contacting her mother. Seeing as the spring break arrangements seemed to work out, how about an extra pair of hands for the summer? I don't know if Miss McGowen's more trouble to you than not, but I thought you might be able to use the help. God knows she could use the attitude adjustment, and maybe a summer's worth of hard labor will do the trick.

What's the word on your peaches?

Let me know.

MA
Judge Miller Abbott
Kings County District Court

Twelve

Georgia hadn't had such a hot June since 1951. All over Bridgewater, you could practically hear air conditioners busting from overuse. All over the orchard, you could hear the creak-creak of the trees drooping in the sun.

Leeda started sweating as soon as she stepped out of her car. She noticed immediately that Murphy McGowen's beat-up yellow Volkswagen, which she'd finally connected with her in the lot at school, was parked on a swath of grass a few feet away. And the first person she saw when she rolled her huge suitcase into Camp A was Murphy herself. She was splayed out on the couch, her right leg hanging over the back, her left hand dragging on the floor. When she saw Leeda, she lifted her head slightly and just said simply, "You."

Leeda didn't need to ask why she was here. Everyone in Bridgewater knew about Murphy's prank with the fountain. After laughing their asses off, all of Leeda's friends had started making fun of Murphy, saying what a burnout she was. Then they'd moved on to Murphy's mom and the different stories they knew about her: She'd shown up to parent-teacher conferences in black leather shorts and a lace halter top; she'd been seen making out with some guy on the picnic table outside Toodles Honky Tonk at three in the afternoon. Then they'd speculated that Murphy McGowen was as much a hopeless case as Jodee. Leeda had felt differently. She hadn't said it, but she'd thought the prank was pretty ingenious.

But now, standing under Murphy's cool green gaze, Leeda just threw back her shoulders and pasted a look of boredom onto her face. "Hey, Murphy."

The whole gang was already here, the same ladies from the spring, along with a few new faces. Everyone greeted Leeda with cool politeness as she yanked her suitcase up the stairs one step at a time, and down the hall.

She stared at the empty room and felt her resolve waver. And then her pride reared up, causing red-hot tears to pop out along the edges of her eyelids. She unzipped her suitcase and dragged out all the comforts she'd brought from home—pictures of her friends, a photo of Rex in a silver Tiffany's frame, one of her mom and dad, a Swarovski crystal swan her mom had given her for her birthday last year. Danay had picked it out.

The next morning Leeda rolled out of bed at dawn with every-body else and stumbled out onto the lawn to await the big talk from Uncle Walter. She hadn't noticed the night before, but the smell engulfing the orchard was heady and sweet. The trees had sprouted green, droopy leaves, and of course, peaches dangled like bubbles—bright orange and everywhere. The peaches all looked fine from where Leeda stood, but that wasn't saying much. What meant more was that her parents had said that *Walter* was *optimistic*—two words that didn't fit together in Leeda's mind. Word was that the first few peaches had been culled, and that there was no sign of brown rot yet, and that the Darlingtons were planning to move forward with the summer harvest in the hopes that the rest of the peaches would follow suit.

Still, if it was possible, Uncle Walter looked even older than he had in April, the gray at his temples having grown up the sides of his head like fungus.

Standing up on the porch beside Walter, Birdie looked the opposite—she looked fresher, a little thinner, and excited. Her eyes scanned the group in front of the porch frenetically. Leeda looked behind her to see who Birdie might be looking for. Instead, her gaze landed on Murphy, skulking in the back, dark circles under her eyes and her arms crossed around her waist.

Leeda turned back around, pulling her fine-mesh sun hat tighter down over her eyes to keep the glare from giving her a migraine.

"We'll be picking Empress, Sunbright, Springprince, and Candor for the next two weeks," Walter droned flatly, "then we'll move on to Goldprince, Summerprince, Gala, and Rubyprince. Birdie will take you out and show you where to get started. We'll harvest the trees in three rounds—please be careful about picking only the ripe peaches on each round."

Leeda felt like he was speaking Greek. Coming out of his mouth, the colorful names of the peaches sounded like a joke.

"Pick up your harnesses by the supply barn. That's also where the bins are and where some of the women have already set up their tables to start sorting. Dump your peaches there and

Poopie will give you your tokens to mark how many bushels you've done."

Walter paused for a moment, looking uncomfortable. "Thank you to all of you who helped with the fires in April. We'll be checking the peaches as they come in for signs of brown rot. If this harvest is successful, it will be thanks to everybody's hard work." Leeda picked at her nails, uncomfortable with the memory of the night of the fires. It hadn't been one of her shining moments. She didn't really have shining moments. Walter's mouth turned down slightly, and the rest of him turned and walked back into the house.

Birdie looked around. "This way," she said, so low Leeda had to lip-read to make out what she'd said. But everyone followed anyway.

Leeda, uncomfortable in the crowd, walked up beside Birdie.

"You're supposed to go work at the sorting tables," Birdie said. Just as she did, Murphy caught up.

"Hey, Birdie, what do the tokens mean? Does that mean I have a quota I have to pick?"

"Murphy, you too. Most of the women are at the sorting tables because it's easier. The stronger women pick if they want. Poopie'll explain everything to you if you go over there."

"Walter doesn't think I'm a stronger woman?" Murphy demanded, her curly dark hair flying around her ears as she walked.

"Well." Birdie looked wide-eyed and nervous again. "You're *small*."

"Whatever. I'm picking peaches."

"Murphy . . ."

"It's my choice, right?"

"Yeah, but . . ."

"I'm picking."

Leeda looked between the two of them, tensing up. "Well, if Murphy's picking, I'm picking."

Suddenly Birdie stopped in her tracks and gave both of them a death glare. It was the first time Leeda had ever seen such a look from Birdie, and it surprised her so much she stumbled back a foot.

"Fine. Whatever." Birdie threw up her hands, then walked on ahead of them, leaving both of them to follow her.

Murphy looked at Leeda. "See, you pissed her off. Your cousin's a total powder keg."

Leeda scowled at her back as she walked on ahead. Birdie wasn't a powder keg. She wasn't even a firecracker. She was maybe, at most, a sparkler.

It was past nightfall by the time Birdie started toward Camp B, her last stop of the day. She strapped on her Tevas and stepped off her porch and onto the front lawn, swiping her arm across her face to rub off some of the sweat that had gathered on every bare inch of skin, making her feel like a salamander. Honey Babe and Majestic nipped along behind her, catching bugs in their teeth.

The crickets chirped at her from the trees as she dragged across the grass, more exhausted than she'd ever been in her life, and also more drained. Her mom had always done so much with the workers—getting them settled in, getting them supplies for picking, keeping an eye on the different areas to see if everything was running smoothly. Birdie was sure she was a poor substitute. She hadn't spoken to Enrico once, one-on-one, since he'd arrived back at the farm. He'd been part of the group she'd led to pick the Springprinces, but they'd barely met eyes. And Birdie had been so focused on combing through the peaches, looking for signs of rot with her paring knife and a worried flutter in her throat, that she had hardly noticed.

But now, on the stairs of Camp B, she tightened her ponytail and stuck her sweat-slicked hair back behind her shoulders. She rubbed the sweat off her face one more time, her heart pounding, and looked at her dogs. "Stay." And then she took the last couple of steps and knocked on the door, calling through the screen. *"Puedo entrar?"*

One of the men, Fonda, appeared at the door and pushed it open slightly, smiling.

"I just want to make sure you have everything you need." Birdie stepped in and the door hissed closed behind her. Immediately, she was bowled over by the foreign smell of the dorm. It smelled like *men*.

Birdie could feel herself blushing. "Is everything okay? *Necesita más?*"

Fonda just smiled at her and shrugged, then turned and led her into the common room, which was disgusting compared to the women's—the couch was in a shambles with cushions lying all over the floor, empty beer cans and soda bottles were strewn about, a pair of tighty whities lay across the top of the TV. Five or six guys were sitting on the floor, a card game spread out in the middle of them. Everyone was covered in the same glistening layer of sweat. Enrico wasn't among them.

"You can check," one of the guys said. "I think we have everything."

"Okay, well . . ." Birdie took a step backward, thinking that she would just take their word for it. The dorm felt too manly for her to be standing here. It felt like she'd invaded forbidden territory.

She glanced down the hall and swallowed. "Well, maybe I'll just take a quick look. . . ." The men's house was much bigger than the women's, with a long downstairs hall that held eight rooms, four on either side. It was filled with a blue glow from a light that was coming from one of the open doorways. Birdie padded down the hall, peeking in through the door as she passed.

Enrico was lying on the bed by the window, watching a tiny TV, his arms glistening beneath the sleeves of his T-shirt.

His eyes shot up to hers and widened. "Birdie." He sat straight up, looked around, and straightened the covers around him. He ran a hand through his hair, which was all messy.

"Come in."

Birdie shuffled in and took the seat Enrico offered beside him on the bed.

The room smelled better than the rest of the house—more like boy than man. His bed smelled like boy. It was beginning to make her giddy. She peered around the room nervously—noticing several books lying all over the place, open and facedown—then glanced up at the TV.

"What're you watching?"

"*The O.C.*"

"Oh."

At the moment a local commercial was on. *"Are you tired of riding around in that old hooptie? Come see the Credit Doctors, where we make buying a new car easy."*

Birdie tried not to laugh, but a small snort slipped out. Enrico shoved her playfully on the shoulder.

"You think I drive a hooptie?"

"I can't believe you even know the *word* hooptie."

"I know many English words," Enrico said, grinning at her.

In an effort to look casual, she leaned back so that her back curved and her head rested against the wall.

"Here, pillow," he said, holding up a pillow as if it were a lesson. *"Almohada."*

"Almohada," Birdie repeated.

He settled the pillow down behind her head.

"Thanks."

Then he lounged back beside her.

"This girl is very pretty," he said, nodding to Mischa Barton on the TV.

Oh. Birdie sized up Mischa. She was skinny, for one thing. And delicate. Birdie wondered if she was his type.

They lounged like that until the end of *The O.C.*

Birdie thought she should go, but she couldn't get herself to move. She stayed through the mini–news update and still didn't move. They stayed put through the next couple of shows.

During each commercial break Birdie tried to think of something to say. She'd look at Enrico and he'd look at her, his eyebrows rising expectantly, and then, when she didn't say anything, he'd turn back to the TV, unconcerned.

Their thighs touched a few minutes later, but Enrico pulled his away.

Finally the nine-thirty news came on, and a hot weight descended on Birdie's chest. The news was hardly a pretense for staying. She could feel Enrico's breathing change from slow and deep into a nervous, uneven rhythm. His arm pushed against hers gently, almost imperceptibly, so that the fine brown hairs on it tickled her. Birdie listed ever so slightly to the left, toward him. She studied what she could of him sideways—his tan legs, his hands. . . .

Her elbow came to rest on his—just slightly.

He sat up. There was an open Coke can on the windowsill, and he leaned forward and grabbed it, taking a sip. Then he started playing with the mouth of the can with his thumb and forefinger. Birdie watched his fingers make the slow circular motions. She had a vision of him cutting his thumb on the lip of the can. She would kneel beside him and put a Band-Aid on it for him and then look up at him and they'd just move toward each other easily in a kiss.

"Oh!" Enrico jerked his hand into the air. A thin trickle of blood ran down not his thumb, but his forefinger.

"Oh." Birdie shot up. Did she have ESP? Telepathy? "Um." She felt her stomach flop nervously. "Let me get a Band-Aid for you."

She hurried down the hall to the first aid box hung by the door, grabbed a bandage (the pinky kind), and walked back slowly, knowing she'd been given a sign and if she let the moment slip past, she would be pathetic in the eyes of herself and the fates.

Enrico was still sitting on the bed. He had the edge of his forefinger in his mouth. Oh God.

Birdie walked up to stand directly before him. She pulled the outer wrapping off the Band-Aid. Enrico looked up at her under his eyebrows.

"Here you go!" On reflex, she tossed the Band-Aid at him across the few inches of space. It fluttered madly, listing sideways and landing on the floor. Enrico bent down to pick it up, awkwardly.

"Thank you," he said, looking at her unsurely, like she might have lost her mind.

"No problem." Birdie watched him peel off the waxy white strips and apply the Band-Aid, realizing at that moment it was the wrong size and didn't even cover the cut.

"Thanks," Enrico said again.

Birdie shifted from foot to foot. "No problem."

The discomfort between them was so thick Birdie felt she could step forward and bump her head on it. The skin under her armpits was tingling and itching. Finally Enrico stretched his arms back, which pushed his ribs forward against his shirt. "Well, I am going to bed, I think."

Birdie could have been knocked over with a feather. "Oh. Oh yeah. Sorry."

Enrico's dark eyebrows descended worriedly over his pretty eyes. "I am just suddenly tired," he said, smiling nervously. "See you tomorrow."

"Yeah," Birdie said, blushing. "Sure. Good night."

Enrico closed the door behind her and Birdie walked down the hall, feeling like her body might sink into the cracks in the cool, creaky wooden floor and drip down into the dirt underneath.

When she stepped out onto the porch, she put her hand to her forehead and muttered, "Why?"

When she looked up, her dad was at the bottom of the stairs.

"What are you doing?" he demanded.

Birdie froze. "Um, just . . . making sure everybody has what they need. What . . . are *you* doing?"

Walter relaxed a bit. "I came to look for you. I need you to come up to the house at five tomorrow morning. I need some help in the office."

"Okay, Dad."

"Birdie, I don't want you in the men's dorm. It was all right when you were a kid, but . . ." His mouth settled into a thin, awkward line. "I'll take care of it from now on."

Birdie swallowed. "But I wasn't . . ."

"You should be in bed."

"Okay."

Walter turned his cheek for Birdie to kiss. She did and then headed toward Camp A. But she didn't go to sleep.

She flopped into every angle, hoping to find one that would send her off to sleep. She turned so that her head was at the foot of the couch.

She'd never felt more desperate for someone to talk to. And there was no one. Not her dad. Definitely not her mom.

It seemed like whatever had been building in her since the spring was making it impossible to stay inside herself. It was too big to contain.

Leeda was lying on her bed, her feet up on the wall with the door open to catch the breeze. She was resting her sore muscles and facing the facts. She was never going to make it this summer. That was the facts.

The day had been hell, picking peaches all morning, dropping them into her harness basket, carrying them, dumping them. She hadn't seen Rex all day. She'd gotten a fifth of the work done that anyone else had, and she'd actually *tried*. She'd wanted the workers to start being nice to her again, like they had at the beginning of spring break. But at this rate, that seemed impossible.

The air was so sultry that she was covered with sweat. She'd never felt so hot and miserable. Leeda rolled off her bed and pulled on her turquoise silk robe. It was almost ten. Not too late to call home and ask them to come get her. Leeda got up, feeling the ache in her muscles, and decided it was the only way.

By the time she made it down to the front stairs, she could already feel the softness of her huge pillow-top bed and the little plastic straps of the pool lounger pressing gently into her suntanned skin while she sipped a sloe gin fizz brought up by the help. She tip-toed past the couch, where Birdie appeared to be already sleeping. The dogs perked their ears at her as she creaked out the door.

She forgot to think about critters lurking in the grass as she rushed across the lawn toward the supply barn. It didn't even occur to her someone else would be on the phone until she saw Murphy hunched over the box in the dim glow striping the grass from the light on the Darlingtons' porch. Leeda came to a stop and waited for Murphy to turn around, but apparently she hadn't heard her.

"It's *our* house, Mom. I live there too." Murphy had the phone tucked between her ear and her shoulder, and with her free hands she was scratching at the soft skin on the insides of her forearms with nervous energy. Her voice crackled and cracked, like someone on the verge of crying from sheer frustration—contradicting her body language, which was strung out and defeated.

"I don't want him using my stuff," she said coldly.

Silence. And then, "Fine. Whatever."

Murphy slammed down the receiver and, to Leeda's shock, plopped down on the grass and began ripping up handfuls of grass, throwing them over her left shoulder.

Leeda felt like a voyeur, like she was seeing Murphy naked. She tried to take a silent step backward.

Murphy jolted and looked in her direction, swiping quickly at her eyes. She took so long to gather herself that Leeda thought she should say something.

"Are you okay?"

"How long have you been standing there?" Murphy finally growled.

"Um, just a second?"

"Ha, right." Murphy snatched up another handful of grass, gripping it this time instead of throwing it. "Don't you have a life?"

Leeda scowled and crossed her arms. "Don't flatter yourself. This phone's for everybody."

Murphy rolled her eyes. And then she began sifting the grass between her fingers, almost seeming to forget to be mad.

Leeda softened again. "What's wrong?"

Murphy ignored her. She reached into her pocket as if looking for something, then pulled out her empty hand and sighed. She looked up at Leeda. "Jodee's having a guy move in."

"Oh." Leeda didn't know what to say. Jodee McGowen had always sounded like an exotic creature to her—someone definitely not of the same species as the Cawley-Smiths. It was hard to think of any sort of comforting words about somebody like that.

But Murphy didn't seem to be hoping for any. "I can't believe it. Every time I think things can't get worse, they do." Murphy shook her head.

Leeda searched for something to offer. "How long have they been dating?"

Murphy laughed under her breath. "Like, two seconds."

Leeda didn't know what to say. She wanted Murphy to know she wasn't too sheltered to get it. "God, I know, my sister and her fiancé only dated for six months. And now they're getting married. It's *so* weird."

Murphy stared at her incredulously. "I'm talking about my *mom*."

Leeda stiffened. She was only trying to help. "Well, maybe you should try to be happy for her," she shot back.

Murphy laughed. The laugh sounded like rocks in a rock tumbler. "It'll crash and burn like everything else. My mother is so predictable."

"You don't know. Maybe it'll work out."

"You don't know my mom."

Leeda felt like she did, a little, from everything that she'd heard. She certainly knew Jodee better than Murphy knew Lucretia Cawley-Smith, but what could she say?

"It sucks, Murphy. I'm sorry." She waited for Murphy to come back with something rude, but instead she just slumped over. Again, Leeda got the voyeur feeling. She never would have imagined that Murphy could look so defeated or that she would want anyone to see her that way. It was like seeing a hermit crab without a shell. Rex had shown Leeda one once at the pet store, which he'd dragged her into, and it had looked all wrong.

"God, I hate this. I hate her. Life is not enough for her unless there's some jerk around to treat her like crap. And she rolls over for them. A guy comes in, and suddenly it's his house, and ..." She looked up like suddenly she realized she was talking out loud, and her eyelids drooped. And then she leaned to the left, peering beyond Leeda's calves. Leeda turned to look.

A shadow was crossing the grass toward them.

Birdie stopped several feet away, her dogs at her feet, her hair down from its usual ponytail and all ratted up around her face. Leeda's first instinct was to check her watch, knowing they were out past curfew. She started to pluck up an excuse.

"I've been looking for you guys." Birdie swiped the ratty hair back, but some of it stuck to her temples wetly. She looked very serious and nervous, and her chest rose and fell unevenly. Which made what came out of her mouth next sound out of place, and funny, and formal. "I was wondering if maybe you'd take me to sneak out."

Leeda looked down at Murphy, who stood up and brushed herself off, eyeing Birdie suspiciously but also with a slight smile creeping onto her lips.

"I know you think I'm a spy," Birdie said. "But it's not my fault." Her big brown eyes scanned their faces. "If I don't do something ... I don't know...."

Leeda didn't know why, but she felt the decision was Murphy's, as if some kind of unspoken agreement had already been struck between them, and they were two against Birdie's one, and Murphy was the boss of the two.

"I'm going to explode," Birdie blurted, making them both look at her again. She blushed. "Seriously," she added. "I thought you guys might ... help...."

It took a few seconds, but Murphy's face took on an amused, eureka expression. Like of course Birdie was here to sneak out. And of course she, Murphy, got that. Murphy transformed in front of Leeda like a hermit crab getting its shell back. She was suddenly the girl from that night they'd gone swimming, tough but irresistible. "I told you," she said, pointing to Birdie but looking at Leeda, "this girl is a powder keg."

"I know where we can get some booze," Birdie offered. And then her eyes widened in surprise, as if a lightning bolt might strike her. But it didn't. There wasn't a cloud in the sky.

"You guys, I've gotta take them. They'll start barking if I try to lock them up."

"Oh God," Murphy said. "Let's go."

They had already made it halfway across the orchard when Murphy realized Honey Babe and Majestic were still trailing them. The dogs had stopped when she'd turned, while they were still several feet behind, and now they both tilted their heads at the same exact angle, looking at her woefully as if they sensed her hatred.

"They look like cartoons."

Birdie smiled sappily. "I know, aren't they cute?"

"Damn yippers," Murphy said. She glanced at Leeda, embarrassed about her little breakdown by the phone. But Leeda seemed to have forgotten it, and already she felt she was recovering impressively. With her mom, mental distance was best. Sometimes her guard went down, but it never took long to resurrect it.

It helped to have a distraction.

"We have bichons," Leeda whispered, "because they're

non-allergenic. Danay's allergic. I don't like dogs because they lick."

Murphy and Birdie both looked at Leeda quizzically.

The orchard smelled thick, even thicker than it had in the day, maybe because what little breeze there had been had died. Murphy felt like she could get a toothache from breathing the air, it was so sweet. Leeda, who'd insisted on going back to the dorms for a flashlight this time, shone her Maglite on the trees and the ground, searching for danger. It looked to Murphy like a disco.

"Can you stop with that thing? You're gonna get us caught."

"Hey, look!" Leeda hissed.

The beam had paused on one of the trees, lighting a section of it in a big white circle. A tiny brown bird sat on the branch, but it wasn't moving. They all stepped closer.

"Is it dead?" Murphy asked.

Birdie laughed. "It's sleeping."

"Sleeping?"

They all crept right up to the tree, Birdie leading the way. The bird was perched on one foot with the other tucked into its belly, its eyes closed.

"Shouldn't the flashlight wake him up?" Murphy looked at Birdie. She felt like she had to be careful—like a thin thread was holding Birdie with them and she didn't want to break it.

Birdie shook her head. "They sleep through noise and light but not motion. So if a snake or something comes after them, they wake up."

"Wow." Murphy's hand shot out and shook the branch slightly. With a squawk the bird shot off the branch and flapped away. Birdie and Leeda looked at Murphy, who looked between both of them for a moment and shrugged. "Sorry."

Murphy skipped ahead of them toward the lake, peeling off her tank top and then stopping to take off her shorts. She felt like she hadn't seen the lake in a hundred years. She hadn't realized that it had become epic in her mind.

"Ah, it's great." Leeda quickly stripped down too, to her silky hip-slung boy shorts and demi-bra, and walked up to the edge to dip a toe in. Birdie hovered self-consciously behind her.

"Watch this," Murphy said, climbing the tree from before.

"Oh, Murphy, please . . ."

Murphy ignored Leeda. There was nothing she could do to hold her energy back. The feeling of the lake she'd gotten the first time she'd come seemed to have intensified exponentially in the heat of summer, and Murphy couldn't contain herself. And maybe it was partly that all the energy of being angry had to be transferred somewhere.

She cannonballed.

Birdie walked up beside Leeda, making sure not to compare herself to either her willowy cousin *or* curvy Murphy, who had surfaced onto her back, breathing hard.

"Thank God. This feels incredible." Murphy sighed.

"Did your feet touch the bottom?" Leeda asked. "Is it slimy?"

"Was it slimy last time?" Murphy asked. Leeda frowned at her.

Underneath her clothes Birdie wore a tankini she'd changed into at the dorms. She pulled off her shirt, then shimmied out of her knee-length dungarees, glancing at Leeda and Murphy shyly.

She felt dazed and hopeful and happy. Birdie couldn't believe that she had just foisted herself on her cousin and Murphy, and that it had been so easy, such a nonevent. She had sought them out once she'd seen Leeda sneak out of the dorms, with her pulse pounding. And now she couldn't understand why it had seemed so risky.

She looked around to make sure Honey Babe and Majestic were settled and accounted for (Honey Babe was itching his back on the grass, Majestic was biting at invisible bugs), and then she jumped in.

When she popped up again, spitting water, Murphy was doing laps, and Leeda was sitting on the edge of the lake, letting her legs loll so that the water was up to the bottoms of her knees. Honey and Majestic had both come to the edge of the lake and were sniffing at the water.

Honey put a paw to the water gingerly, then pulled it out and shook it.

Murphy paddled up and rested her elbows on the grass beside Leeda's thighs.

"Come on, Leeda."

"Mm, I don't think so. . . . If Rex were here . . ."

"Are you guys together?" Birdie asked, feeling left out. She knew Rex was the guy her dad had hired part-time for odd jobs. She knew he was very meticulous and very easy on the eyes and that was about it.

Honey Babe whimpered.

"Yeah," Leeda said casually, swirling her feet in the water, seeming a world older than Birdie.

"So, Bird, do you ever bring guys down here?"

Birdie shook her head. "Nah." In the silence, it hung in the air. "My mom and I used to have picnics down here. I come down here alone a lot."

"My mom would never be caught dead eating sandwiches where the bugs might get on them," Leeda said.

"She sounds like you." Murphy splashed water onto Leeda's knees.

Leeda scowled, but Birdie knew Murphy was right. Leeda was the spitting image of her mom in a lot of ways. She had the same habits and manners. But it always seemed to fit a bit awkwardly on Leeda, like the wrong pair of clothes.

Murphy drummed on the ground with her hands. "Being with *my* mom is like watching makeover TV. Every time she meets a new guy, it's like she's looking in the mirror and they lift the curtain and she goes, 'Ooh, I'm beautiful!'" Murphy did the imitation, clasping her hands. "And then she cries a lot. Then the guy dumps her and she's back to the ugly duckling."

Leeda cleared her throat uncomfortably. So did Birdie. Murphy's face fell for a moment.

"You know, she dated that guy Horatio." Murphy looked from Leeda to Birdie, blinking. "Balmeade?"

Birdie nibbled her lip. She remembered her mom and dad talking about some woman Mr. Balmeade was seeing on the side. They'd talked about her like she was a joke.

"He told her he was getting divorced. My mom wouldn't date a married guy. Well, a married guy who was *happily* married . . ." Murphy looked unsure. "I mean, that's bull probably. She'd probably hook up with anybody with two legs and a heartbeat. Of course," she continued, "he dumped her eventually."

Birdie didn't know what to say. Apparently neither did Leeda. Murphy tugged out tufts of grass from beside Leeda's leg. "The difference between me and my mom, I guess, is that she gets used by all these guys. For me, it's the other way around."

"Well, whatever works . . ." Birdie ventured. She felt in her heart it couldn't work, but maybe she was just naive.

"Oh my God." Leeda pointed to the water. Honey Babe had come around to where the shore angled into the lake at its lowest and was pushing away from the shore, paddling his minuscule legs.

"Honey!" Birdie laughed. Majestic, always the follower, was creeping in after him.

Murphy and Leeda both chuckled. "That is the most ridiculous thing I've ever seen," Murphy said, deadpan. "I didn't know your dogs had it in them."

Honey Babe and Majestic were now side by side, paddling slowly toward Birdie, their giant ears bobbing in rhythm above the water. They looked like tiny synchronized swimmers.

Birdie laughed, loud and long. For the first time in a long time, she didn't have the sense that life was passing her by. Whatever had been building up in her didn't disappear. It also didn't explode. It stayed the same. But inside, Birdie felt like she expanded. For now, she was big enough to hold it.

Thirteen

Murphy wiped the sweat off her forehead and reached up to pick another peach, tightening her grip around it and plucking it off its branch with a tiny snap, then lightly pressing it in her hands before dropping it into the basket harnessed to her front. It had been a couple of days since the girls had snuck out to the lake, and since then she'd been working harder. Not for Walter or for Darlington Orchard, but because of Birdie.

She could see her through the trees, talking to a pair of workers by the house, looking unsure of herself as usual, her big eyes thoughtful. Murphy ruminated that she might be the first really nice person Murphy had ever met and actually *liked*. It was something about the way she was so sweet but so rugged when it came to the farm stuff—knowing all about the farm and the animals, like with the sleeping bird the other night. Yesterday she'd driven by in a rusted-out red tractor, spraying the trees. She was sweet. But she wasn't soft. Murphy could respect that. And she had the uneasy feeling that she didn't want to let her down.

Leeda, just down the row beyond two men, seemed busier

too, though it was pretty comical watching her work. She liked to put each peach to her nose and sniff it, then wipe off the fuzz, then look at it as if it were a work of art, then drop it into her basket. Freckles had popped out lightly on her pale shoulders and across the bridge of her nose, and her hair was a sweaty mess, which she constantly tried to straighten out. It made Murphy smile.

Emma stood on Murphy's left side, picking steadily and expertly, passing up the less-ripe peaches for the ones that were ready for harvest. Murphy hadn't gotten the hang of that yet.

She tried to watch Emma sideways to get her technique. When Murphy actually put effort into something, she liked to do it right. But Emma caught her and smiled. It was quite a switch from the coolness with which the women had treated her at spring break.

"The trees are so crooked," Murphy said, dumbly trying to cover up why she was staring. "It looks like someone wrestled with them. *Estan*"—she searched her mind for the word for ugly—"*feo.*"

Emma smiled bigger. "We clipped the branches for the new branches to grow."

"Oh." Murphy stared.

"New peaches no grow on old wood, you understand?"

Murphy looked at the tree anew and traced the branches with her eyes. She could see how it was sort of beautiful, all the places the tree had been sliced for the new bits of it to grow, creating awkward, stooped angles in the limbs.

"Doesn't it seem like trees should be able to grow on their own, without all our help? You know, Mother Nature and all?"

Emma just shrugged and went back to work. Murphy looked up at her tree again. Rex was standing on the other side of it, grinning at her.

"You have a problem with Mother Nature now, Murphy?" His eyes danced, amused. She hated his constantly amused expression.

"Well." She hoisted her basket tighter against her. "I always pictured Mother Nature as this wise, nurturing woman, didn't you?"

Rex shrugged.

"But now she sort of sounds like my mom. Scattering trees that won't grow right on their own, and spending the rest of her time eating Mallomars on the couch and going to Chili's Bar & Grill to smoke and meet guys." Murphy had actually come up with this comparison a couple of days ago, when she'd meandered back to Cynthia Darlington's garden for the first time since being back on the orchard. The weeds she had pulled had already rerooted and grown back, and Murphy had tackled them again, as a kind of vendetta. She'd gone back yesterday to do more work. She'd probably go back today. It would bug her if she didn't.

"Well, you know we're all doing our best," Rex said.

Murphy rolled her eyes. "Right."

Rex raised his eyebrows. "Don't think so, huh?"

Murphy scowled at him. "You know what, actually." She tugged on a twig. "I really don't care. People want to believe they're one thing and really they're another. My mom thinks she's Aphrodite and she's really Medusa. It's not worth thinking about." She felt like she came off really well saying this.

But Rex's eyebrows remained raised. "Then why are you so pissed off?"

Murphy shot back. A million reasons came to her mind in her defense. "Because—"

"Because if you didn't care, you wouldn't be so pissed off," Rex interrupted.

Murphy blinked at him. He was still smiling.

"I loved Darth Vader, by the way," he said. "It was classic."

Already he was backing away with a relaxed lean in his step. Down the row he leaned to whisper something into Leeda's ear, who'd been watching them, and she slapped him on the thigh.

For some reason, it made Murphy's spirits sink.

Leeda caught Murphy's eye and gave her a bit of a tentative look—as if she was wondering if they were really friends yet or strangers again.

Murphy didn't have an answer for her. She didn't know.

Midafternoon, Leeda hauled her second bushel of peaches toward the bins outside the supply barn, where Birdie and Poopie and most of the other women sat in the square of shade cast by the small droopy building, sorting the peaches into two categories: flawed and flawless. Leeda opened the bottom of her harness gently, which released the peaches into the bin, and then sank forward against the table with a sigh, resting her palms on its cool surface. The air wafting out of the barn was blessedly chill, stale, and sickly sweet with the smell of old metal and old wood. Coming from the white-hot rows between the trees, it felt like being doused in a cold drink.

"Do you guys mind if I come and sort for a while?"

She waited for Birdie to gloat, but of course she didn't. Her eyes lit up, and she simply pushed over on the bench beside

Poopie so Leeda could have a spot. Leeda looked at the two of them side by side. Birdie. Poopie. Birdie Poopie, which was what her grandmom called bird crap in her thick southern accent. Leeda was still too unsure of Birdie to let her in on the joke. She watched her cousin out of the corner of her eye. The past couple of days she and Birdie had crossed paths a lot and Murphy too, but it was hard for Leeda to tell where she stood with them. This was something Leeda was always gauging. She wanted to know where she stood with everyone, all the time.

She listened as Birdie explained to her that the flawed peaches got rolled to one side of the huge table, while the flawless ones went to the other. The flawed ones were sold in local markets and the flawless ones were shipped north.

"Why do the northerners get the good peaches?" Leeda asked.

"They're all *good*," Birdie said, slicing into one and examining its insides, surprising Leeda with her confidence. She seemed more relaxed around Leeda than she ever had.

"They're just not all pretty," Poopie finished, answering Leeda's quizzical expression.

"What're you doing, then, Birdie?" Leeda asked, watching Birdie slice open another peach and search the inside.

"Looking for brown rot."

"Oh." Leeda guessed that meant the farm wasn't yet out of the woods.

Following the others occasionally with her eyes, she started sorting the peaches, moving slow, looking them over, then rolling them to the proper area—occasionally pulling one back from one pile when she felt she'd made a mistake, and assigning it to the other. After a while the rest of the workers tapered off for quitting time, but Leeda remained with Birdie and Poopie, lost in the repetition of the sorting. Eventually Murphy walked up with her final basket full of peaches, dropping them gently into the bin.

"Hey, Murphy," Birdie chirped. Murphy looked at her vacantly for a second, like Birdie was a different creature than the one she expected her to be.

"Hey." She looked at Leeda. "You tired, princess?"

"Shut up," Leeda said sarcastically. She followed Murphy's eyes to where they'd rested behind her. Poopie was staring at Leeda's hands, shaking her head.

"What?" Leeda asked, examining her fingers, which were covered in juice and peach fuzz, her nails ragged.

"Well, I've never seen a girl more useless with peaches. Look, you've thrown several good ones into the flawed pile. What's wrong with this one?" Poopie leaned over the table and pulled one back, holding it out to Leeda.

"It's too pointy on the bottom."

Murphy let out a guffaw, and that made Birdie giggle.

Leeda looked at both of them, frowning.

Murphy scooted in beside Birdie, and Poopie sank down beside Leeda, so slowly Leeda thought she could hear her bones creaking.

"Honey, this is the perfect peach."

Leeda looked at it. "It looks like all the other ones."

Poopie held it up. The peach was completely round except for the little curved point at the bottom. It was flushed red all over with just a little hint of yellow. Poopie traced the cleft that led down to the point with her pinky.

"Poopie, should we leave you alone with that peach?" Murphy asked.

Birdie snorted. Poopie gave her a wry smile and smacked her on the knee.

"Have you ever eaten a perfect peach?"

"I'm not much of a fruit person," Leeda answered tightly.

Poopie rubbed the peach against her dirty shirt and held it out to Leeda, her brown eyes dancing. "Darlington Orchard has the most delicious peaches anywhere on this earth. Try it."

Leeda raised her eyebrows, looked at Poopie's shirt, then took the peach and rubbed it on her own shirt. She bit into the peach, her teeth sinking into the flesh and the fuzzy skin running up between her two front teeth like a sail. She dug it out with her fingernail and swallowed quickly without chewing. The juice ran down her fingers. Leeda stuck them in her mouth meticulously so it wouldn't run down her wrist, and sucked it off, then tried another bite, cleaner and neater.

"Oh, you girls don't know anything. You don't know how to *enjoy*." Poopie shot up from the table, muttering in Spanish. She pounded away, talking to herself, leaving all three girls staring after her.

"Here," Murphy said, looking for a peach from the flawed pile. This one actually did have a little brown mark on it. "Watch the master." Murphy made sure to bite into that area first. The juice dripped right down her chin, landing on her shirt just above her right breast. "I call these babies my juice catchers," she said through slurping.

"That's disgusting," Leeda said, dropping her chin on one hand.

Murphy ignored her. "I think this is the best peach I've ever had."

"Of course it is." Birdie grabbed one and gnawed on it. "Some peaches taste flat. Or they get too stringy. Or oversweet. The fuzz gets too thick. Our peaches are the best. I've already had seven today," she murmured. She too let the juice drip all over.

Leeda eyed the round circle where she'd bitten hers twice. She pushed it back into her mouth and took a ragged, uneven bite, the front of her teeth scraping against the pit. The juice and the flesh of the peach tore and filled her mouth, and she flattened it down with the roof of her mouth, really trying to taste it, like she had never done with anything, like she was getting to *know* it. It tasted somehow like orange and green and dizzyingly sweet, but like Birdie had said, not too sweet. The taste was so rich it made her lips purse. It was different on different parts of her tongue—the tartness hit the tip, the sweetness tingled at the sides and at the back.

This time she let the juice run down her fingers.

"Now you know how to *enjoy*," Birdie said in a perfect Poopie accent, waving her arms in the air in a giant dramatic gesture and taking Leeda enough by surprise that she snorted peach juice into her sinus cavity. Birdie had two bits of peach skin sticking out of her teeth like fangs.

"Great, now I'm gonna get a sinus infection," Leeda said, even though she was still laughing.

"Damn, Birdie, you are full of hidden talents," Murphy said. "Brown-rot queen. Impressions."

"I don't think I wanna be a brown-rot queen," Birdie said earnestly, making Murphy smirk.

"What's your hidden talent, Leeda?"

Leeda slurped, still slightly self-conscious about the juice running down her chin. "I make great *lists*," she said darkly, giving Murphy a look to let her know she knew this wasn't a talent at all.

"That's good," Murphy offered. "I couldn't make a list if I tried. Seriously. It's chaos up here." Murphy tapped her forehead.

"Whatever." Leeda knew Murphy was uncommonly smart. "Oh, I'm also an excellent shot," she added.

"Leeda's good at everything," Birdie said. Leeda eyed her quizzically. She couldn't think of anything Birdie had ever seen her be good at.

"Well, you're definitely not as much of a loser as I always thought," Murphy added.

"Oh, *thanks*." Leeda wanted to be offended, but actually, she felt warmed up with pleasure. Flattered. And she felt something tiny click into place. It made her whole body relax. It was like they had settled it. They weren't strangers again. It had just been decided.

The sun had just dipped low enough to shine into the shade of the barn and it hit her face, but she decided not to worry about UV rays giving her freckles and premature wrinkles. She'd never felt her body relax so completely, resting from the hard work and loosening up in the company of the two sitting next to her. She felt liked. Leeda was liked by a lot of people, but usually for things that didn't matter. She felt she was liked by Birdie and Murphy for no reason at all, and that made the experience, for however long it might last, more real.

Leeda knew friends never turned out to be what you expected. They came and went in waves, pulling away and coming back, leaving you feeling safe one minute and lost the next.

In the movies they always made it look permanent, and for a long time Leeda had expected to find friends like that. But there was always some gap that developed; there was always a glitch.

She didn't really know Murphy, or even her cousin, at all. But for that tiny space of time, savoring the taste of her peach, feeling the sleepy laziness of someone who's earned it, it felt like Birdie and Murphy might turn out to be friends like that. Even though they had nothing in common and there was fuzz stuck under her fingernails and the juice was drying in a sticky mass on her arms, Leeda was happy.

The moment slipped away, but because it wasn't perfect, it was the most perfect one she could remember having.

On a July evening in 1993, synchronous lightning bugs were discovered on the Darlington Orchard property, lighting up the night like blinking Christmas lights. These obscure insects were known among nature enthusiasts for their unique ability to light all at once, unexplainably in sync with thousands of others of their kind. They were known to reside in only a few places on earth, none of which were anywhere near Bridgewater. That week entomologists from far and wide descended on the orchard to see them, but within days they had disappeared, never to be seen in the region again by more than a select few.

Fourteen

Leeda started staying for dinner. The workers always invited her to share, and it was pretty obviously connected to the fact that she'd actually started to really work. At first Leeda resisted out of politeness, but the food was just too delicious.

Every night she was shocked by the many uses of peaches. The women knew how to make anything out of them—peach-and-pecan soup, peach salsa, peach-and-onion fritters, peach-and-amaretto jelly. They combined them with the produce of their vegetable garden, which lay behind the men's dorm. When the men cooked, it was less creative—burgers, sometimes steak. But there was always corn on the cob, cucumber-and-parsley salad with cider vinegar, beans, mild white cheese crumbled on tortillas and cooked over the open fire.

And being outside with the tight-knit group of workers, smelling the grill and listening to all the talk afterward, was so much better than sitting around Uncle Walter's table, which was cool and comfortable, but dreary and dead.

The nights changed too. For the next week, which slumped hotly into July, the girls snuck down to the lake every night.

Once they'd started going, it was impossible to stop. At the end of a long day, the thought of the cool water and the cool wet grass and lying around in the dark, out of the heat of the dorms, became too enticing to resist. One girl would show up in the doorway of one of the others, looking at her with raised eyebrows like someone might proposition someone who might turn them down, and then the two would move unsurely on to the last girl and look at her with the same raised eyebrows. But then it became a non-question, and there was no need to even ask, and nobody raised their eyebrows at all.

Though the other women in Camp A seemed to be on to them, they never said anything. But Leeda felt that since they'd started, she and Murphy and Birdie oozed secret excitement, like the fire ants and their pheromones, and that everyone caught the scent, and it lit up the rooms of the dorm a little more.

Leeda hardly spoke with Birdie or Murphy during the day. Birdie said her dad would probably pull her out of the dorms if he knew they were having too much fun, and if he found out about the lake, he would definitely lock her up, fun or not. When Leeda asked how she knew, Birdie directed her to the expression that had planted itself permanently on Walter's face. It was definitely antifun.

It was like they had double lives, separated distinctly into night and day. But Birdie was the first to break that when she told them about the cider house.

The afternoon was too hot to be real. The white dirt drew the heat in and the trees made a blanket that trapped the smell of the ripe peaches and the ones already rotting on the ground. It made the orchard feel more closed in than ever, like the air caught between the trees was pinning it to the ground and holding it there. Leeda knew she must be on the verge of sunstroke because it had actually started to feel romantic to be so sweaty, and to look around and see the red cheeks of the workers, and to feel how slow and heavy and relaxed her limbs had become. She was wiping the sweat off her neck in a long, languid gesture when Birdie appeared out of nowhere, her big brown eyes on Leeda sympathetically. She didn't appear to be suffering from the heat at all.

"Did you find my note yet?" she whispered.

Leeda squinted at her, her heavy hands sinking to her hips. "Note?"

Birdie raised her eyebrows comically and jerked her head to the left, to a tree Leeda had just picked. There was a tiny white piece of paper tucked into a crotch of two limbs.

Leeda smiled. She widened her eyes and nodded back at Birdie, in mock conspiracy, and waited for her to turn and walk away before shaking her head at her cousin and how goofy she was. She pulled the note out of the tree and unfolded it.

Cider house. See you there. Fifteen minutes.

Leeda kicked a smushy, rotting peach out from under her feet and got a head start.

About half an hour later, she, Murphy, and Birdie were sitting on the cool, smooth concrete of the cider house floor. When they'd met at the door, holding their notes, Murphy and Leeda had teased Birdie about what a kid she was. Murphy had said, "Birdie, do you like me? Check yes or no." But Leeda was grateful. The cider house, as it turned out, and as of course Birdie knew, was the coolest spot in the whole orchard. It sat up on a hill that overlooked the rest of the orchard, where it got a breeze, and it had the most delicious concrete floor Leeda had ever put her butt on.

Leeda had ducked back to the dorms and brought her notebook. Murphy lay flat on the ground, her arms and legs flopped out on the cold concrete, one hand holding a magnolia leaf she'd yanked off the tree outside. Birdie sat cross-legged beside her.

Murphy pulled up her knees and clicked her tongue against her cheek a few times. She looked over Leeda's shoulder. "What're you doing?"

"I'm writing out ideas for my sister's bachelorette party." Leeda had been putting it off forever. Every time she'd even thought about it made her bitter. But August was closer than it seemed—and Leeda was a planner by nature. She fiddled with her pen irritably as she looked at Murphy.

"Ooh. What are your ideas?"

Leeda pulled the notebook closer to her chest. "Just some stuff in Atlanta."

"What kind of stuff? Read me what you've got." Murphy wagged her feet right and left on the floor.

"Um. Okay." Leeda looked down at her list, self-conscious. "Part one."

Murphy laughed. "Ha, part one," she slurred, too tired to speak clearly.

"Dinner. I have three options. The Regal Fez in Buckhead. Bistro Bijou . . ."

"She really likes that crap?"

Leeda stiffened and turned toward Murphy, her gray eyes cool. "It's not crap. For part two," she continued, "I'm thinking of renting out a theater at Phipps Plaza."

"Your sister wants to go watch a movie on the wildest night of her life?"

Leeda sighed. "I can't get into any clubs."

"Sure you can. Just flirt with the bouncer."

"I don't do that." Murphy made it sound so easy.

"Well, what did what's-her-face say she wanted to do?"

Leeda rolled her eyes. She thought about the dinner they'd had at Nikolai's Roof that had landed her here. "Danay wants to ride the *Fur Bus*." She was looking for Murphy to empathize.

"That sounds fun," Birdie piped in. "Maybe you should just do what she wants to do."

Even though it had been Birdie speaking, Leeda looked at Murphy as she defended herself. "But then everybody will be getting drunk but me."

"Why not you?"

"I'm supposed to be in charge of everything," Leeda replied tightly. "I have to be sober."

Murphy gazed at her quizzically for a moment. "Oh, I get it."

"What?" Leeda asked, even though she didn't want to know.

"It's all about you. You don't want anything *she* wants."

Leeda snapped the notebook shut. "I'm just trying to make it good."

Murphy nodded knowingly, her hair rubbing on the concrete while Leeda stared coolly back.

"Why do you hate your sister?" Murphy finally said, so matter-of-factly that Leeda wanted to throw her pen at her.

"I don't." Leeda clicked the pen in and out.

Murphy sat up. "Regal Fez sounds like something you plan for someone you hate."

"Listen, I . . ."

But Murphy's eyes had widened. She nodded over Leeda's shoulder toward Birdie, who was holding a bottle gently on her lap, fondling the label. She appeared to be oblivious to both of them, finally holding the bottle to her face and kissing it.

"Um, Birdie?" Murphy asked.

Birdie jerked, drawing the bottle back down to her lap as she looked at them. Murphy slid the bottle out of her hand and read the label out loud. "Darlington Peach Cider. Fine peach cider—sweet and surprisingly crisp—made from fresh Georgia peaches." She looked at Birdie. "Why were you kissing it?"

No response. Murphy nodded slowly. "Oh. Oh *my*. You're obsessed."

Leeda was confused. "Obsessed with peach cider?"

"You're obsessed with the cider guy. Enrico."

Birdie's cheeks went scarlet. "No, I'm not."

Murphy laughed. "Yep. That guy Enrico. You *love* him. You want to smell his labels. And then kiss them."

Birdie looked mortified. "No, I . . ."

Murphy tackled Birdie's embarrassment the way she had tackled Leeda's defensiveness a moment before, as if she were oblivious to it. "He's really cute. You know, I bet he likes you too. I've seen you guys together."

Birdie laid the bottle down beside her with a clink. "Really?" she asked breathlessly.

"Birdie!" Leeda felt so out of the loop. How had Murphy noticed when she hadn't?

Birdie slid onto her back, sighing. "Oh my God. He's so amazing."

Murphy was grinning from ear to ear. "Have you kissed him on anything but the label yet?"

"Oh nooo." Birdie shook her head.

"Well, why?" Murphy pressed. "Doesn't he go back to Mexico at the end of the summer?"

"He lives in Texas." Birdie said this as if it was the saddest statement she'd ever made in her life. She practically yelped it.

"Same difference. Why haven't you made your move?"

Birdie swallowed. "I've never even kissed *anyone*."

Leeda wasn't surprised at all, but Murphy jolted like she'd stuck her finger in a socket. She was speechless.

"I haven't even really *met* anyone," Birdie explained quickly. "You know?"

Murphy sank back on her hands, rubbing her palms against the dust of the concrete. "Well, we can change that. The thing is, you can't start on someone you really like. It's too intimidating."

Birdie tilted her chin toward her chest, looking confused, and as always, very earnest. "Huh?"

Murphy shrugged. "We're going to have to find someone you don't like. We can do it tonight if you want."

"Do what?" Birdie asked. Leeda was wondering the same thing.

Murphy hopped up and brushed the dirt off her legs. "Go out and get you a kiss," she said.

Somewhere around midnight Murphy, Leeda, Birdie, Honey Babe, and Majestic piled into Murphy's dilapidated yellow Volkswagen, Yellowbaby, and took off down Orchard Drive after having first pushed the car backward down the long driveway away from the house (with Leeda steering, of course). The car was full of the scent of Leeda's perfume, which all five were wearing, Birdie having spritzed both dogs lightly, to their delight. Murphy rolled down her window to clear the air.

Leeda looked around the car nervously. "Is this thing going to explode?"

"It might," Murphy said.

Birdie couldn't help but laugh. It had been one thing to sneak down to the lake. But leaving the orchard property felt so daring and so blatant that Birdie was a ball of nervous giddiness.

"Oh God," Leeda said, leaning her head back against the headrest and holding tight to the handle above the window.

Murphy hadn't told them where they were going yet. They careened down the main drag of Bridgewater, but kept going, past the edge of town where the Pearly Gates Cemetery was, and then onto Route 75 south.

"How far away *is* this place?" Leeda asked.

Murphy shrugged. "About forty-five minutes if we hurry."

"Oh God."

They zipped past a sign for hot boiled peanuts, then several billboards for one of the large orchards, then past several for condos and resorts in Florida, just four hours away. Murphy kept her window down, and the wind blew so hard that Birdie had to hold her hair back on either side of her face to see the signs.

Finally the billboards tapered off, and Murphy pulled onto an exit ramp that led them to a dark, two-lane road. By the lights of the occasional farmhouses they passed, Birdie could see they'd come to a swampier area. The air smelled wetter. Bugs smacked against the windshield in droves. A square green sign jumped into the headlights announcing *Mertie Creek, 5 Miles*.

About ten minutes later, Murphy pulled into a gravel drive and the three of them piled out of the passenger side because the driver's side door didn't work. Honey Babe and Majestic stayed behind, curled up on the backseat.

They were in a parking lot, standing in front of a low, wood-lined building with a high slanted roof. About fifty old wooden chairs hung from the front wall and scattered across the porch all around the door. Picnic tables sat in front of the porch under low-slung crisscrosses of round white lights. But from the sound of it, everyone was inside, laughing and shouting above some loud, twangy music.

"I'm not going in there," Leeda said.

"Well, Bird and I will see you when we come out, then," Murphy said, reaching an arm around Birdie and sweeping her along. Birdie looked back over her shoulder at Leeda and couldn't help but grin at the look on her face as she ran to catch up.

Inside, the smoke was so thick Birdie had to wave her hands in front of her eyes to see clearly. The room consisted of a large square bar and a small dance floor with a corner staked out for a country band that was doing a Kenny Chesney cover.

Birdie and Leeda clustered right up behind Murphy like ducklings. "I don't have ID," Birdie whispered to Murphy, thinking how mortifying it would be if someone asked her for it. But Murphy just turned and gave her an *oh, please* look. She breezed right along up to a lone free stool at the bar. The two men on the stools next to it looked her up and down. "Can you spare those stools for a couple of thirsty teenagers?" Murphy asked, a sly, charming smile on her lips.

The men stood up as fast as if Murphy had cracked a whip. Neither of them bothered much to look at Birdie or Leeda. Birdie didn't blame them. She figured that for any guy, Murphy would be hard to look away from.

"What'll y'all have?" the bartender asked as they climbed onto their stools. Sloe gin fizz for Leeda, Jack on the rocks for Murphy, and Birdie had to think for a few seconds, so Murphy ended up ordering her Jack on the rocks too.

When the guy returned with their drinks, he waved off their money. He placed the drinks next to the ancient yellow phone sitting on the bar in front of them.

"Compliments of the guys across the bar."

They all peered across the way. Two men, they had to be in their late twenties at least, with huge bushy beards and beer guts, waved at them with their fingers, smiling. They each wore a big squared-off cap. One said *I Brake for . . .* And then it had a picture of a beaver. The other just said *Destin, Florida.*

"Ew," Leeda whispered.

"There you go, Birdie," Murphy said, whipping out a ciga-rette. "We're gonna get you kissed good and proper." Leeda took a desperate swig of her drink.

"I just love crazy people like this," Murphy said. "Jack Kerouac people. Mad to live, mad to die, that kind of thing. My mom met my dad here. He used to work here as a bartender."

Birdie thought Murphy said it with a certain air of BS, but she nodded and sucked her drink through the tiny red straw.

By the time they finished their first round, the band had launched into a David Allen Coe song and Murphy jumped up to dance, pulling Birdie and Leeda with her. She looked funny in her Mick Jagger T-shirt, grooving to country. It seemed to Leeda like Murphy would have danced to just about anything, she had so much energy. When they came back to the bar again a few songs later, both Birdie and Murphy were covered in sweat. Leeda was still cool as a cucumber because she'd danced stiffly and slowly, sipping her sloe gin.

As the girls waited for more drinks, the phone next to Murphy rang and Murphy picked it up. "Hello? I don't know. Hold on."

Murphy stood up on tiptoes. "Don Martin?" she yelled as Leeda and Birdie watched in awe.

Nobody answered. "I'm sorry, but I don't think he's here." Pause. "This is Murphy." Pause. "Okay, if I see him, I'll tell him." Murphy hung up and looked at the girls and shrugged. They all cracked up.

"Would you girls care to dance?"

The two men from earlier were standing behind them and looming above them.

"Leeda and Birdie would," Murphy said, pushing Birdie forward into the arms of the guy with the beaver hat. She shoved her drink into Murphy's hand as she was dragged away.

They jostled out onto the dance floor. Leeda danced stiffly at first. But then the guy started dipping her and showing her all these two-step moves, and as she seemed to relax, she started to dance fabulously. She seemed to have an innate sense of rhythm and her body moved like a bird. Birdie watched her smile melt from tight and polite to genuine.

Birdie smiled too. Leeda and Murphy were both dazzling. For the moment, being here with them made her feel happy being Birdie, and not so stuck inside herself like a pea in a pod. She forgot to think about the orchard completely, which was a miracle. The weight of its problems slid off her shoulders to the rhythm of the music.

Even being here with . . . "What's your name?" Birdie asked.

"Saddle Tramp," the guy answered, grinning at her through his beard. "That's what everybody calls me. It's my CB handle."

Even being here with Saddle Tramp made her feel bolder. Or maybe it was the whiskey.

Birdie could see Murphy on the sidelines, watching them both proudly, like an evangelist staring at her converts. Birdie felt a wave of affection for her. And Leeda too.

She was so engrossed in the feeling that she didn't see Saddle Tramp's puffy, hair-ringed lips making a beeline for hers until it was too late.

Out in the parking lot the air—normally hot but cool compared to the temperature inside the bar—carried their voices into the empty lot. Murphy reveled in the feeling of sweat cooling on her body. It wasn't often she felt sated.

"What time is it?" Leeda asked, swiping her hair from where it was stuck across her forehead.

"Damn, it's nearly three," Murphy said, looking at her wrist.

"My dad'll be up in two hours," Birdie said gleefully, a happily scandalized look on her face. God, Murphy couldn't remember ever being as innocent as Birdie. When Birdie had been kissed by the trucker out on the dance floor, she'd frozen like a statue for a moment, then darted away as fast as she could. Now she was absolutely giddy.

About half an hour ago Leeda had stumbled into some guy holding a pitcher and now it was all down the front of her flimsy turquoise tank top on her white tennis skirt. She plucked at her clothes, disgusted.

"My underwear is soaked." Leeda's eyes arched pleadingly at Birdie and Murphy. "I can't ride all the way home in wet skivvies."

"Just take 'em off," Murphy suggested.

"But what'll I do with them?" The question came out in a slight slur. Which sounded funnier than usual coming from someone like Leeda.

"I don't know. Just bring them with you."

"I don't want to carry around beer-soaked skivvies."

Murphy shrugged. She really didn't care either way. Leeda ducked behind a baby blue Chevy pickup while Murphy and Birdie continued on to the car. They stopped when they heard a snicker behind them.

Leeda was still standing next to the pickup. Her black thong, on the other hand, had found its way onto the middle of the pickup's windshield. Leeda had her hand stuck in front of her mouth and she leaned forward, clenching her knees and laughing drunkenly.

Birdie and Murphy both guffawed loudly, and then Birdie ran across the lot, scooted behind a car, and whipped out her skivvies, flinging them onto the windshield too. They were pink and said Sunday across the front.

"I'm ready to go home now." Birdie stuck her chin up in the air and then laughed. "I wonder what they'll do when they see them."

Murphy followed suit, though she hated to part with her favorite monkey undies.

Finally, they piled into the car, wet and sweaty and sticking to the ripped vinyl seats. Honey Babe and Majestic were thrilled to see them.

Murphy turned the key in the ignition. The car rumbled and died.

Murphy and Leeda looked at each other and then Murphy tried the ignition again. Nothing happened this time. Damn.

"Well, car's broken," Murphy said, throwing her hands up and letting them fall on the dashboard.

She looked at Leeda and Birdie.

"How will we get back?" Leeda asked.

Murphy thought. "I guess we'll have to call someone."

Silence.

Birdie's eyes widened. "My dad's gonna kill me."

Murphy thought about her mom, but she'd definitely be asleep right now. And Richard would probably be the one to pick up the phone.

"I'm sure someone can come pick us up, Bird. Don't worry."

Finally she looked at Leeda. Birdie did too.

Leeda had never thought Rex's car could look good. But when he pulled over in his beat-up Ford pickup, she wanted to kiss the hood.

It was close to four when he got there, barely giving them enough time to get back to the farm before sunrise, but Rex didn't just pull up and throw the door open for them to hop in. He turned off the ignition and got out of the car.

Leeda crossed her arms over her chest instinctively.

"Thanks, baby." She walked up to him and stuck her hand into his. He didn't look happy. In fact, he looked pissed. He looked at Birdie, then at the bar behind them, then at Murphy.

Then he looked over their shoulders at the cars. Damn. She'd forgotten.

"Did you guys put that underwear there?"

Murphy and Birdie cracked up, but Leeda shrank, embarrassed. "Um . . ."

"Your idea, right, Murphy?"

"Actually, that was all Leeda." Murphy was giving him her patented dead fish look.

Rex sighed. "I mean the bar."

Murphy bristled. "So?"

"So number one, you guys shouldn't be drinking and getting on the road in the middle of the night. And number two, I don't want a bunch of drunk rednecks hitting on my girlfriend. You guys shouldn't come to a place like this alone."

Murphy leaned heavily onto one hip, yawning. "Birdie, we should have called Walter after all. If we were gonna have a dad, it might as well have been yours."

Leeda had to agree that the whole speech was pretty ridiculous coming from Rex, who'd had his share of wild nights. Leeda met his eyes. Many times she'd felt like he was more of a big brother than a boyfriend. She felt like that now.

"Next time we'll call someone else," Leeda muttered.

"Please do."

He ducked into Murphy's car through the open passenger door and tried the ignition. "I think the bushings are out on the clutch," Murphy said. Rex just shook his head and climbed back into his own car.

They rode in silence for several minutes, all smushed into the bench seat, with Leeda next to Rex and Murphy at the window. Birdie sat in the middle with both dogs on her lap. "It's the starter that's out, not the clutch," Rex said.

"Actually, Rex, I've had it happen before, and it's the clutch." Murphy rolled down her window and stuck one hand out.

"The clutch wouldn't keep it from starting," Rex said evenly, with steely calm.

"I think I know my car better than you do, Dad."

Leeda sat curled up next to Rex. "I know it's crazy," she interjected, "but I'll be damn happy to see the orchard after sitting here with you two."

Rex seemed to soften as he drove, but he didn't say anything else. Everyone sat silently, even Honey Babe and Majestic, whose eyes were wide and mournful, as if they sensed the tension in the cab.

When Rex dropped them off, the air had just turned gray. There was a stripe of light right along the horizon of the orchard, and the first birds were just beginning to chirp. The rumble of the car wheels at the bottom of the drive, though quiet, seemed to stand out.

Rex dropped them off without another word. They all stood looking across the grass. The lights of the Darlington house were still dim, and this drew a relieved breath from Birdie, who leaned her shoulder against Murphy's.

Leeda looked at them. Bits of their hair had stuck together and dried against their foreheads and the sides of their faces.

Birdie had a sweat stain right down the middle of her top. Leeda knew she must look equally bad.

She wanted to initiate a talk about what a great night it had been, all in all. Already, now that it was getting light, Mertie Creek seemed like it had happened years ago, and it made her sad. But maybe she was just tired. In any case, she got the sense she shouldn't say anything. It was better not said.

They straggled into the dorms for a precious half hour of sleep without a word.

Fifteen

On Sundays, if there hadn't been much rain to ripen the peaches, the workers harvested until eleven and had the rest of the day off. Each week for Murphy's first three weeks Poopie pulled a beat-up white van to the front of the dorms and everybody who wanted to pile in for a trip to Wal-Mart did. Murphy never went because she wasn't allowed off the premises. Still, she looked forward to Sundays because it allowed her to have the orchard mostly to herself, and because it was fun to watch the workers return.

She'd learned last week to make it a point to be back at the dorms around the time they were supposed to come back so she could watch them piling off the bus. Inevitably, the workers would go crazy buying things to bring back to Mexico at the end of the summer—clothes, candy, but also inflatable pools, board games, toys. Murphy didn't know how they were going to carry it all. But everybody was so thrilled when they poured off the bus, laughing and chatting, showing off their purchases, that Murphy never wanted to miss it.

The bus had left at about ten A.M. Leeda and Birdie had gone to Leeda's house to see Leeda's parents and have lunch. Though she knew it was silly, that she wouldn't have been allowed off the orchard anyway, Murphy felt slightly left out and slightly pathetic for feeling slightly left out. It felt weird to have Birdie and Leeda go off without her.

She spent the morning lying in her bed reading, then ate cereal for lunch, then trailed out to the garden and weeded, clearing away the areas surrounding the first buds, which were popping up everywhere like wildfire. Yesterday, she'd discovered a nectarine, but it was filled with bugs, just like Birdie had predicted. No miracle yet.

When she got hungry, she walked into the orchard and picked a couple of Rubyprince peaches, which had just ripened this week. She was already able to tell the difference in taste between these and the other varieties of peaches that they'd harvested. Candor was her favorite so far. She now kept a peach in her pocket at all times to snack on, the juice soaking into the fabric of her shorts.

With time to relax her muscles, Murphy was bored. She wasn't even sore anymore, except for the very dull, satisfying ache that she went to bed with each night. She thought about calling her mom, but the thought gave her such a heavy feeling in her gut that she immediately tried to forget it. She peered around, wondering where Rex might be. With so much of the orchard equipment falling apart he was always somewhere, fiddling with something. Murphy started looking for him without really noticing she was looking. She found him with one of the rusty green tractors by the barn.

"I think you're right. I think it's the starter."

Rex stood up and turned. He was all sweaty and an oil streak lined his neck. There was oil all over his hands.

"I know." He smiled and wiped his hands against his stomach. "It's still at the bar in Mertie Creek, huh?"

"Yeah, I don't have any way to get down there."

Rex rested his hands on his hips and looked down at the tractor. "I'm just about finished with this. You want me to take you?"

Murphy squinted at him. "Really?"

"Any friend of Leeda's is a friend of mine, no matter how much of a pain in the ass she is." Rex grinned sarcastically. "We can stop at the junkyard and get you a new starter."

Murphy put her own hands on her hips, mirroring him. "You're not getting anything in return," she joked.

"Please," Rex said, rolling his eyes.

She met Rex at his car ten minutes later and they started down the road.

"Your garden's looking good," Rex said after a few minutes of sitting in the breeze in silence.

Murphy sank back in her seat and looked at him. She wondered how he knew. She hadn't realized until that moment that she'd even begun to think of it as *her* garden.

"I think it needs something. A bench or something."

Murphy nodded. "Yeah. You know, there's even a nectarine tree in there? But the nectarines are all buggy."

"Too bad," Rex said.

Murphy had rarely sat in a car with a guy who (a) wasn't dating her mom or (b) wasn't hitting on her. She didn't know quite what to do. She just leaned back and looked out the window and listened to Rex's music. His taste was superb. The day, which was a little hazy, started to feel surreal. The grass was fluorescent. The smell of the air was dizzying. Murphy stuck her hand out the window like the wing of an airplane. The music coming from Rex's speakers got under her skin and made her feel like that was what was pushing them forward.

When they got to the junkyard, Rex sifted through several cars for a starter, digging in them with his deft hands until he'd finally found one. Murphy crouched beside him while he extracted it, breathing in the smell of motor oil. They drove on to Mertie Creek. In the light of day it looked different, like the knots on the back of the needlework that had made up the other night—all messy and slapdash. Yellowbaby was still there.

Rex ducked inside through the passenger door and fiddled for about fifteen minutes, starting and restarting the engine until it hummed to life, and finally emerging with a concentrated look on his face.

"We can get you a new door handle at the junkyard too. And I can tighten your clutch. I'll try to do it sometime this week."

"Thanks."

He stood back so Murphy could crawl in toward the driver's seat under his armpit, then leaned down to look at her. He blinked at her a few times, and Murphy pasted a nakedly friendly look on her face. "Yep." She nodded, stiffening her body and hunching up her shoulders intentionally. It would be too easy to flirt with Rex. "Well . . ."

"I still have some work to do back at the orchard. See you back there."

Murphy turned the key in the ignition and didn't look at him again. "Sounds good."

Back on the orchard, Murphy walked back to her garden and did some more work. A few roses had snuck out of their buds since this morning. Murphy dug a hand shovel out of the toolshed and turned the soil around; though she didn't know quite what that was supposed to do, she'd seen it done.

When she walked back to the dorms about an hour later, she ducked behind the faucet partition and washed her face, getting her hair soaked. She rubbed at the dirt on her cheeks and rinsed. Then she faced the wall, pulled her shirt over her head, and rinsed her armpits and her chest and her back. She held her shirt back to her front and turned to look for the soap.

Rex was standing a few feet behind her, staring—not at her body, but at her face.

"Oh. Hey." Murphy crossed her arms tightly against her, which was a rare modesty for her. Rex stared at her, then looked at the ground.

"Hey."

Murphy's heart started to pound out a rhythm. Not like the rhythm she usually got with boys who saw her breasts. It was sort of bigger and more unpredictable at the same time. Holding her shirt tight against her chest with one hand, she ran her other hand through her hair, slicking it back.

"Can I have some privacy, please?"

Rex rubbed the back of his neck with his left hand, scratching it hard, and looked hard at her face but nowhere else. "Yeah. I was wondering if Leeda was back yet."

"Nope." Murphy frowned. He wasn't going anywhere.

"Rex?"

"Yep, sorry." He turned his back to her so that she had a view of his sunburned neck as she moved around the corner of the dorm. The water was still running behind her, but she was focused on that neck, that head of his, wondering what was going through it.

Murphy pulled her T-shirt on tight, crossing her arms over her chest again. For a moment she felt wide open, and it was an achy, horrible feeling. Murphy searched herself for some reliable emotion to tackle this strange, unsteady one. She knew there was a reason she could find to be angry. And it took only a fraction of a second to find it.

Rex had been watching her. Like any other guy would have.

The open spot in the inside of her chest closed with a snap, and the anger settled over her like a fog. Rex was like every other guy. In the end, that was it. He was the same as anybody else.

Murphy breathed a sigh of relief. It felt good to be let down.

Compared to the heat and dirt of the orchard, the inside of Breezy Buds Plantation, the Cawley-Smiths' mansion, felt pristine and deliciously crisp and cool. Leeda laid her sunglasses down on the banister and looked around. She had never looked so disheveled—her Sweetee shirt was unbuttoned at the bottom; her shorts hung slackly off her hips. "Mom?"

"Did you tell them what time you'd be here?" Birdie asked.

Leeda nodded, not surprised but hurt all the same. She hadn't seen her mother in three weeks.

She sighed. She wanted to look for her mom, but she didn't

think she should have to. "I'm gonna take a shower. Meet you at the pool?"

Birdie started toward the back of the house.

Upstairs in her bedroom, Leeda basked in the pleasure of her own bathroom and all the good smells of her soaps and shampoo. When she emerged, surrounded by a cloud of steam, after an incredibly long shower, she slipped into her favorite pink, low-hipped bikini and wrapped a towel around her waist. A pile of mail was scattered on her bureau, and she sifted through it—a bunch of magazine subscriptions she wanted to renew, a few outfits she'd ordered from girlshop.com. A thick, square envelope was at the bottom of the pile. It was addressed *To Miss Leeda Cawley-Smith* in black calligraphy.

Leeda slid her finger through the seal and opened it, pulling out a card wrapped in tissue paper. It smelled like lilacs and had lilac petals stamped into the card stock. It was Leeda's invitation to the wedding.

She walked downstairs into the family's huge living room, then the parlor, then out onto the grass. The pool was large and completely square, with a rock wall built into the back of it, which cascaded a steady, clear stream of water into the pool. The patio was large and Italian tiled and glowing in the sun. There, stretched out on their stomachs, were Mrs. Cawley-Smith, Danay, and Birdie.

Birdie had pulled her recliner a little to the side, closer to the pool. She was dripping wet and drinking a Diet Coke, and she smiled at Leeda as she came out. Mrs. Cawley-Smith and Danay had their faces turned toward each other and their sunglasses on. Danay was topless.

Sometimes Leeda was stunned at how perfect her sister

was. And how much she and their mom looked alike. Lying side by side, they looked like a before and after of the same woman.

Leeda tugged on her bikini bottom and dragged a chair up to the pool.

"Are we allowed to go nude at the pool now?"

"I need an even tan for my dress. It's backless," Danay mumbled, not moving an inch except for her lips. Leeda hadn't even known she'd gotten a dress yet. Wasn't the maid of honor supposed to know these things?

"What about lunch?"

Leeda's mom scratched an itch at her waist. "I'm sorry, honey. We got hungry. You and Birdie tell Lydia what you want the next time she comes up."

Leeda clenched her teeth. She sank back on her chair and looked at Birdie, who shrugged at her. She hated how hurt she felt. But she was above saying it. She turned to her sister and said airily, "I got my invitation. You forgot to add the 'and guest.'"

"What do you mean?" Danay lifted her head slightly.

"Well, for my date."

Danay sank back down flat in an "is that all" gesture. "Lee, it's a small wedding. A lot of people aren't bringing dates. Unless they're married or engaged."

Leeda felt her heart sinking. "But what about Rex?"

"Leeda," Mrs. Cawley-Smith said, "you can do without him for one night."

"But I'm the maid of honor."

Silence from both Danay and their mom. Birdie had reached

the bottom of her Diet Coke and made a sucking sound with her straw, then looked at Leeda self-consciously.

"That's not fair. Mom?"

Lucretia merely rolled over onto her back and pursed her lipsticked lips.

"Leeda, the maid of honor usually partners up with the best man," Danay said flatly.

Leeda winced. Brighton's best man was Glen, his bald, gay cousin. The few times they'd met, he treated Leeda like a princess, to the point of it being embarrassing.

"But . . ." Leeda felt desperate. It went beyond feeling shafted. She didn't think she could take the hours being trapped with her family in such a major act of Danay worship without Rex at her side. She would shrivel into nothing. She would lose herself. She would get the feeling she was getting right now, only times ten.

"Birdie got an invite," Danay interrupted, "and it didn't allow for a guest either, and you don't hear her complaining."

Birdie looked up, startled.

"Birdie doesn't complain. Ever." Leeda made sure to keep her voice even.

Danay turned to Birdie. "Birdie, help me out here. You're not upset you're not allowed to bring a date, are you?"

Birdie looked at Danay, then at Leeda nervously. "Um. I don't know." She stood up, walked to the base of the diving board, and pin-dropped into the pool, then surfaced and swam as far away from them as possible, treading water. Leeda felt too persecuted herself to notice Birdie's obvious discomfort.

Danay stood up. "I'm going to find Lydia and get her to

bring us some snacks. What do you want?" Danay rubbed the top of Leeda's head in her affectionate, oblivious, condescending way.

It gave Leeda the same feeling she always had with her family, of pounding against a giant wall. She looked at her mom. And it hit her like a brick. She really did love Danay better. Maybe it was just by a fraction, but she did. Leeda watched Danay disappear into the house.

Both Cawley-Smith daughters had been named after goddesses, in the pretentious Cawley-Smith way, though neither of their names had been spelled correctly since Lucretia didn't know as much about mythology as she wanted to act like she did. Only Danay seemed to merit the allusion—sliding in through the glass door, trailing that extra fraction of love behind her like a yo-yo.

Leeda picked at a nail, wanting badly to go inside and call Rex because that was what she always did. But she knew, grudgingly, that Birdie would hate to be left alone with her mom. Instead she tried to tell herself the things Rex would say to calm her down. But she couldn't think of an excuse he could give her for the reason she wasn't good enough for her family.

Murphy was sitting on the front porch when they got back.

"Are you waiting for us?" Birdie asked.

Murphy looked around and shrugged. Clearly she was. She looked like a little lost puppy.

"I thought you guys might have drowned in the jacuzzi or something," she murmured sarcastically.

"It's too hot for the jacuzzi," Leeda joked back.

"You guys wanna go to the lake?"

They plopped down on the grass by Smoaky Lake, stretching out on their backs. Leeda felt so helpless, but she also somehow felt like she didn't have to say it. Watching the clouds go by with Birdie and Murphy was very Zen.

"Will you guys come with me to the engagement party?" Leeda asked suddenly, surprising Birdie and Murphy and even herself. "I don't think I can take it by myself."

Silently Birdie and Murphy nodded.

"That one is Danay getting jilted at the altar," Leeda finally said, pointing to a fat white cirrus that was drifting by.

"That one is Danay and your mom tied to some train tracks," Murphy added.

Birdie searched the clouds too. "There's a big chocolate Easter bunny," Birdie said. "Sitting next to the Virgin Mary."

They all laughed.

Sixteen

It drizzled all day the next day, so peach picking was called off. Birdie walked around the orchard in the rain, looking for ripe blackberries along the perimeter. The cider house was at the far back corner of the farm, and Birdie could see from under the hood of her sweatshirt that the door was open, an orange glow coming from inside. She pulled her hood back and gave herself the breath test. If Enrico was inside, she was not going to do what she'd done last time, with the Band-Aid. She wasn't going to screw it up. She walked up to the threshold.

Enrico sat below the bare lightbulb, reading. When he saw Birdie, he didn't smile, but merely nodded to her. She straightened out her sweatshirt and ran her fingers along her denim shorts to smooth them out. They hung low on her hips, like either Birdie had shrunk or she'd been wearing them for too many days.

"What're you reading?" she ventured, stepping beside him and behind him so she could look over his shoulder. The smell of sickly sweet cider and sawdust filled up her nose. *Love in the Time of Cholera,* by Gabriel García Márquez.

"I already read this in Spanish," Enrico said. "I think this will help me with the English book."

"Oh."

Birdie knew she was breathing warmly on his shoulder. She backed up a step.

"What do you read?" Enrico laid his book down on his lap and turned to look at her. Though it was raining, it was still sticky and humid, and sweat had collected above his lips.

"I watch TV," Birdie said, smiling sheepishly. She tugged on the cord that the bare bulb was hanging from, letting it swing back and forth. "Aren't you lonely out here?"

Enrico smiled softly. "No. I like being alone. Too much talking at the house."

"I know what you mean." Birdie leaned against the cider press, watching his big serious eyes, her stomach starting to ache. "I like being alone too. I can get away to my room sometimes, but . . ."

"These rooms are too small to do."

"I know." She sighed unevenly. "Sorry."

Enrico shook his head, still smiling. "Not your fault." He looked down at his book, then up at her. "Maybe you help me with a few of these words?"

"Sure."

Enrico flipped through the pages of his book, frowning in concentration. He opened a page and held it out toward Birdie. The word *frivolity* had been marked with a pencil.

"Oh," Birdie said, thinking of the right way to put it. "That's, um, having fun."

Enrico nodded and sucked his bottom lip into his mouth,

chewing on it thoughtfully. This alarmed Birdie. It made her feel like she was going to cease to exist. *Something* was going to happen to her. She couldn't go on this way.

"This one?" He thrust out another page with another word: *shrouded.*

Birdie looked at it. It danced on the page in front of her like something in the wavy hot air of the desert. She could swear her pulse was loud enough for him to hear. "Um, I think that means covered up, hidden."

When Enrico pointed to the next word, Birdie's finger darted out to touch the page and slid next to his.

"Um, I think that means ... um ..."

Birdie looked up at Enrico. His face was just inches from hers. Her first instinct was to look away, but bravely she kept her eyes on his profile, forcing herself to stay still. He didn't notice for a second. He was still looking at the page and the place where their fingers were touching, and then he tilted his face toward her, sending the shadow cast by the lightbulb on a slow trek from his forehead to his jaw.

Enrico jerked slightly and cleared his throat. Then he pulled back, fanning the pages of the book against his fingers. "Maybe I look in the dictionary," he said faintly, apologetically.

Birdie was suspended in space. She could feel her skin flushing, radiating prickly circles. She sank back on her right foot, retreating, but trying not to retreat idiotically fast. "Well, um, I guess I'm not sure." She hadn't even seen the word.

Crap. Crap crap crap.

Maybe he hadn't even noticed that a second ago she'd been trying to be kissed.

"Okay," she said breezily, clutching to this possibility with all her might. "Well, I gotta go get some blackberries for Poopie." She showed him her teeth, and for a second she felt like Horatio Balmeade—fake. "She makes great pie." Her voice caught embarrassingly, so that it actually came out "pi-ie." *God.* "But if you need any more help, let me know."

Enrico watched her as she backed up, his eyes wide. He looked like an onlooker at a train wreck.

At least she didn't trip on her way out.

Back at the house, Poopie was waiting patiently with her pie crust for Birdie's berries. But Birdie had forgotten all about them.

"Birdie, where is your head?" Poopie asked, shaking hers in aggravation.

Birdie ignored her, digging into the fridge for something crunchy to take out her aggression on. The only thing they had was a bag of carrots. No cookies in the freezer. No nothing. When had she stopped buying snacks?

"Your father wants you to take some papers to Mr. Balmeade tomorrow," Poopie said behind her, but all Birdie heard was "your" and she assumed Poopie was still getting on her about forgetting. She whirled around, slamming the fridge door behind her.

"Who cares about the goddamn berries!" she yelled at the top of her lungs.

Poopie's face twisted to a look of comic shock. She shook her head and gazed up toward heaven. And then she went out for the berries herself, tapping Saint Jude on her way down the porch.

•   •   •

"I don't even know why I'm going with you. I can't stand the sight of this guy."

"You're going *because* you can't stand the sight of the guy. So you can make fun of him once we get there," Leeda replied to Murphy, who was trailing behind her and now stuck out her tongue.

"You can read me like a book," Murphy said, deadpan.

Birdie tossed the manila packet of papers over the fence that separated the Balmeade Country Club from the orchard, then began to climb, sticking her toes between the metal squares, swaying slightly, and slipped over effortlessly, bouncing on her feet as she hit the ground. She wore an uncharacteristically pissed-off look, one she'd had on all day. And the minute she landed on the Balmeade grass, it seemed to Leeda to settle harder onto her features.

"Hey, Birdie, you're having a skinny day," Murphy said, sounding like she noticed the look too. Leeda always cringed when Murphy said things so bluntly, but Birdie smiled distractedly.

"Thanks."

Birdie was actually in short overalls and a flowy orange top. And she did look skinny. But she also looked miserable. She had told them about her incident with Enrico in the cider house. And now they were headed into enemy territory. Birdie shuffled her feet, waiting for them like a person standing on a deserted alley at night rather than on a bland lawn in the middle of the day. She looked distinctly threatened.

"Thanks for coming with me, you guys," she said, her face softening for a moment.

Walter, Birdie had said, had asked her to bring the packet of papers to Horatio Balmeade, who was supposed to be in his office to receive them at two o'clock. He had asked her to go alone. He had also asked her to walk in through the front entrance like a civilized human being. But Birdie was taking Leeda and Murphy with her and—thanks to Murphy's needling—she was going over the fence.

"What's in the envelope?" Murphy asked.

Birdie shrugged.

"Aren't you curious? Maybe it's naked pictures of Mrs. Balmeade."

Birdie didn't even crack a smile at the joke. "I don't think I should look. It's private." She let out a soft, distressed sigh. "You guys are going to behave yourselves, right?" she asked Murphy diplomatically.

"Tweety Bird," Murphy answered, gnawing on a peach she'd pulled out of her pocket, "Leeda will do her best."

Leeda had stopped at the fence, not quite sure how she was going to get over. Since they were going to the country club, she'd worn a skirt. And Leeda had never climbed a fence in her life, except the time her friend Alicia's party got busted and she ended up with a huge bruise from when Rex had pulled her over.

"Go on, Lee," Murphy said, catching up.

Leeda looked at the fence, then stuck a foot in one of the gaps in the wire. It hurt. Her toes jammed together. She pulled her foot out and put it down.

"Just climb it," Murphy ordered.

"I'm wearing a skirt." She knew as she said it that Murphy wouldn't let it drop. Which made her feel embarrassed and annoyed.

Sure enough, Murphy looked at her like she was an alien. "Oh my God. Birdie, I can't believe we brought Leeda all this way so we could see her undies, and now our plan's not going to work!" Leeda blinked at her, confused, but Birdie giggled half-heartedly. Murphy turned a duh face on Leeda. "Who *cares*? It's just Birdie and me."

"It's a thong," Leeda said tightly.

Murphy fish-eyed her.

Finally, frustrated, Leeda made Murphy wait on one side and Birdie on the other to catch her in case she fell. She climbed over, her thong showing itself in all of its baby pink glory, and came down with a soft thud on the other side. They started across the grass, which was short and fine and perfect, sloped here and there to admit a sand trap or a tiny, perfectly shaped pond. The clubhouse up ahead practically gleamed with the whiteness of its walls. A golf cart zoomed past them, carrying an older couple in all white.

For Leeda, coming to the club had used to feel like a great way to spend the day, but now it was like stepping into a mind-numbing TV show instead of real life. She glanced at Birdie to see how she was dealing.

"Those trees are so ugly," Birdie said distastefully, pointing to the skinny Italian pines. Leeda had always thought they were pretty, but now, she realized, her taste had shifted. They didn't look ugly to her. But they didn't look right either.

"I'd like to stick one of those trees up Horatio Balmeade's butt," Murphy said casually, and Birdie giggled.

Leeda had to admit, Murphy knew how to put things into perspective. But she made Leeda nervous. It had taken all of Leeda's sweetest, eyelash-fluttering persuasion to get Uncle Walter to let

Murphy off the orchard for Danay's party, and she didn't want her to screw it up. Already Uncle Walter had started to look at Leeda suspiciously, like he was beginning to figure out that she wasn't quite the good influence on Birdie he had assumed she would be, though he still seemed to mostly lay the blame on Murphy.

And seeing the way Murphy strode beside Birdie, like she might kick Horatio Balmeade in the shins if he looked at her sideways, was enough to make Leeda wish—half guiltily—that they'd left her in the dorms.

Inside the clubhouse the blandness of the grounds extended itself and hitched up a notch. Leeda felt a little dizzy from the coolness of the air conditioner, the neatness of every person who passed by, the clean, empty smell of the air after the heady, earthy smell of the orchard, which clung even to the inside of the dorms. Leeda looked for Rex but didn't see him.

"You guys stay here," Birdie said.

Leeda and Murphy sank onto the leather couch by the door as Birdie crossed the room like a convict approaching the electric chair.

"I wonder what those papers are," Murphy said darkly, tapping her feet against the marble of the floor.

"It can't be good," Leeda said, eyeing her meaningfully. "Do you think she knows?"

Murphy stared across the wide floor as Birdie was reapproaching them. "Yeah, she knows," she said quietly. "Did you talk to him?" she added brightly as Birdie approached. Birdie's chest was heaving in tight bursts, and she looked like she might cry.

"He wasn't there."

"Didn't he tell you to come at two?"

Birdie looked back over her shoulder. "Yeah. I just put the papers on his desk." And then she looked at Murphy and Leeda. "Let's get out of here."

"Hey, Birdie, where we going?" Leeda asked.

Birdie didn't answer. She didn't know. She took long strides in a straight line, trying to put the clubhouse as far behind her as possible. Everywhere, the Balmeade Country Club appeared to be thriving financially. There were gardeners out trimming the shrubs to perfection and tons of shiny white golf carts criss-crossing the grass. Beside the new condos on the north side there were even newer condos going up. Here everybody was white, wore white, drove white golf carts. There were SUVs parked in discreet lots beyond the course so nobody would have to walk too far. All the golfers were men.

"Birdie, are you okay?" Murphy called out from behind her.

Birdie turned back to Leeda and Murphy and swallowed, trying to talk herself out of all the anger she felt. She took a deep breath. "Those papers were specs. For the orchard. Acreage, tree count, land surveys. I peeked."

Leeda and Murphy both stared at her solemnly.

She crossed her arms and stared around, blinking. She wasn't surprised, but she was still shocked. "I just . . . I want to knock everything down."

They were standing near a couple of boxwood shrubs, close to the first hole. She was about to kick one of the shrubs when Murphy grabbed her arm and gave her a hard yank. She, Murphy, and Leeda went tumbling behind the bushes.

"What?" Birdie hissed, looking for whatever it was that Murphy had seen. Her eyes lit on Horatio Balmeade, strolling across the grass with another man about fifty yards away.

"Why are we hiding?" she whispered to Murphy. Murphy didn't answer. Her green eyes narrowed for a moment, and then she seemed to remember something, and she reached her hand into her pocket, pulling out a very ripe, half-eaten peach.

"Here." Murphy held the peach out, a few drops of juice landing on Birdie's knuckles. "When he comes by, you should nail him with this."

Birdie looked at her, wide-eyed. "No!"

"Murphy," Leeda said, low and tense.

"Come on." Murphy shoved the peach into her hand, grinning. It squished against Birdie's fingers. "You know you want to."

Birdie looked at Leeda, who shook her head. "We'll get busted," Leeda hissed. Birdie felt the texture of the pit in her hands, buried in the thickness of the meat of the peach.

"Trust me, you'll feel much better," Murphy said.

The men continued to approach. She could see the gleaming white of Horatio's outfit through the holes in the bushes. Birdie gripped the peach in her fist. She felt a giddy nervousness that made it almost impossible to keep from laughing out her anger, especially when she looked at Murphy's expectant, gleeful face. "The pool will be Olympic standard," Horatio was saying.

"Birdie, don't," Leeda whispered.

Birdie acted fast. She stood up, lobbed the pit over the bush toward Horatio's back, and ducked.

"Eugh!"

Murphy snorted and clapped her hand over her mouth, then

clutched the branches as they stared through the spaces in the bushes.

Horatio had his hand on the back of his head and was leaning forward slightly. He clasped the back of his head, then looked up toward the sky, then around at the bushes, then down at the ground. He smiled at his friend and laughed fakely, and it came out so awkward that Birdie cringed for him. He picked up the peach and looked over toward the bush again, then the paltry patches of shrubbery and small trees in the opposite direction, his face going fire-engine red. He shook his shoulders, straightened them, and walked over to a caddy who was on his way across the grass. He started pointing around the area.

Murphy burst away from the bushes, keeping low to the ground. Birdie and Leeda followed, stumbling over themselves, moving on inertia.

They sprinted across the grass, breaking through the small patches of trees, and though they veered behind the clubhouse and out of Balmeade's sight, they didn't stop till they'd reached the road that ran along the back of the resort. It wasn't until they got there that Birdie realized she had peed her pants. And then it was only because Murphy fell on the ground, laughing hysterically and pointing, while Leeda hovered over her, panting and strained, looking like she wanted to step on Murphy's head.

On February 14, 1988, Lucretia Cawley-Smith and her huband, both drunk on too many sloe gin fizzes, accepted her cousin Cynthia's offer to stay the night at Darlington Orchard. A few weeks later, Lucretia, who wanted only one child and was more than satisfied with the one she had, reacted to her first wave of morning sickness in the same way she met most of life's surprises—with a raised eyebrow and a feeling of discontent that fate hadn't checked with her first.

Seventeen

Leeda checked herself one last time in the bathroom mirror, smoothing out the lines of her silver dress and running a few curls around her fingers to make them curvier. Out in the hall Murphy and Birdie were leaning against a wall, waiting for her—Birdie in a typically understated loose cotton dress and Murphy in one that was typically juicy, skimming her thighs in tiny pleats. They both looked beautiful.

Of course, at the moment it pissed Leeda off that Murphy looked beautiful. Leeda had been giving her the freeze-out since the peach incident, but by all appearances, Murphy couldn't care less. She'd given up teasing Leeda about it. At first Murphy had called her a priss, pointing out several times that they hadn't gotten caught. But Leeda almost wished they had, just so Murphy would be wrong.

"You look nice, Bird," Leeda said, shooting Murphy a cool glance. Murphy seemed unfazed.

Outside, the workers were still gathered around the barbecue. As the girls stepped outside, everybody turned to look at them. Several people let out wolf whistles. The women all smiled. Leeda shifted awkwardly, but she was pleased and touched. Just by the smiles on their faces, she could tell Birdie and Murphy were too.

As they started across the lawn, two faces loomed out at Leeda. One was Rex, who hadn't even showered yet. He was driving separately because Leeda had insisted it would look suspicious for them to arrive together since she was coming from the orchard and the last thing she needed was for her parents to make the connection that Rex worked at the orchard. And though he'd said she was paranoid, he'd gone along. Leeda had been pushing her family's buttons by inviting him in the first place. When they met eyes, she communicated with hers that he should get his butt ready to go.

The other face was Enrico. He was staring at Birdie as if she were a ball of light, his face illuminated, his mouth hanging slightly open.

"Hey, Birdie," Leeda whispered, leaning forward and pinching Birdie's butt. "Your boyfriend's catching flies."

Birdie snaked a hand out stealthily, smacking her low and hard on the upper thigh.

"Ow." Leeda shot her hand to her skin, surprised at how much it hurt.

Walking across the grass all dressed up felt strange—but special. It felt like being dressed up at the orchard, you glowed extra bright. The car arrived to pick them up exactly on time.

The Grand Ballroom of the Bridgewater Plantation View hotel was festooned with wine-colored candles that matched Danay's lipstick. Leeda's mom and dad stood by the big white doors proudly, greeting guests as they came in. Leeda drifted up to them with Murphy and Birdie at either side. Her mom kissed her like she was one of the guests.

"Hi, honey. Hi, Birdie."

She kissed Birdie lightly too.

"And who's this?" she asked Murphy's cleavage.

"That's ... Murphy, Mom."

"Hi, Murphy," Mrs. Cawley-Smith said fakely. Her mom could be so embarrassing sometimes. "Do you work at the orchard?"

Murphy crossed her arms over her chest defensively. But she managed to answer very politely. "Yep."

"Can you find your sister and send her over?" Lucretia asked, turning to Leeda. "I need to ask her something."

Leeda's special feeling from back at the orchard immediately disintegrated. She'd barely seen her mom all summer. "Yeah," Leeda said, "I'll find her."

The party was in full swing half an hour later, with a twelve-piece Zydeco band that Danay had requested after hearing them at Jazz Club in New Orleans. Rex arrived around that time, saying hi to the girls and then dragging Leeda out onto the dance floor. Rex didn't dance like some guys, showing off, or like others, who danced like spazzes. Rex danced nicely, solidly, dashingly, but without so much dash that he came across as less than the *guy* guy he was. Leeda was proud of him.

"Your sister's a good dancer," he said, nodding to where Danay and Brighton were keeping perfect rhythm.

"I know. I hate it," Leeda said, knowing she sounded bratty. Rex rubbed her back at the waist, where his hand was holding her.

"The audacity." He smiled. Leeda did too. Good old Rex.

He swung Leeda around a few times. They brushed past Horatio Balmeade, who was dancing with his much-younger wife but who eyed Leeda all the same as they crossed paths. Murphy was also not far away, dancing with one of the waiters.

Birdie stood on the sidelines, sipping champagne in fast little spurts and looking like if she kept going at the pace she was, she was headed for the night of her life.

After giving the cute waiter her number, Murphy drifted up to the bar and ordered a Manhattan, disbelieving that it could actually be free. "You look a little young to be drinking," the bartender said, still handing her the drink but doubtfully.

"Thanks," Murphy said, flashing a seductive smile and sipping on her way to join Leeda, Rex, Birdie, Danay, and Leeda's mom. Mrs. Cawley-Smith was in the middle of listening to herself talk about the migrant workers at the orchard. Murphy immediately wanted to turn around and hightail it elsewhere. But even though she was annoyed with Leeda for being so nitpicky about Birdie's beautiful peach pit attack, she didn't want to embarrass her by being rude. In fact, she'd never managed to act this mannerly for this long in her entire life.

Leeda stood listening, looking small. Murphy had never seen her tuck her shoulders or look so unsure of herself.

"It is really sad," Danay said. "They don't have any rights. No way to get around. It's total exploitation. No offense, Birdie."

"But," Leeda ventured tentatively, "everybody's fine with it. You should meet some of the workers. They work hard, but they have a good time. And they can make enough in one summer to live on in Mexico for two or three years."

Murphy watched the exchange, keeping quiet for once. Birdie, who knew more about the subject than anybody, was twirling an olive around and around in her martini, looking dazed. Occasionally she exchanged a look with Murphy and rolled her eyes. The only person Murphy didn't observe was Rex. She was careful to keep her eyes off him.

Time and again when Leeda spoke, Mrs. Cawley-Smith's eyes glazed over. It was really unbelievable. It started to irritate Murphy, the way she would start looking around as if she had somewhere to be or glance over at Rex like he was some kind of pest that had made its way into her party by mistake.

Leeda was in the middle of saying something about how hard the work at the orchard was when her mother looked at Rex coolly and drawled, "You know my Leeda, Rex, she's never really worked a day in her life." She said it as if she was bestowing Rex with a gift by saying something so chummy.

"Actually, that's not true."

Everybody in the circle turned to Murphy.

"Have you been to the orchard to visit her?" Murphy went on.

Mrs. Cawley-Smith tugged on her solitaire necklace. "I haven't been to the orchard in years, actually. I'm not much into nature." She smiled dryly.

"Are you much into Leeda? Because you could have come to visit. I mean, if you had, you'd see how hard she's been working."

Murphy looked at Leeda, who mouthed at her to be quiet. But once Murphy got started, it was hard for her to stop.

"It's like you've typecast your own daughter."

Mrs. Cawley-Smith's mouth had straightened into a thin, perfectly lipsticked line. "Excuse me?"

"Murphy." Rex had sidled up to her and was tugging at her elbow now. Murphy yanked it away.

"You and Danay are standing here, laughing about how Leeda is this and Leeda is that and you don't even know her." Murphy spat the words. She didn't know why she was suddenly so pissed off, but she couldn't control it.

"Murphy..."

Suddenly Rex was physically dragging her away from the group. Murphy caught Leeda's eyes as she was pulled across the dance floor. Rex didn't stop until he'd dragged her through a pair of white double doors out onto the huge, red-tiled balcony of the hotel.

When they got to the wall, he turned her around to look at him. "Stay here," he said sternly.

"But I don't..."

"Stay." Rex pushed her back against the wall gently but firmly. Murphy stayed, shocking even herself.

He disappeared inside, and a minute later he emerged with a bottle of Voss. It figured the Cawley-Smiths would only serve designer water.

"Drink."

Murphy did, looking up at his stern gaze and glowering.

"I was just sticking up for her. It wasn't fair."

"You weren't thinking about Leeda. You were thinking how pissed you are at the world. You were thinking about Murphy, as usual."

"But Leeda..." Murphy faltered.

"Look, I know her mom is crappy. But she needs to figure it out on her own. Embarrassing her isn't going to change anything."

Murphy crossed her arms over herself, thinking. She could see his point.

"But she looks at you like you're a bug. Doesn't that piss you off?"

Rex shrugged. "It's not about me. I just want Leeda to be happy. And if that means swallowing my pride every once in a while, fine."

Murphy sank back against the wall.

"She's a good girl." Rex's features had softened, and he looked at Murphy intently.

"I know." Murphy felt like she knew her more after an hour with her family than she had the whole time they'd spent at the orchard. It was like putting a piece of Leeda where it belonged in a bigger picture. Murphy had assumed that Leeda's perfectionism was as natural-born to her as her pinky finger, just part of her perfect life. It was funny how it only took seeing another part of the picture to realize it was the opposite.

Leeda *was* a good girl.

But it made her heart throb painfully to hear Rex saying it. She tried to look as casual as possible, crossing her arms over her stomach. That seemed to make her cleavage poke out too much, and she didn't want Rex to think she wanted him to look at her cleavage, so she uncrossed them again.

"Leeda will figure it out. She just doesn't fit with them. She *tries.*"

"I always thought she was a total cardboard cutout."

Rex shrugged. "She wants to be. She doesn't realize she's better than that."

"She's lucky she has you." Murphy was thinking about how wrong the Cawley-Smiths were about him. It was amazing how wrong.

"She needs me," Rex said, this time sounding a little wistful.

"Is that bad?"

Rex shook his head. "Not at all."

With nothing more to say, they both looked out at the parking lot.

"I love the south of France, don't you?" Murphy nodded toward the square of concrete as if it were the Mediterranean.

Rex grinned at her and patted the top of her wrist. His touch felt warm and sweet.

"Love it. I knew July was the best time to come."

Brighton and Danay stood in front of the orchestra. A moment ago Brighton had tapped the microphone and the whole room had quieted. Now all eyes were on Danay and her fiancé.

Leeda milled nervously beside her parents, uncomfortable about what Murphy had said. She was dying for her mom to say something, anything, about it. Just so she could know what she thought. But Brighton was going on and on, thanking several of the guests by name, then thanking Lucretia and Phil for raising such a smart, beautiful, thoughtful daughter. He dug out the line about how children were a reflection of their parents and that if Danay was a reflection of hers, they must be two very incredible people.

Leeda wanted to keel over. Until Danay took the mike and

added a special thanks to her, Leeda, her maid of honor. This made Leeda's heart warm up just a bit.

"Guys, she's single," Danay added. Leeda's heart turned back into ice. She scanned the room for Rex, but he wasn't in sight.

When the speech was over, she felt her mom's eyes on her and turned. "Well, Leeda, I have to say your friend is colorful."

This was what she'd been waiting for. "Murphy just gets . . . passionate about things, Mom. Anyway, I think she's right. I don't think you—"

"Birdie, you don't hang around girls like that, do you?"

Birdie looked strangely tranquil, not fidgety at all. She swayed a little, the chocolate martini in her hands sloshing up the side of the glass. She grinned. "Murphy's one of my best friends."

Leeda blinked at her a few times. Then she turned to her mom defiantly. "Me too, actually. Murphy's one of my best friends. So you should just try to accept her." It sounded weird that it had come out. But the more Leeda thought about it, the more it felt true.

Leeda's mom frowned, looking over Leeda's shoulder, then back at her, then touching her lightly on the shoulders and turning her around. "Well, she does seem very passionate about Rex."

Leeda's eyes lighted on Murphy and Rex, standing out on the balcony, looking out at the view together. She turned back around.

"Oh, please, Mom. They're my *friends*."

"Well, they make a neat pair," Mrs. Cawley-Smith said. "You

have excellent taste." She wagged her cocktail napkin, showing that she was empty, and headed back toward the buffet table.

Leeda stuck her tongue out at her mom's back, then looked back toward the balcony. It was nice that Murphy and Rex were finally getting along a little. It was.

"Your mom's kind of a bitch," Birdie said, her words long and drawn out.

Leeda looked at her. "Thanks, Bird."

"Sorry." Birdie smiled apologetically.

"She thinks she's looking out for me."

Leeda peered out at Murphy and Rex, talking earnestly with each other. She swallowed the tiny lump in her throat.

"Well, she's wrong about Murphy and Rex. They can't stand each other."

"I know."

Birdie followed her gaze thoughtfully. The view on the balcony told a different story. "Even if they do start getting along, it doesn't make your mom any less of a bitch."

Leeda agreed completely.

"I'm starving." Birdie was good and woozy, and her stomach felt achingly empty. "I think I drank too much."

"Maybe you have an oral fixation," Murphy suggested.

"I was just nervous," Birdie moaned.

They were sitting on the steps outside Camp A, talking in low voices. Murphy and Leeda were sitting close to each other, their fight apparently forgotten, though neither of them mentioned Murphy's display at the party as the reason why. To Birdie, it was obvious.

"We'll go into the kitchen and wrassle you up some grub." Murphy popped up, looking no worse for the wear for all the Manhattans she'd drunk.

"I have some Girl Scout cookies in my closet upstairs."

"You can't go in the house," Leeda warned.

"Aren't you eager to be reunited with your doggies?" Murphy asked. They'd left Honey Babe and Majestic with Emma, who adored them, for the night.

Birdie shook her head and stared at the house. She had never wanted a Thin Mint more in her life. "He's sleeping. C'mon," she begged. "Will you guys walk me up to the door?"

While the girls waited, Birdie let herself into the house and crept upstairs to her room, then padded down into the kitchen. She emerged onto the porch with not only two boxes of Thin Mints but a bag of salt-and-vinegar potato chips and a six-pack of beer.

"Birdie," Leeda said. "Your dad'll find out you took that."

"Trust me, he's so depressed I could take the *fridge* and he wouldn't notice."

"But I thought you said you drank too much."

"Apparently not." Birdie plunked down on one of the rockers. She pulled a beer out of the plastic ring and held it out to Murphy, who looked at her thoughtfully.

"You all right, Bird?" She took the beer.

"Sure."

They all began sipping their beer. For a while they just took in the sound and smell of the orchard at night.

"Maybe since you're feeling so bold you should make your move on Enrico right now while he's in his bed."

Birdie stiffened. She knew Murphy was joking, but even the *idea* made her nervous.

"I'm not making any move on Enrico." Birdie gulped at her Bud. "He's not interested anyway."

"Why wouldn't he be interested? Of course he's interested." Murphy sounded like she was saying that of course the sky was blue.

"Oh, he is definitely interested," Leeda added. "Did you see the way he looked at you tonight when we were leaving?"

Birdie thought back to it. She'd been too busy avoiding looking at him to look at him.

"Yeah, but earlier, in the shed . . ." Birdie stopped. She was too embarrassed. "God, he's hot."

Leeda and Murphy snickered quietly.

"Thanks." Birdie coiled up defensively.

"Sorry." Leeda blinked up at her, patting her thigh. "Birdie, he *likes* you. Why wouldn't he? You're beautiful, you're funny, you're sweet."

"You have the best hair," Murphy added.

Leeda nodded in agreement. "You pick a mean peach. You know how to do all this farm stuff that makes you look cool. You're a steel magnolia."

"Oh God." Birdie waved the compliments off with a weak wrist. But secretly, she was touched.

"Birdie, you have to go after what you want," Murphy said. "How do you expect to get it if you don't?"

"Well." Birdie looked from one to the other unsurely. Their faces sort of swam in front of her. "What do you think I should do?"

"Just bend over a lot in front of him."

"Murphy!" Leeda slapped Murphy on the thigh. "Maybe you

should just invite him to hang out down at the lake or something."

Birdie tried to picture herself doing that. "It's impossible. Saddle Tramp will be the only man I've ever been with." With those words, her stomach had started to do something odd. She put down her beer. "Um. I don't . . ." Her sentence trailed off. She wasn't sure it was a good idea to open her mouth anymore.

"I can tell him." Murphy played with the top of her can. "I'll be very subtle."

Leeda laughed. "You don't know how to be subtle."

"Shut up."

Birdie tried lying back on her back, but that was a mistake. The ceiling of the porch was spinning.

"You okay, Tweety Bird?"

Birdie shot up and lunged for the porch railing, retching with a loud groan. She felt someone's hands on her back and her hair being lifted. She retched several more times and then took a deep breath.

"Birdie?"

The lights above snapped on. Birdie saw her shadow suddenly materialize on the lawn beneath her. *Oh God.* She stood up and turned, Murphy's hands still on her, but Murphy and Leeda had turned also.

Her dad was standing on the porch in just his boxers. His belly hung over his shorts slackly and palely. As he took in the empty beer cans and food lying on the porch, his expression changed from one of concern to something else entirely.

Birdie felt the world spinning beneath her. It took only the look on her dad's face to tell her it was the end of summer as she knew it.

Eighteen

Bird, Poopie says your tail is stuck in a crack. What exactly does that mean? And what are you doing in there? x! Leeda

Dad made me dust everything. Body has gone numb from depression. Even cookies do not have the same appeal they used to. Have you seen E.?

*D*uring the first week of August the orchard work began to slow. Everyone trickled out of the trees imperceptibly earlier each day until Leeda realized that they were actually making it in before noon every time. There just weren't that many ripe peaches to pick.

It wasn't until then that Leeda looked around at the trees and noticed how empty they were. Only the Jefferson and O'Henry rows were left, the very last peaches to bloom. Another twelve days and that would be it. There was a sense of relief that so far the peaches had been free of brown rot, but everyone could tell the orchard wasn't yet out of the woods.

The orchard was strange without Birdie appearing everywhere you looked. She'd been restricted to the house for a week, working in the office and cleaning, helping Poopie cook. Most of this information Leeda and Murphy got from Poopie herself, who sat on the porch with her and Murphy from time to time, her eyes round and sympathetic, her cross glinting in the sun, rocking back and forth and filling them in.

It was harsh. There was no other word for it. And when Murphy pointed this out to Poopie, she closed her mouth and refused to comment. But it was obvious she agreed. And when Leeda asked her to tell Birdie to open her window between three and four every day, she didn't say she would.

But on the second day, when Leeda looked up at the window, it was open.

Leeda was an amazing shot. Always had been. She got it in the first try, setting off a flurry of barks and two butterfly-eared dogs peering down at her, their front paws up on the window defensively. And then Birdie appeared in a silhouette, waving to her.

"Don't you feel like a huge piece is missing without Birdie?" Leeda asked, lying on Murphy's bed. They were listening to the Libertines, which Leeda hated. "And can we change the channel?"

Murphy shrugged. "Sure." She didn't talk about Birdie the way Leeda did. But Leeda knew she felt the same way; she'd at least figured out that much about Murphy. It wasn't the same without Birdie. Even she and Murphy didn't seem to have quite the same connection as when Birdie was around. It was like it all didn't work quite right without the three of them.

•   •   •

*E. is lost without you. So are Murphy and me. But Murphy says
E. looks like he's been hit by a tire iron, whatever that is.
Murphy says hi. How much longer is your tail going to be stuck?*

*Three more days. If haven't succumbed to despair by then. Dad
is killing me. Have buried myself alive in a crust of disdain.
That's García Márquez.*

Murphy was walking across the grass one afternoon when
Honey Babe and Majestic appeared, sprinting toward her, jumping at her ankles and licking all around her lower legs.

"You guys are disgusting," she said with a smile, crouching
and pushing them away. She stood and started back across the
grass alongside the dorms toward her garden. Honey Babe and
Majestic ran on ahead of her on the tiny footpath, turning
around from time to time to wait for her. The three of them
broke through the last few feet of brush together.

Over the past few days the garden had exploded. The roses
were vibrant and red and luscious and velvety, lining the edges.
The hydrangea glowed neon blue. Murphy stood on the edge of
it, sizing it up. Other than a few weeds she planned to pull
today, it was perfect. She couldn't remember anything she'd
done that she felt more proud of.

Honey Babe and Majestic lay down under the trellis while
she knelt and dug up the last few strings of grapevine, occasionally resting back on her heels and gazing at the dogs or up at
Birdie's window.

"Aren't you supposed to be keeping her company?" she asked.
The dogs tilted their heads at her quizzically. "Dumb dogs."

Murphy hadn't tossed any messages up to Birdie. She hadn't stood outside her window, trying to catch her attention like Leeda. With the end of her sentence approaching, Murphy felt herself closing up like petals at night, thinking of going back home to life as normal. If she let her mind calm down and really thought about it, she realized how fearful she was starting to become.

She let her eyes drift up to Birdie's window again, and this time there was Birdie's silhouette in the window. Murphy raised a hand to wave sedately. Birdie waved back, then disappeared.

Murphy looked back at the dogs, who were leaning against each other, eyeballing her. She wanted to share her success with someone other than two papillons.

She stood up, brushed the dirt off her knees, and walked back to the dorms. She knocked on Leeda's door, but there was no answer. Murphy grabbed a pen and a piece of paper from her room and wrote on it: *Dinner in the garden, 7 o'clock. Bring gifts.*

That evening she put together sandwiches in the kitchen and made lemonade. She set out toward the garden with her blanket rolled under one arm to use as a picnic blanket. She dug a Wilco CD out of her collection and hauled her CD player down the path. Halfway down, she ran into Rex.

"Rex, hey . . ." Murphy hoisted the CD player up tighter under her arm.

Rex had a couple of peaches in his hand and he held one out toward her. "Hey. Have a peach."

"Thanks." Murphy stuck the peach in her pocket.

"Your garden looks really good."

Murphy smiled. "What were you doing in my garden?"

"I don't know. I've kind of been keeping an eye on it. And I'm out of here tomorrow, so I wanted to get a final look. You did a good job."

Murphy's heart sank. "You're going already?" She was as surprised at the question as Rex appeared to be. It didn't sound like her at all.

Rex stuck his hands in his pockets and looked around. "They don't really need me anymore. I guess everybody'll be trailing off from here on out."

Murphy kicked a toe in the dirt. "Yeah. I keep forgetting. I keep thinking it's only me that's leaving. It's weird."

Rex looked at her seriously and didn't answer. Finally he said, "Leeda and I just took a nap down at the lake."

"Oh."

They looked at each other.

"What's with all the goods?" Rex said, indicating the stuff in her arms.

"Oh, I'm having a picnic. Me and Leeda."

"Sounds great."

"Um."

"I'm so glad you invited me." Rex gave her his cocky grin.

Murphy sighed and let her shoulders sag. "Fine. Whatever. See you at seven. You've got fifteen minutes. Clean yourself up a little, huh?"

"No problem." He continued on down the trail.

Bird, try to come to the garden.

Leeda crumpled up the note into a ball and lofted it into Birdie's window, then walked through the trail to the trellis. When she got there, Murphy and Rex were laughing about something, sitting cross-legged, Murphy with her back against the trunk of the nectarine tree, her cupped hands resting on the grass between her legs, and Rex resting back on his hands.

"Hey, baby," Rex said, smiling up at her and patting the grass beside him. Leeda tried to ignore the tiny voice that was telling her he didn't seem one hundred percent happy to see her.

The food—just sandwiches—tasted more exotic in the garden, and the lemonade was sweet and cool. Leeda relaxed, picking flowers from where she sat and sticking them all over Murphy's curly hair.

"I guess Birdie isn't making it," Leeda said when she'd finished her second ham and cheese.

"Poor Bird," Murphy said, stretching out on her back and smushing most of the flowers.

"Moment of silence for Birdie missing the picnic," Rex said, and they all bowed their heads, Murphy bowing hers against her chest where she was lying. When the moment of silence was over, Rex turned to Murphy.

"What're you going to do when you grow up anyway?" Rex asked.

"Move to New York."

"Ooh, that sounds good," Leeda said. "Maybe I'll come. We can go to NYU."

Murphy tucked her hands behind her head. "Nah. I don't know. I think I'll get a job as a waitress. Something romantic like that."

Rex frowned. "What about school?"

Murphy shrugged. "I'm not so into school."

"Don't you think that's kind of a waste?" Rex sounded concerned enough to make Leeda feel a little jealous. Murphy sat up.

"What, do you think waitresses are stupid?"

"No, I just think you're stupid. Aren't you a genius or something?"

"You just said I was stupid."

"I think anybody who has something good and wastes it is stupid."

Leeda looked back and forth between the two of them, feeling like a spectator to their conversation. Rex was gazing sternly at Murphy and Murphy was narrowing her eyes at him in return, and neither of them seemed too concerned about what Leeda was doing when she grew up.

"Yeah. You're crazy, Murphy," she piped in, wanting to be part of the discussion and also knowing Rex was right. Leeda knew that if she had Murphy's brains, she'd be using them for something—like surpassing her sister.

"Oh, please stop. I feel like I'm back in school."

They all lapsed into silence for a moment and suddenly Rex looked at Leeda, as if he'd just remembered she was there.

"What do you think Leeda will be?" he asked Murphy, wrapping his arm around Leeda's shoulders contritely. She braced herself for disappointment.

Murphy nodded definitively. "A movie star."

"Queen?" Rex suggested.

"Queen sounds fabulous," Leeda said flatly. But Rex poked her ribs and, like a little kid, she laughed and felt stupid for being jealous.

"You can be queen of Darlington Peach Orchard. Here." Murphy pulled a peach out of her pocket and tapped Leeda on the top of the head with it. "Rex and I declare ourselves your loyal subjects."

"That's a paltry offering. The Darlington Orchard is almost extinct."

This made everybody silent, and Leeda felt bad again. Murphy plucked grass and scattered it on Leeda's knee.

There was a shadow over the rest of their picnic. Leeda felt softly worried, like the worry had settled in at the edges of her mind. It only reminded her that she'd never felt more accepted or loved, and that she was happy. And it couldn't possibly last.

From her window, Birdie watched the festivities in the garden. Rex, Murphy, and Leeda looked like a cozy threesome without her. In fact, it looked like they didn't miss her at all.

Since Walter had locked her away, she'd cleaned the whole house from top to bottom. She'd talked to her mom twenty million times and passed messages along to her dad about things Cynthia wanted from the house for the new one she was moving into.

Birdie had maintained her sanity with her little notes from Leeda, and the knowledge that they were out there miserable without her (like the notes had said). But now she could see how obvious it was that life outside was moving on without her, and she was beginning to wonder if it wouldn't always be that way.

She'd spotted Enrico once, when she was down in the kitchen washing dishes, glancing out the window over the sink. He'd been hauling a bushel of damaged peaches off in the direction of the cider house. It had made Birdie even more keenly aware that the last days of the harvest were passing her by. Sitting up in her window watching the picnic, she nibbled on her nails, agonizingly restless. Already she had lost too much time.

"They could hear that sigh clear across Bridgewater," Poopie said, standing in the doorway. "What's wrong, Birdie?" She walked across the room and sat on the window seat beside her. She shook her head. "It's sad, I know. The orchard . . ."

Birdie picked her fingernails. "Dad sent over papers to Mr. Balmeade."

"I know about them," Poopie interrupted. Birdie wasn't surprised. Poopie knew about everything. "The workers think this is the last summer."

"You won't leave Dad, will you?" Birdie had never even considered this a possibility. Her skin prickled as Poopie shrugged.

"I need to work."

Birdie breathed raggedly. She tried to change the subject because she couldn't handle this one anymore. "I'm sick of being inside, Poopie." Honey Babe was on a pillow on her lap, and Birdie ran her silky tail through her hand, twining it around her fingers and clenching it in her fist.

"I just don't understand why Dad thinks this is good for me. I'm gonna end up like that lady in *Jane Eyre*." Birdie was referring to a character in the story who was locked away in the attic because she was insane and finally ended up lighting the house on fire. She and Poopie had watched the movie on A&E.

"You're not gonna be like the lady in *Jane Eyre*, honey."

"How do you know? People just get more eccentric as they get older."

"You should tell him how you feel."

Birdie stiffened. For a moment she thought Poopie was talking about Enrico.

"You never tell your father what's going on in your head. He needs to hear it, even if he doesn't want to."

Birdie's shoulders drooped. "He doesn't listen. I mean, I do everything right." Birdie's voice cracked. "But it doesn't matter. I mean, even when I'm *not* locked up, I'm locked up. And you might leave ..." Birdie swallowed.

Poopie frowned and stood up, looking annoyed. Birdie gulped. Was she being too whiny? Before she could say anything else, Poopie walked purposefully out of the room.

A few minutes later she reappeared in the doorway. "I talked to your father." She smiled. "You can go."

"Really?" Birdie hopped up.

Poopie nodded.

Birdie threw her arms around Poopie's neck and gave her a big kiss on the cheek.

It was just approaching dusk. The smoke coming from the dorm area smelled of barbecue. When she'd started down the stairs, Birdie had been planning to make a beeline for the picnic, but now, with her heart pounding, she let her legs carry her in the direction of the dorms.

She walked past the barbecue area, scanning the group for Enrico but not slowing down when she didn't see him. If she slowed down, she'd give up. She tromped up the stairs of Camp B and knocked on the door, not waiting for someone to answer before pushing it open.

Birdie didn't have a strategy. She just knew that if she didn't do this now, she *would* end up like that woman in *Jane Eyre*. She would stay an old lady in a young body. She would always be locked up.

She stopped just a few feet before Enrico's open door, her heart thumping so loudly she could hear it. And then she had a brief talk with herself. She was confident. She was brave. She was all the other things Murphy and Leeda had told her she was.

She took the last few steps to the doorway and turned the corner.

The room was empty. The sheets and blanket had been rolled up at the foot of the bed. The mini TV was gone. The books were gone. Everything was gone.

Enrico was gone.

Murphy swirled a fried mushroom cap around in a tiny tub of white sauce. Richard was feeding her mom a buffalo wing, which hardly made the special permission Murphy had gotten to leave the orchard worthwhile. Murphy would have begged to skip the free day and go back to work rather than watch the two of them act like teenagers. But she was already occupied thinking about Rex.

She loved him. That was the conclusion she'd arrived at sometime between the picnic last night and waking up this morning. Only *she* could have managed to get in her own way like this. It was the crappiest, stupidest thing she'd done yet. Murphy lifted the mushroom to her lips and ripped off the cap with her teeth, sucking the juice out of the little pool of it under the cap. She looked up to see the TGI Friday's waiter, who was staring at her suggestively, and frowned at him.

"Honey?"

"Yeah." Murphy stuffed three more mushrooms in her mouth and washed them down with a swig of sweet tea.

"Richard and I want to tell you something." Jodee twined her fingers through Richard's and stared at Murphy nervously. Murphy felt the mushroom caps congeal into a sickening glob in her stomach.

"I don't wanna know," Murphy said.

"Murphy."

"Look, I gotta go to the bathroom." Murphy fled the table. In the bathroom she rubbed at her tight throat, took a few deep breaths, and then washed her hands compulsively twice. She looked in the mirror and shook her head. "Please, God, don't do this to me." Then she rolled her eyes bitterly, immediately realizing she hadn't racked up enough good karma to ask God for much of anything.

There was a pay phone in the vestibule just outside the bathroom door. Murphy had painted over the tiny holes of the receiver in black nail polish once, so people could hear through the phone but not be heard. Now she ducked out of the bathroom and picked it up, praying that someone had fixed it since then, and that today wasn't the day her karma had caught up with her. She dialed information and got them to dial the Darlingtons' home number.

"Hello?"

"Poopie," she croaked. "Is Birdie there?"

There was a silence on the other end. "Honey, I haven't seen her in a couple of hours. You okay?"

The lump in Murphy's throat was so big that she couldn't

speak. She shook her head until she finally got the words out. "I'm okay. Thanks. Bye."

"Honey . . ."

Murphy held on to the receiver after she'd placed it on the hook, thinking of who else she could call. The only way she could reach Leeda would be through the phone by the barn. She tried that number, but it rang and rang. How had she lived in this town her whole life without racking up one person she could really talk to? Leeda and Birdie felt like a life raft that was floating too far away. She wanted to scream.

If either of them had been there to hear her, she would have told them that Jodee had done a lot of stupid things with stupid guys, but she'd never married one of them. She would have said that it felt like the last measly surviving thread of the rug under her and her mom's life was being yanked out from under her.

When Murphy finally emerged into the dining area, she had managed to paste a look of cool indifference on her face. Jodee had paid the check and she and Richard were both waiting just outside the front doors. They climbed into the car.

"Murphy . . ."

"Let's just act like you already told me, okay?" Murphy croaked, then cleared her throat.

Jodee looked across at Richard in the driver's seat. He just shook his head. Then she looked back at Murphy, her eyes big and sad. "Okay, baby."

Murphy spotted Birdie on the porch when they pulled up the drive and headed in that direction. She almost sprinted across the grass. But she made herself walk, and the closer she got, the more sure she became that something was wrong with Birdie. The area around her eyes was all puffy, and she was stroking her dogs like her life depended on it. Immediately all of the things Murphy had been waiting to spill sank under the surface.

"You okay, Bird?" Murphy asked, climbing the steps.

"Yeah." Birdie's voice came out thin and warbly.

Murphy put her hand on Birdie's knee and shook it. She knew she should ask what was wrong, but Murphy wasn't that kind of girl. She didn't really know how. "Hey, Walter let you out?" she said instead, trying to sound cheery.

Birdie turned her big eyes to Murphy, her breath fluttering between her teeth. "Enrico left."

Murphy's heart gave a heavy thud. She crouched down beside Birdie's rocker and laid her arm on the armrest, not knowing what to do. Being a shoulder to cry on was something Murphy had never done in her life.

"It's okay. It's not a big deal," Birdie was saying. She stood up from her chair and plopped down on the deck beside Murphy. Honey Babe planted her two paws on the side of Murphy's leg and licked her arm. Murphy barely noticed.

"When?"

"Last night." Birdie sniffed. "Poopie got Dad to let me out early, and I was gonna come to the garden, but . . ." Birdie didn't finish.

They stared out at the grass for a while.

With a long sigh, Birdie spoke. "It's not just Enrico. It's just I'm such a coward. I let everything pass me by. I don't know if I'll ever . . . not . . . do that."

Murphy patted her back awkwardly. "That's not true, Birdie."

Birdie's silence said she didn't want to be coddled. Finally she dropped her head softly on Murphy's shoulder.

"I should have gone for it."

"Well, how could you have known the dummy was leaving?"

"That's no excuse. I suck."

"Everybody sucks," Murphy offered.

"Oh, Murphy." Birdie lifted her head, smiled at her, and rolled her eyes. They were quiet again. And then Birdie sat up straighter. "You know what? Can you change the subject?"

Murphy nodded. The words about her mom rose to her lips. But then, that wasn't exactly a pick-me-up. She tried to think of something else, interesting but not heavy. Something they were both invested in.

"Hey, Bird, what do you think about Rex and Leeda?"

As soon as it was out, Murphy wished she could take it back.

"They're cute together, huh?" Birdie asked, rubbing the back of her hand along the bottom of her nose.

Murphy considered. "Yeah." She told herself not to say it. "Do you think she loves him?"

Birdie considered. "I think they're good friends." She pulled back, resting her hands behind her on the deck and tilting her head. "Why?"

Birdie's face was so open and sweet that Murphy thought for a minute she really could tell her about Rex and she would understand. Didn't she at least deserve that? Wasn't Birdie her friend as much as Leeda's?

Murphy shook her head. "It's just I was thinking the same thing. I think I'd like that kind of thing someday."

In the end, it seemed disloyal to Leeda to say anything at all.

Loyalty was a funny thing. So was love. They both bit you when you least expected it.

At age seven, Enrico Fiol found a peach blossom blowing across his front yard in Northern Mexico near the Texas border. There wasn't a peach tree within eight hundred miles. Knowing his friends would make fun of him for admiring the flower, Enrico snatched it up and hid it in a book. It sat there forgotten, dried and mummified, for the rest of his life.

Nineteen

Leeda's two huge suitcases lay in the middle of the floor, half packed. She'd taken down her curtains and folded up her blankets, stowing all her breakable knickknacks inside. Sitting on the bed and looking around, she couldn't believe how different the room felt. She couldn't believe she'd lived here for a whole summer. It just looked so unlike anyplace she would spend her time.

In the hallway the women were packing too, dragging things down the stairs and piling them up outside for the bus. Poopie would shuttle them in the bus to the Greyhound station and help them get everything on when the bus arrived. Leeda watched boxes and boxes of stuff go by and smiled. Greyhound didn't know what it was in for. If Leeda were from Mexico, she mused, she would have done the same thing.

She began pulling her clothes out of the dresser, packing them carefully: shirts on one side, shorts on the other. But her limbs felt heavy.

Across the hall Murphy was blaring her music and lying on her bed. The last time Leeda had peered in, she hadn't packed a thing. Now Leeda ripped a piece of paper out of the notebook on her desk and folded it into a paper airplane. Then she unfolded it, wrote on it, folded it again, and sent it sailing across the hall.

A few seconds later the airplane came back. Leeda unfolded it.

In her writing it said, *Get to work, slacker.*

In Murphy's it said, *Come over here and do it for me. Pretty pleeease?*

A second later Murphy herself appeared in the doorway, her eyes sorrowful.

"Poopie's here with the bus."

They walked out toward the drive, where everyone had gathered, including Birdie. Poopie had already taken a load of the men over, so already the group seemed small. The rickety white door of the bus hissed open, and suddenly everyone was piling on Murphy and Leeda and Birdie, hugging them.

Next to Leeda, Emma squeezed Birdie's chin and kissed her cheek. "Thank you, Birdie." A tear trickled out of her eye. This was not like other good-byes at the orchard, though Leeda had never witnessed one. This was people saying good-bye forever.

As the bus pulled away, Leeda gently patted Birdie's back. They watched it disappear down the long drive. Birdie turned, smiling, but with tears in her eyes.

"Oh, honey." Leeda hugged her, and Murphy stood behind her, rubbing her shoulder. Birdie pulled back and swiped at the rims of her eyelids.

"It just feels like the world's ending," she said through a smile.

They walked back to the barbecue pit.

"Where will you go?" Murphy ventured, cupping her hands thoughtfully. "If you guys ... have to sell?"

"I don't know. Dad talks about moving to California."

"California?"

"What about Aunt Cynthia? She's moving here, isn't she?"

Birdie shook her head. "Yeah. I don't know. I don't know how we'll work it out."

Leeda began ripping apart a long blade of grass. "Well, maybe you won't have to sell...."

Birdie let out a long sigh. "We can't keep up with other farms with better equipment, more land, better connections to the grocery chains. Dad was never good at any of that stuff. He's just good at growing peaches."

"But couldn't you get all those things?"

"We don't have the money."

She was interrupted by the sound of a car pulling up the drive. All three girls turned to see Horatio Balmeade's black Mercedes slinking its way toward the house.

"Buzz kill," Murphy said.

Leeda too felt like it was a total reality check. But Birdie didn't look fazed. For once she looked excited.

"Do you guys know we have a huge freezer in the back of the house?"

"Are we gonna put his body in it?" Murphy joked.

Birdie looked at her mysteriously.

"Not quite."

Squid was Birdie's dad's favorite. He liked to buy it fresh from a guy who caught it in the Gulf and then freeze it in the giant freezer out back. Murphy gave Birdie a boost above the toilet seat as she took a handful of the frozen fish and stuffed it into the ceiling tiles of the Magnolia Lady's Lounge at Balmeade Country Club.

"Birdie, be careful."

"Blah blah," Birdie said, sliding the foamy square of ceiling back into place. She'd never done something this bad, ever, but she felt like an old pro at it. Her heart was racing but in a good way. This, she figured, must be what Murphy got off on, and now she understood why.

Leeda had explained to the girls that there were actually four lounges, the Magnolia, the Jasmine, the Bougainvillea, and the Rose. Murphy had thought it was hilarious that they were called lounges and had said she had drunk too much water and that she had to lounge right then and could they please excuse her.

They finished with the Rose, which they'd chosen to be last because it was the most remote, in the back of the fitness hall. By that point the fish had started to melt already and was giving off a slight odor.

They chose to crawl over the fence back into the orchard a few minutes later. Birdie and Murphy had to hold the old barbed wire open for Leeda to crawl through slowly. Once they were across the property line, Birdie jumped up and down a few times, giddy and breathless. She couldn't believe they'd done it.

"I wish we could see his face," Murphy said, also moving around restlessly. It was just dusk, and it gave the whole event a surreal glow.

"You two stink," Leeda said, holding her hand over her nose and then yanking it away. "So do I."

"You guys are going home tonight?"

Murphy and Leeda looked at each other. One more night wouldn't hurt.

"I guess not," Murphy said, waggling both of her hands in the air. "How about the lake?"

One last time. Birdie didn't say it, but she knew that was what they were all thinking. They could pretend it was just another night.

Up ahead of them Murphy had begun stripping off her clothes, and suddenly she was down to nothing.

"Murphy, please put your clothes on," Leeda called ahead. "Nobody wants to see that."

Once she reached the edge of the lake, Murphy looked at them over her shoulder. "I love this lake. I plan to honor it this last time by swimming in it naked."

Leeda and Birdie exchanged looks, turning when they heard the splash of Murphy jumping in.

Leeda had been skinny-dipping before at a couple of parties, but only when she'd had a bunch of drinks. Somehow swimming naked with just girls seemed more intimate. But she stripped off her tank top anyway, and then her bra.

Naked, she toyed with the idea of dipping her toes in first.

"Oh, what the hell." She dove, the water blanketing her softly. It felt like bathwater. When she surfaced beside Murphy, Birdie was standing on the shore, looking nervous.

"C'mon, Bird."

"Oh, I don't know. Okay, fine, just don't look."

Leeda and Murphy giggled but treaded water, turning their backs.

There was a *swish swish zip* and then a splash as Birdie too got into the water.

Leeda swam on her back. They gathered and splashed around for a while, talking in low voices as it got darker.

"It's night," Murphy whispered, looking up. Sure enough, a couple of stars were peeping out above them and the crickets had started in singing without anyone noticing. "Can you smell peaches?"

They were far away from the trees, but Leeda sniffed the air, thinking she did too.

"I smell peaches in my sleep," Birdie offered.

Leeda sank onto her back and backstroked away, then rested her arms and let herself float out into the middle of the lake. She couldn't remember anything feeling more gorgeous. And maybe it was partly because this was the last of it, and it would never happen this way again.

Splash. Leeda righted herself. Murphy had climbed out of the water and, without any self-consciousness whatsoever, was skirting the lake to a high rock on one side. She went in with a splash, disappearing underwater for several seconds. And then Birdie let out a whoop and went plunging under.

When they surfaced, they were both spitting water and laughing. Leeda was struck by just how stunning her friends were. They looked like mermaids, treading water and splashing around.

Murphy climbed onto shore again, her skin glowing.

And then she stopped. "Oh." She stood stock-still for a second, then threw her hands over her breasts and her crotch, walking backward. "Hi."

Leeda paddled up to the side of the lake, where a figure had emerged. She felt her heart sink into her abdomen. "Rex?"

Rex was looking at the grass at his feet very carefully. He glanced up again at Murphy.

"Rex!" Leeda cried, her voice cracking with jealousy. "Turn *around*."

Rex obeyed, and Leeda and Birdie scrabbled out of the water. All three girls yanked on their clothes.

"I thought I'd find you guys here," Rex explained when they let him turn back around. "I saw your stuff back at the dorm."

"I bet you say that to all the naked women," Murphy said, like she was trying to sound casual. She didn't sound casual at all.

"I seem to be seeing a lot of you lately," Rex replied.

Leeda didn't laugh. She felt like a statue. Paralyzed.

Rex kept staring at Murphy. And frowning. And still staring. And Leeda felt all the blood drain out of her feet. Because his eyes weren't heavy lidded right then, like they always were with her—heavy lidded and sleepy and kind and reassuring. They were wide open and unguarded. And all over Murphy.

Tweet tweet tweet.

Murphy sat up in bed and looked at the window. It was only barely light, but there was her little friend, sitting on one of the branches of his tree and staring at her with his beady eyes.

She closed her window, then fell back in bed and pulled her

pillow over her head. But it was too late. She was already awake and too fully aware of the day. And the night before.

She rolled out of bed and pulled her boxers on over her bikini underwear, her curly hair so heavy on the side she hadn't slept on that she felt her head might flop in that direction. She pulled it into an elastic so that it lay in a lopsided bun at the nape of her neck and shuffled into the hall.

Birdie had gone to sleep in the newly vacated bedroom at the end of the hall the night before. But Murphy could see now that the door was open and the bed was empty. She slid her slippered feet up to Leeda's closed door and tapped on it gently, scratching it with her fingers. "Leeda," she whispered. "Lee?" Nobody answered.

Murphy sighed. She wanted to see Leeda, to reassure herself that they were still good. She'd been so quiet on the way back from the lake. Murphy knew she hadn't done anything wrong, but the moment with Rex had been palpably tense. She felt like Leeda might have somehow seen into the deepest, darkest part of her heart and seen that Rex was there. She just needed to know that wasn't true. But she guessed she'd have to wait for her to wake up first. The old Murphy would have pounded on the door anyway. But this one shuffled back into her room.

Without bothering to change, Murphy slipped into her Dr. Scholl's sandals and walked outside, turning left to go visit her blue jay. He stared at her from his branch, a wriggling worm stuck under his skinny black foot.

"Look," Murphy said, "I know this should be where I tell you that all those times you annoyed me, you were actually growing on me, and that I'm really going to miss you."

The blue jay tilted its head as if it could actually understand her.

"But it's not going to happen. I actually just came by to say that I hope the winter takes you."

Murphy turned and started back around to the other side of the dorm, toward the garden. She was fully aware she was moping along like somebody with an extreme hangover. She was also aware that it was sort of an act, for her own sake. It felt good to walk like she felt.

At the edge of the clearing she surveyed her work, looking at it with a fresh eye. It really was stunning. The yellow roses were in full bloom and majestic. The azaleas were vibrant and healthy.

Murphy took a deep breath of satisfaction and ducked under the trellis, then came to a stop.

There was Rex, kneeling in front of a wooden bench that sat back against one of the rosebushes. He was looking up at her, surprised.

"Hey," Murphy whispered.

"Hey." Rex stood up. "I thought you'd be sleeping. I wanted to just leave it here."

Murphy swallowed, then looked behind him at the bench. She didn't want to look at his eyes. "You know that's a terrible place for that. Right up against the prickers."

Instead of coming back with some remark the way Murphy expected, Rex's eyebrows descended. "Oh yeah." He tapped his forehead.

"I'll help you move it," she offered, walking up to one side of the bench and lifting it. "How about under the cherry tree?"

Rex nodded, lifting his end, and they moved it the few feet and put it down. Then stood back.

"Wow. Thanks, Rex. That's . . . really cool. Did you make it?"

Rex nodded. "No problem. It was supposed to be a surprise. I finished it a couple of days ago."

"It is a surprise."

"I actually thought about not bringing it after the weirdness ... last night...."

Murphy didn't want to acknowledge last night. She clicked her sandals back and forth against her feet.

"You get any fruit off that nectarine tree?" Rex asked finally, covering up.

Murphy shrugged. "Nope. The damn bugs. I haven't gotten one nectarine."

Rex laughed. It hurt Murphy to hear his laugh come so easy when she felt so tense. He was always so easy. He was the only guy she'd ever known who acted like she thought a guy should be.

Rex scanned the tree up and down. "Well, there's that one up top."

Murphy was about to tell him he was full of it when she caught sight of it too. "Oh my God, you're right."

She and Rex looked at each other, and Murphy's smile grew huge. "I grew a beautiful nectarine."

"The tree had nothing to do with it."

"Nothing."

Rex walked up to the tree and hoisted himself, reaching for the nectarine with a leap.

"Here you go," he said, tossing it at her. Murphy caught it against her stomach. It was completely perfect, not one bug. She rubbed the fruit against her shirt, then took a bite.

"Thanks, Rex."

"Yeah."

But Murphy could hardly chew.

"Is it bad?" Rex asked, looking concerned.

She shook her head. "No . . ."

Rex stepped up close to her. "What's wrong?"

"Nothing. Don't look so freaked out."

She blinked at him several times, then twisted her lips toward the shelter of a sarcastic grin. But the grin hadn't made it all the way onto her face before Rex reached out and put his hands against her shoulders. Murphy's heart leapt into her throat. In another moment his lips pressed into hers, forcing the smile away completely, fitting like the nectarine had, like the ripest softest sweetest thing in the world. His tongue found its way inside her mouth, pressing against her nectarine-covered tongue. And then he pulled away. She realized his hand was on the back of her hair, and he kept it there, stroking her. The way he looked at her was thoughtful, gauging. Not excited or passionate, but like a friend's gaze, trying to figure her out.

She let herself feel his fingers there for a moment, overwhelmed with joy.

And then the thought of Leeda hit her like a hammer. And all of the joy was replaced by ugly, heavy dread. She nodded forward and pulled out of Rex's grasp.

They stared at each other. Murphy had the feeling of being in a dream and out of control, the kind where you woke up and hoped you hadn't just done what you thought you had. But Rex was real, standing in front of her. He looked exhausted, his eyes directly staring into hers, unashamed.

"Leeda's my *friend*," Murphy said low.

Rex was silent. It was all the fuel she needed. She felt her anger drumming up so that it almost felt like it was real and that it was really him she was mad at. She met his gaze with all the disgust she could muster.

"M-Murphy," he stammered. "I'll tell her. Leeda and I shouldn't even be . . ."

Murphy squinted at him as if she had no idea what he was saying. Like the whole moment was a foreign concept to her. She shook her head. "I don't even *like* you."

"Murphy . . . we have this . . . thing. . . ."

"Thing?" Murphy searched the sky, faking astonishment, disgusted with her own insincerity. "You're crazy."

When she looked back down, Rex's confidence had flickered. She could see it in his eyes. Murphy felt her own hurt was too naked, and she looked away, and her eyes lit on the house. A movement drew her eyes to Birdie's window.

A silhouette—Birdie's silhouette—stood there for a moment, the shadow hand flying up to the shadow mouth. The whole figure swayed slightly and then slid to the left, vanishing out of sight. Murphy felt the blood drain out of her face and a sick thudding in her abdomen.

Rex reached toward her waist, touching it gently. It felt like a lifeline to her. "I want to be with you."

Murphy pulled back and glared at him. She was panicked now, her head spinning. She tried to harness the misery she felt and direct it toward him. Her voice came out strangled and hateful. "I don't want you. Don't you get it?"

Rex finally took a step back, and this broke Murphy's heart. He looked at the house, then back at her, confused and dazed. He shook his head, grinning ruefully, painfully. "I'm an idiot. God, I'm sorry."

Murphy felt tears springing to the edges of her eyes. She balled her fists, twisted them in her T-shirt, and croaked, "Leave me alone."

Rex nodded and stuffed his hands into his pockets. He turned and walked down the trail.

Murphy looked up at Birdie's window desperately, but her silhouette didn't show up again. Murphy ran her hand hard through her frazzled hair. She could still see Rex walking down the path, not looking back.

In helpless rage she hurled her nectarine at his heels, but it missed, bouncing along the ground and disappearing into the underbrush.

Honey Babe and Majestic met Murphy halfway down the stairs, jumping at her legs and licking her hands as she bent down to pet them.

"Birdie?"

She could hear VH1 burbling softly out of Birdie's room but no other sound.

"Tweety Bird?"

She'd already been back to the dorms to splash her face and calm down enough to talk to Birdie. When she'd gotten there, she'd seen that Leeda's door was open, and the thudding inside had gotten worse. Walking over to the house, she felt like she had a fever. She kept on sending up one thought. *Please don't let her tell Leeda. Please please please.*

Now the rag rug on the landing slid slightly under her feet and Murphy pushed it back, swallowing. She padded to Birdie's door and looked inside, feeling her skin start to prickle all over, hot and cold. There were Birdie and Leeda, sitting on the bed facing each other, one of each girl's legs hanging off the side of the bed, the other tucked up under them.

They both stared at Murphy. Birdie, with a half-open mouth and big, unsure eyes. Leeda's eyes were red around the edges and ice cold. Murphy felt both looks like a slap.

"Hey, guys . . ." she murmured.

"Hey, Murphy," Birdie muttered, picking at her quilt.

"Uh, what are you . . . what are you guys doing?"

Murphy slid around the edge of the door and leaned against Birdie's wall.

Birdie's eyes darted to Leeda. Murphy felt a wave of nausea. "We're just . . . watching TV."

"Oh." Without meaning to, Murphy looked down at her shirt, noticing how much cleavage was poking out of her tank top.

Suddenly Leeda stood up. "Well, see you, Birdie." Without looking at Murphy, Leeda started toward the door. Murphy felt herself wince, and tried to iron her face into a cooler expression. But Leeda seemed to have the monopoly on iciness. She breezed right by Murphy into the doorway.

"Leeda, wait . . ." Murphy said, reaching her hand toward Leeda's waist. Leeda jerked away, fast as a rattlesnake.

"Don't touch me."

Murphy's mouth dropped open. For the first time in her life she was speechless. Her heart began to thud in her ears, her toes. That was where Leeda's words hit her. They hit her everywhere.

Leeda looked wounded too for a moment, and Murphy swallowed, trying to regain her composure enough to string a few words together. She wanted to deny it had happened at all, which would have been the way she used to do things; a few months ago she could have slid out of anything, usually by turning it on the person who'd accused her. But this was too important to lie about.

"Leeda, I didn't kiss—"

She'd been about to say she hadn't kissed Rex back, but Leeda cut her off.

"It's actually sad that you have to do so much for attention. Rex *said* you were all show."

Rabbit punch. Murphy hadn't seen it coming.

"Do you think it's all that hard to turn a guy on? Anybody could dress like you, and walk like you, and get a guy's attention eventually. You walk like you're easy. Any girl could do that. I could do that. *Guys* are easy, Murphy."

Leeda glared at Murphy. Murphy had seen jealousy a million times before in other girls, but jealousy was only part of Leeda's look right now. The other part was Leeda's mother's look—disgusted, bored, condescending. It made Murphy back up against the wall harder. "But I didn't mean . . . I tried not to give him the . . ."

Leeda rolled her eyes and waved one palm in the air like she was brushing away a fly. "Please. Even Birdie noticed the way you were flirting with him at the engagement party, didn't you, Birdie?"

Murphy looked, flabbergasted, at Birdie, who sat on the bed giving them the fish eye and looking like she might pass out. Murphy tried to see herself through Birdie's eyes, and she could see how wrong the vision was—Leeda the wronged saint and Murphy the painted floozy—and it twisted her. She fought back the tears that rose up now because she felt like everything good was crashing around her.

"I thought you were my friend." Leeda's voice cracked, but her eyes stayed cool.

Murphy tried to keep her voice calm. It was a break in Leeda's armor, and a wave of relief washed over Murphy. It was a million times better for Leeda to look at her like she was a human being and not an insect.

"Lee, I *am* your friend. Rex . . ." She wanted to tell Leeda that her loyalty had been tested, and passed, and how much that meant. But the words got stuck in her throat. She didn't know how to say it. She had done the right thing! She, Murphy McGowen, had done the right thing!

She almost smiled.

"You're gonna end up just like her, you know, begging guys to love you, sleeping with other people's husbands. . . ."

Murphy swayed on her feet. The almost-smile felt slapped away.

She held up her hands as if to shield her face, feeling her blood come to a simmer. "Leeda, you should stop talking now. You don't know what you're talking about."

"Oh, I do, believe me." Leeda seemed on the verge of leaving the room, but she stopped and looked at Birdie. "Birdie and I want you to leave."

Now in anger, Murphy couldn't keep her tears back. They popped out on her eyeballs and hung there, but she wouldn't let them drop. She looked at Birdie, who had pulled her covers over her head and curled herself in a fetal position facing the other way.

Then she looked at Leeda.

"If I leave, you won't get the secret." Murphy smiled, reeling Leeda in, slippery as an eel.

Leeda looked flustered. Her gray eyes fluttered. "What secret?"

"The secret of what I have that you don't."

Murphy pursed her full lips, put her hands on her hips.

"I'm dying to know," Leeda said sardonically, but Murphy could tell by the way her eyes grew big and a little soft, she really wanted to know.

Murphy shrugged, as if the answer was obvious. "I'm just more than you. More person. More life. You're boring and uptight. Anybody who really gets to know you ... Anybody who is around long enough will find out you're just ... bleh."

Leeda took off down the stairs two at a time and slammed out onto the porch. Murphy stood in the doorway, dazed, hurt more by the things she'd said to Leeda than the things Leeda had said to her. Birdie sat up on the bed, watching her, in shock.

Murphy looked at her and felt the sting of her betrayal, of them ganging up on her, and glared at her. "Thanks, Birdie. Thanks a lot. Have a nice life, wherever you end up." Murphy knew how to twist the knife, dragging herself to the ugliest level possible.

A few minutes later, her stuff packed into the trunk, Murphy peeled down the gravel drive, her car clunking along, the orchard passing by on either side. She didn't look in the rearview mirror to see it fall away.

$\mathcal{B}$irdie was lying flat on the kitchen floor. She'd never done it before, and it seemed like a good diversion. Her dad had gone out, and she couldn't take the quiet. No workers outside, no work to do. After all the stress of rushing around trying to keep everything running, the downtime felt empty and useless. And there was no hope of Murphy or Leeda or Enrico showing up on the porch.

The only sound was the phone ringing. It had rung like this once every ten minutes for the last hour. Caller ID announced it was her mom. Birdie was studiously trying to ignore her. She didn't have the energy today to navigate her mom's feelings while simultaneously protecting her dad. Or deal with the idea of moving in with her.

The phone went silent, then rang again, and Birdie's guilt finally got the best of her. She watched her feet as she walked and lifted the receiver blindly.

"Hey," she breathed.

"Hey, Birdie, it's Leeda." Leeda's voice was high and lilty, like someone trying hard to sound great. Birdie breathed a sigh of relief. She wanted to reach through the phone and hug Leeda.

"I'm sorry I haven't returned your calls. I've been so busy. Getting ready for the wedding is hell. And we had the bachelorette party last night."

"Oh? How was it?"

"Danay *loved* it."

"Oh yeah?"

"Yeah. She was completely happy. Stupid happy. She got so wasted. She puked on the marquis at the Fox Theater."

"What were you doing at the Fox?"

"It's her favorite bathroom. She wanted to puke in there."

Birdie laughed. "Didn't make it, huh?"

Leeda laughed back, but her laugh sounded forced.

"So I guess you knew better after all," Birdie offered.

"No, I didn't." Leeda paused. "I used your ideas. I mean, I used your idea to use Danay's ideas."

"Oh. That's good."

"Yeah."

They both let the awkward silence stretch out.

"Birdie?"

"Yeah." Birdie swallowed the lump in her throat.

"I miss you. I miss the orchard."

It was such a relief to hear Leeda say it. Birdie smiled into the phone. "I miss you too. Life is so boring here right now."

"Yeah. I wish you were coming to the wedding. It would be a lifesaver."

Birdie's mom had gone through with plans to move into her condo on the same day as Danay's wedding, and Birdie hadn't been able to wiggle out of it. She hadn't even had the heart to try. Birdie swallowed. "I wish that too."

Another long silence.

"Have, um, have you talked to Murphy?" Birdie asked.

"I don't want to talk about her."

"Okay." Birdie's voice came out guilty. She still felt somehow responsible. Like if she hadn't looked out her window, Murphy and Rex wouldn't have kissed. She had read somewhere, in one of the books her aunt was always giving her, that cells behaved a certain way when they were being observed, a way that was different than they would behave normally. Maybe Birdie was responsible for all the ills of the world just by somehow being around to hear about them and watch them on TV.

"Anyway, Danay was so damn grateful she invited Rex to the wedding. Last minute."

Birdie figured she wasn't supposed to ask about that either.

"That's great, Leeda."

"Well, listen, I'll call you after."

"Okay."

"Okay."

The receiver went dead. And Birdie lay back down on the kitchen floor.

In the family's penthouse suite at the hotel, Leeda tugged at the straps of her dress and stepped out onto the balcony. The temperature had reached ninety-nine degrees in the limo on the way from the church and Leeda felt every degree of it making her bridesmaid dress, which was strapless, salmon, and not half bad, stick to every centimeter of her.

"Hey, Lee. They want you downstairs."

Leeda turned to see Rex standing in the wide living room

with his hands in his pockets, looking at her seriously under his dark eyebrows. Rex had given her this look many times since the last day in the orchard. Every time he saw her, he acted like a lead weight. And Leeda always reacted in the same way.

"Okay, sweetie." Leeda swiped at the sweat under her armpits and turned a full-watt smile on him, linking her fingers through his.

In the elevator they fell silent. Leeda played with her fingernails so the silence wouldn't feel like the kind that was asking to be interrupted. But Rex interrupted anyway.

"Lee . . ."

Leeda looked up at him. "Please, Rex. Not today."

Rex's shoulders fell, but he obliged her. When the elevator doors opened, Leeda felt like she'd made a narrow escape.

The room was packed with over five hundred guests. Leeda grinned and touched a few on the elbows or shoulders and smiled at them as she made her way through. In the center of the dance floor Danay and Brighton and the wedding party were dancing to the wedding song. *Oh crap*. Leeda was supposed to be dancing with her in-law Glen. She scoped around the room for him, but he was hitting on one of the waiters. Thank God.

Unfortunately, her eyes then immediately found her mom, who made a beeline for her.

"Leeda, we were looking all over for you."

"Yeah, I couldn't find Glen, though," Leeda fibbed, scanning the opposite side of the room as if she were looking for him.

"Honey, this is your sister's day. Remember that."

"How could I forget?"

Leeda watched her mom walk to join her dad, king and

queen of the party. Leeda wasn't interested in taking anything away from Danay at the moment. She just wanted to make it through the day in one piece and do what she needed to do. And that was going to take some effort. She felt like her whole being was being held together by Jell-O.

Through a loose gaggle of people Leeda made out a familiar face. Horatio Balmeade was staring at the breasts of her cousin Margarita. Rex had drifted away to the side of the dance floor, where he stood darkly, nursing a glass of champagne, which she knew he hated.

Leeda wanted to go stand beside him. It would make her feel safer, like it always did. But she held herself back, because in a way it was *less* safe too, now. There was too much danger in talking with Rex—they hadn't talked about Murphy and she didn't want to. She circulated among the guests instead, smiling at everyone the way she was supposed to, making small talk, being the perfect daughter, and giving off the impression that nobody's life was as seamless or as sweet as hers.

Ding ding ding. Leeda turned to see Glen standing at the front of the room. "Now we'll hear from the maid of honor."

Leeda's pulse spiked instantly. *Oh God.* She had totally forgotten she was supposed to write a speech. How could she forget something like that? As everyone looked at her, she pasted a smile on her face, but her stomach throbbed. She was so unprepared. She walked up to the bridal table and took the mike from Glen.

"Um . . ." The room of five hundred people stared back at her. "Uh, my sister, Danay . . . is . . . my sister. . . ."

Oh God. The whole feeling of the room seemed to be urging

her to pull it together. She said the first thing that came into her head. "She's, um, pretty perfect."

There were a few chuckles. "It's easy to be jealous of a sister like that," Leeda added, and then regretted it. She spotted Rex across the room. And instead of making her feel safe, it reminded her of Murphy. "But the thing is, I'm stuck with her." A murmur from the audience. "Oh, c'mon, that's not such a bad thing." Leeda started this sentence irritably, but as she finished it, she felt her body relax. There was a long pause, and then what she wanted to say came to her, like she was riding a wave. "Maybe it's lucky when we're stuck with someone we love. Because it gets hard, and then it gets easy to give up on someone. And I guess that's what makes a marriage . . ." Leeda searched for the words ". . . so special. Is that you choose to be stuck with somebody, even through the hard times. It's like a pact. It means the good times are just so good, and it means you love that person so much that you're willing to stay through all the bad." Leeda scanned the faces for Danay. Tears were glistening in her eyes. Leeda cleared her throat. "I guess what I'm saying is we're lucky to be stuck. I'm glad I'm stuck with Danay, and Brighton—" All eyes in the room looked at Brighton. "I'm glad you're stuck with her too. I hope you don't forget how lucky that makes you. She's perfect." Leeda stopped herself abruptly, embarrassed.

Brighton shook his head. "I won't let him," Danay said loudly, grinning through her tears.

Everyone looked at Leeda expectantly. "That's it." She smiled.

Amid the applause she felt a hand on her back. She turned to look—Rex.

He hugged her, tight. She sank into him and let go.

Murphy and Gavin lay crashed out on the couch, Gavin's head against Murphy's chest. A few minutes ago he'd tried to unzip her shorts, but Murphy had shut him down, and now she could tell he was wondering why he was here at all. Murphy thought it was nice to have a warm body just sitting next to her. It didn't really matter who it belonged to.

"You got anything to eat?"

"You can check in the kitchen," Murphy said, keeping her eye on the TV. *A Hard Day's Night* was playing on VH1. This was the twenty-sixth time she'd watched it. Same as the number of letters in the alphabet. That was worth celebrating. Murphy cheers'ed herself with her can of Dr. Thunder and took a sip.

Outside, a car pulled into the driveway.

"All right, Gavin, you gotta go. My mom's home."

"Really?" Gavin looked shocked and disappointed. He had just found a bag of Combos and was holding it to his chest proprietarily.

"Door's that way." Murphy pointed with a limp wrist.

"Okay. See ya, Murph."

"Murph-y," she shouted at the screen door as it hissed closed. A moment later it hissed again, admitting Jodee and Richard.

"I never knew I was your meal ticket," Richard was saying.

Jodee turned to Richard and touched his shoulder gently. "You know I don't see you that way. I don't think it's too much to ask for you to pitch in for groceries."

Murphy pulled her arms over her stomach protectively. She decided to count the number of seconds it would take Richard to plunk down beside her on the couch and change the channel. It took seven.

Jodee disappeared in the bedroom for a moment, then started puttering around, tidying up the mess that Murphy and Richard had left behind.

Murphy sat up stiffly so that no part of her body would be touching Richard's. She watched her mom cleaning up with a pinchy feeling of guilt.

"Well, what're you gonna do with yourself?" Richard asked. "Two whole weeks off?"

Murphy shook her head. She didn't know. Go back to the usual. That was what you did, right? You stretched out your life, then realized life wasn't stretchable, and so you went back to the way things were before.

"Are you gonna keep in touch with the girls from the orchard?" Jodee asked.

"They hate me." This was a rare intimacy for Murphy. She waited for her mom to ask questions. She wanted for the two of them to go into her mom's room alone so she could pour the whole thing out and hug her mom and cry and have her get her a tissue and some hot tea. But her mom waved a hand at her lightly.

"Oh, honey, they don't hate you. Girls are just hard to be friends with in high school. It gets easier when you're older."

Murphy wondered what women friends her mom actually thought she had. Women all over Bridgewater were probably breathing a sigh of relief Jodee wasn't single anymore so that they wouldn't have to lock up their husbands and boyfriends.

"Right."

Murphy watched Richard's stupid football game until the light outside started to fade. Then she just couldn't stand being indoors anymore.

She got in her car and turned the engine. Ever since Rex had fixed it, it had been starting fine. She stepped on the gas and turned left out of the development, not sure where she'd go. She knew she should call somebody, there were tons of people who would be around to hang out with, but she just couldn't think of anybody she wanted to see.

Finally she turned toward the orchard.

She parked the car near the railroad tracks and walked along the perimeter of the property so that nobody would see her, sneaking into the garden from behind it, approaching it from the side coming toward the house. She looked up at Birdie's window, but the lights were out. For all she knew, Birdie had gone to live with her mother. It didn't matter.

At the garden a few weeds had crept toward the roses, and Murphy yanked them out, surveying the area for more weeds, more threats to her precious flowers. It would all be bulldozed eventually anyway. Finally she gave up.

She sank onto the bench and ran her fingers along the wood, tracing the little patterns that Rex had carved into the armrests. He hadn't had to do these little delicate patterns. He could have made her a normal bench, and it would have been more than enough.

Murphy knew she was feeling sorry for herself, and she also knew that she wasn't going to cry. She refused to be a victim.

Murphy, the martyr. Murphy, the wronged. Murphy, who'd thought she had friends.

A figure appeared beside her on the bench and sat down.

"Hey, Birdie."

Birdie looked around, plucked one of the dead flowers off a branch, and started picking it apart, all the while staring at Murphy with her doe eyes.

"I was just checking on stuff," Murphy said, nodding toward the garden.

"I know. I figured."

"I hope you won't report me for trespassing." She couldn't help throwing it in.

Birdie sucked in her breath. "You know, they're calling for a tropical storm?" she said quietly. "So much of this summer without any rain. But peaches taste sweeter when there's less rain. Rain dilutes the sugar."

"Huh."

Birdie folded her hands on her lap.

"I thought you were going to live with your mom."

Birdie sighed. "I'm kind of straddling houses at the moment."

Murphy didn't reply. She knew how hard that had to be for Birdie, but she was too angry to offer any kind of sympathy.

"Murphy, I shouldn't have gotten involved with you and Leeda. I didn't mean to."

Murphy nodded and pressed her lips together, staring up at the sky. "No big deal."

Birdie seemed on the verge of tears. "I'm such a bad liar, and she asked me what was wrong. And she guessed, you know. She guessed it was something about you, then she guessed it was something about you and Rex. It was like this psychic premonition she had. If you knew how sorry I was . . ."

"I said it was no big deal. I gotta, um—" Murphy hooked a thumb over her shoulder.

"Murphy!" Birdie leaned forward and threw her arms around Murphy's neck. "Please please please forgive me. Please. It was none of my business, what happened with you and Rex. Well, I should have talked to you, but then Leeda came in. . . ." Birdie pulled back and blinked her brown eyes. "I don't care what you did as long as we're friends."

Murphy shook her off, frowning. "I didn't even *do* anything."

Birdie stared. "What do you mean?"

"Birdie, Rex kissed me. But I told him off."

"Really?"

"I did all the righteous stuff. I was a good girl."

"You never had sex with him?"

"Jesus, Birdie."

"Well, I don't understand why you didn't tell Leeda."

"I tried. You heard all the stuff she said to me."

"But you could have sent her an e-mail or written a note or something."

"She already thinks she knows who I am. She did before she knew me."

"But you guys love each other."

"Birdie." Murphy leaned back on her hands. "It's not gonna happen. And I don't want you to say anything to her about it. Promise me."

Birdie looked dubious. "But I could . . ."

"Birdie, promise me."

Birdie blinked a few times. "Okay. Okay. But you're friends with me, right?"

Birdie hugged her around the waist.

"It's hard to be mad at you, Bird."

"I know. I'm so sweet."

"You are."

Murphy hugged her back, feeling the defined spaces of her spine.

"I hadn't really noticed, but you're getting your birdie legs back, Bird."

Birdie shrugged and smiled, pushing her hair behind her ears. "Am I?"

Murphy couldn't believe how much better she felt. She was buzzing with electricity to have Birdie back in her life. It felt like a miracle. She wanted to do something for her.

"So things suck with the farm, right?"

Birdie nodded, unable to speak.

"I guess there's nothing we can do about that."

Birdie shook her head, her lips trembling. "No."

"Well, you should have a vacation, then."

Birdie half laughed. "Yeah. How about the Greek isles? Let's leave tomorrow."

Murphy smiled. "My car won't make it to Greece, but I think it has enough juice for a shorter trip."

"To where?" Birdie asked softly.

Murphy grinned. The idea had taken hold like a vision. Of course, it had to be done.

"My dear, duh. My car can make it all the way to Texas."

Twenty-one

"You turn here."

Murphy peered through the right corner of the windshield toward where Birdie was pointing.

"No, you don't."

"Yeah, it's here."

"Bird, seventy-five is straight ahead."

"I know the back way."

Murphy looked at Birdie, whose wide-set brown eyes were staring at her placidly, and pressed the corner of her lips down to communicate that Birdie didn't know what she was talking about, but what the heck. She took the turn. They passed a pecan farm on the right and then a few open fields.

"Left on Mossy Creek."

Murphy looked at Birdie again, and Birdie smiled innocently back at her. Behind them their stuff was covering the seats—Murphy's army bag and Birdie's matching teddy bear suitcases her grandmother had given her. Also, a jar of dill pickles Birdie had brought and two bags of pretzels, along with two bottles of strawberry cider. One of Murphy's bras had found its way out of her bag and wrapped itself around the pickles.

Birdie had told her dad she was with her mom. She'd told her mom she was with Leeda. Murphy still couldn't believe she'd had the guts to do it. Already Birdie had gotten a look of terror on her face three or four times—never mind the look on her face when she and Murphy had gotten Enrico's address from her dad's office—and mentioned to Murphy that maybe they should turn around. They hadn't even gotten to the highway yet.

They were definitely coming at town a back way from the orchard, and it was starting to get familiar. Murphy leaned forward and peered far over the steering wheel.

"Birdie."

Murphy tapped her foot on the brakes, which squealed as the car slowed. They came to a stop a couple hundred yards before the driveway of Breezy Buds Plantation, aka the Cawley-Smiths' mansion.

Birdie had her feet up on the dash and her eyes straight ahead, her eyes big. "I told her she could come with us."

"Oh Jesus."

"Murphy, come on. I need you guys to get along. I need Leeda to come too."

Birdie saying she needed Leeda felt like tiny Charles Manson fork stabs in Murphy's heart. She wanted to make it somehow so that Birdie didn't need Leeda.

"Well, maybe if you'd rather hang out with her . . ." Murphy didn't expect this tack to work, it was so obvious, but Birdie looked at her with her upper lip slightly puckering and then disappearing into her mouth. She looked wounded and sorry, which made Murphy wounded and sorry.

"God." Murphy felt her chest filling up with warm fuzzies for Birdie, who couldn't fathom manipulating people the way Murphy had just tried to do.

"She might be really sorry," Birdie suggested.

Murphy considered this. Maybe Rex and Leeda had talked about the kiss. Maybe they'd even broken up. If Leeda knew it wasn't Murphy's fault, she probably felt terrible. She would probably grovel. And Murphy would have to think about whether to take her back or not.

"Do you think so?" Murphy asked, hating to sound so unsure and pathetic. She nibbled on a hangnail on her thumb.

Birdie nodded.

"Did she say that?"

"She used our advice for the bachelorette party."

Yellowbaby clunked into the semicircular driveway of the Cawley-Smith house, where the crepe myrtle made a crimson soldier's bridge over the road, dropping tiny fuchsia petals onto the windshield and on top of the car.

"I'll go get her." Birdie went up to the door and disappeared inside while Murphy sat with a butterfly in her stomach and tried to look careless. Never, never, never would she let Leeda see her rattled. She was the last person who would ever see that.

The door cracked open a few minutes later, but it wasn't Birdie or Leeda who exited. Rex emerged from the door and walked up to the car. Panicked, Murphy looked in the rearview mirror. There was his car parked behind her, in the alcove in the bushes.

Rex came up to the car and bent down to look through the passenger window. Murphy didn't bother rolling down the window or leaning over to open the door. He looked at her sadly and gave her half a wave, pulling his hand out of his pocket only for a moment before he tucked it back in. Murphy looked down at the door handle, then gently waved back and let herself meet his eyes for a moment. Looking at him through the glass felt like being an animal in the zoo. Murphy would probably be a python.

Rex looked thoughtfully at her for another moment, and then he stood and walked toward his car.

A few minutes later Leeda and Birdie emerged carrying enough luggage to fill two Yellowbabies.

"Hey, Murphy," Leeda said coolly, opening the door.

"Hey."

"Where am I supposed to sit?" The question was clearly directed at Birdie.

Murphy rolled her eyes.

It was going to be that kind of trip.

"No matter how many times you press that button, the AC is not going to work."

"Oh." Leeda pulled her manicured finger away from the snowflake-marked button below the radio, then fiddled with the tweezers that stuck out of the tape deck. "We should have taken the Beemer."

Murphy's shoulders, which Birdie had a great view of from the backseat, stiffened so visibly she looked like a football player. Birdie could *feel* the negative energy oozing from the front of the car. She sighed and leaned closer to the open window, feeling the breeze on her face. They had crossed the border into Mississippi about an hour ago, and the air had gotten both thicker and smellier.

"It smells like bayou," she said, hoping to spark a conversation. "I bet there's alligators."

Both Murphy and Leeda were silent.

"Have you guys been counting the armadillos?"

"No, Birdie. How many have you seen?"

"Twenty-three. All dead."

Silence.

"It's so mysterious. I never see live ones on the highway. It's like they arrive from the woods already dead." Birdie knew it was a stupid thing to say, but she was desperate.

"Maybe the noxious fumes from Yellowbaby are poisoning them before we can get to them," Leeda offered.

"Ha. Maybe," Murphy said, very pissed off.

Birdie turned her focus back to the dusk rushing up on the car outside and the sound of the swamp bugs hitting the windshield. She had the surreal feeling that she wasn't here at all. Not in this car with Murphy and Leeda. Definitely not on her way to go see Enrico. She doubted that was going to sink in until she actually saw him. And *then* she would freak out.

The thing was, once she stood in front of Enrico, there was no going back. It wasn't like at the orchard, where she could make some excuse for bumping into him. This was what she needed. A no-escape clause. She only wished she could have brought Honey Babe and Majestic. The silence in the car was oppressive and it made Birdie feel lost and sad. She leaned between the two girls, determined to change this.

"I hear iguanas love it when people pet them. Can you believe it?"

Neither girl even bothered to answer.

"Well, wake me when you want me to drive." Birdie, annoyed, but decidedly above showing it, cradled her soft squash blossom cardigan between her cheek and the window and let the buzz of the tires underneath her and the soothing hiss of the night air put her into a half-awake coma.

Somewhere in the middle of the night she woke up to see that Leeda had taken over driving. Birdie fell back asleep and didn't wake up until the sun was out.

"Where are we?"

Leeda looked back over her shoulder, her face drawn and pale.

"Louisiana."

Birdie took over the driving, and Leeda moved to the back, her long legs crunched up like the curls of a pretzel as she lay across the backseat. Murphy sat reclined on the passenger side with her head back, her mouth hanging open.

Birdie turned the radio on low to weatherband. It was a habit, living on the farm.

Scattered showers throughout much of the Southeast, the results of tropical storm Jude moving toward the coast of Florida. And then nothing. The radio had crapped out.

Birdie looked at Murphy, who shrugged. "Sometimes you get lucky. Sometimes you get unlucky."

They switched again in the early afternoon, Birdie moving into the passenger seat. She didn't know why she was so tired, but she conked out again, waking only when she heard the engine stop much, much later.

She looked up, expecting it to be another gas station, and then her stomach lurched.

They were at a row of two-story, redbrick apartment buildings. The area was kind of dingy, mostly pavement, surrounded by a Krystal and a Krispy Kreme. Everything looked like it had been built in the seventies.

"Here we are, Bird." Leeda turned around in her seat and grinned at her blearily. Birdie was suddenly touched. Both of her friends looked so tired. And it was because they were doing something nice for her, Birdie.

She told the girls she wanted to freshen up first, so they headed over to Krispy Kreme. She walked into the bathroom and locked the door behind her, then looked in the mirror.

She looked terrible. She splashed cold water on her face and finger-combed her hair, then tried to smooth out the crinkly crushed wrinkles in her gauzy white embroidered shirt. Actually, cleaned up a little, she didn't look so bad. Her lips were pink and rosy and the sleepiness seemed to make her eyes bigger and softer looking. She almost looked sultry. And she looked thin. Thinner. The summer's hard work had paid off on her body, and she hadn't even noticed.

Birdie took the barrette out of her long auburn bangs and readjusted it. She looked clean and pure and pretty. She was ready.

She walked back into the main area, where Murphy and Leeda were sitting across a table from each other but facing the counter, parallel. Birdie decided to take half a dozen doughnuts to Enrico and chose carefully the ones she thought he might like. Then they walked across the street.

"It's number twelve," she said, scanning the doors. She

almost hoped that there was no number twelve and that they were in the wrong place entirely. But there it was, to the left. Murphy and Leeda followed her to the concrete stoop.

"Um, do you guys mind waiting in the car?"

"Sure," Murphy said, smiling at her encouragingly. "You can do it, Bird."

"Do I look sweaty or anything?"

Both Leeda and Murphy shook their heads.

Birdie turned back to the door, listening to the sound of her friends walking away. She raised her fist to the door and knocked. No answer. She looked back at Yellowbaby. She knocked again.

Then she tried the knob, not expecting it to give, but it did.

The living room she entered consisted of cream carpet, a tan couch, a La-Z-Boy, and several books, in Spanish and English, lying open on the floor, on coffee tables, on the staircase. It was no mistake. Birdie smiled nervously.

"Enrico?"

She walked into the hallway. "Hello?"

She peered into the two doorways. The bathroom and the bedroom. Enrico's bed was there, all messed up. The whole room smelled like him. It made Birdie's knees wobbly. But he wasn't here.

Then she heard the music. Birdie turned and walked toward the sliding glass door, which was open. Her heart jumped into her temples. She approached the threshold of the door.

There were two loungers on the concrete patio. One of them was empty. Enrico was lying on the other one, a book resting on his side.

On his lap was a girl with short black hair.

Birdie took a step backward, her instincts kicking in.

And then the girl bent forward, and Enrico's face appeared over her shoulder, and his eyes met Birdie's. He squinted for a moment, like he couldn't quite make sense of what he was seeing. Then the girl on his lap turned around.

"Birdie?" he asked, sliding the girl up and standing.

Birdie scratched her chin hard. "Hey, Enrico. Hey . . ." She nodded at the girl, trying very desperately to make it look like she was happy to meet her. But the girl smiled weakly, unsurely.

"Birdie, what are you . . . ?"

Birdie laughed. "Oh, ha, you know, we're on a road trip. And I . . . brought you these doughnuts." Birdie's eyes were welling up with tears.

"I . . ." Enrico's dark eyebrows descended low in concern. It was obvious he was faltering between asking her if she was okay and pretending he didn't notice she wasn't.

"So, um, hi . . . Actually, we . . ."

Birdie couldn't get the rest of the lie out. It would have been ridiculous anyway. She closed her mouth instead. She laid the box of doughnuts down gently next to where she stood. And then she turned and ran.

Leeda was sitting in the driver's seat and Murphy was sitting against the hood of the car when they saw Birdie run out of Enrico's town house, her hair flopping behind her and her arms pumping.

"What the hell . . . ?" Murphy and Leeda caught each other's eyes. It was probably the first time they had actually made eye contact the whole trip. And then they watched Birdie cover the rest of the parking lot in a sprint.

She came panting up to the car and leapt in through the open passenger door. Behind her, appearing on his stoop, was Enrico.

"Let's go!"

"What?"

"Get in the car, Murphy!"

Murphy did what she was told, looking dazed, and Leeda turned the key in the ignition.

"Birdie, what's going on?"

"Just drive!" Birdie groaned.

The engine was turning over and over. While it did, Enrico jogged up to the side of the car. "Birdie?" he called through the window, his voice muted by the glass.

Behind him Leeda could see that a pretty Latina girl had emerged from the front of the house. Her heart flopped. *Oh, damn.*

Murphy turned around in her seat. "Birdie, can I roll down the window? The guy clearly wants to talk to you."

Enrico was crouching and staring in the window. Leeda looked over her shoulder. Birdie had dropped her face behind her hand.

"Please just drive."

As soon as she could get the car in gear, Leeda threw it into first. The tires peeled in the gravel and they jerked forward and stalled.

"Oh God, kill me. Please kill me," Birdie said from the back.

"Sorry!" Leeda started the car a second time, throwing it into first again, and this time pulling away with a jerk.

Birdie was saying it over and over again into her hand. "Please kill me."

"Bird? Bird?" Murphy was now leaning over the back of her seat. "Don't say that, Bird."

Leeda couldn't help looking in the rearview mirror as she squealed out of the parking lot. First at Birdie, still hiding in her hands. And then, in the background, at Enrico, standing in a cloud of dust, coughing, and looking as love struck as anyone she'd ever seen.

Thirty years after Georgia's last devastating tropical storm, its land-locked acreage braced for another pounding from Mother Nature. Bridgewater's stores taped Xs on their windows, and in an unprecedented maneuver, the twenty-four-hour Kuntry Kitchen closed its doors. Yellowbaby, an aging Volkswagen, whose radio was held together by a pair of tweezers, failed to report how serious things had become. Its driver, Murphy McGowen, tuned in once, but all she heard was salsa music.

Twenty-two

"**W**e should probably stop here for gas," Murphy said, nodding to the gauge.

Leeda kept her eyes straight ahead on the road. "I can see for myself. And I don't like Exxon. I like BP."

"You think you can tell the difference between Exxon gas and BP gas?"

"I think I'm driving and therefore I get to pick where we get our gas."

In the backseat, Birdie clenched and unclenched her teeth. She had used to think hell was being in a room full of people she didn't know. But now she realized hell was actually being in a small car with Murphy and Leeda, two people she knew better than anyone.

"Hey, why don't we go to Shell and split the difference," she said tightly, as kindly as she could. She didn't think what type of gas they put in Murphy's clunker mattered much anyway; it drove like it was running on grape jelly. *This thing is a piece of lemon*, she thought. And then she wanted to cry.

Murphy shifted her feet along the dashboard. "Well, we'd better do it soon because you're gonna run out of gas."

"I get the concept of a gas gauge, thanks," Leeda said airily. This made Murphy glare at her, then shake her head and laugh.

"What?" Leeda asked.

"Nothing. It's just you're funny, that's all."

A piece of tape had come undone from one of the holes in Murphy's backseat and was sticking to Birdie's thigh. Her hair kept getting in her eyes. She was beginning to think she knew what the inside of a volcano might feel like. She felt like something was going to explode out of her. It started as a rumble way down at the base of her gut.

"What do you mean?" Leeda snapped, obviously seething.

"You're just so petty. It's great."

"*I'm* petty?"

Birdie clenched her fists against her thighs. But it didn't stem the tide. She slammed one into the back of Murphy's seat. "You're both petty! You're both the pettiest, most selfish people I ever met in my life!"

Murphy turned to goggle at her. The look of astonishment on her face made Birdie want to scream.

"All you think about is yourselves. You know what? I don't care if you guys ever make up! Just leave me the hell out of it! I don't need it from you."

Birdie was breathing hard. Leeda had slowed to granny speed and shot nervous glances back at her.

"Birdie, I . . ."

"Murphy didn't even kiss Rex back, you know. She told him off!"

Murphy whipped around in her seat. "Birdie!"

"And the thing is, she's in love with him. And you're not. He's just your crutch. And she still didn't kiss him back. Because she loves you more."

Birdie turned on Murphy now. "And you're loyal enough not to hook up with her boyfriend but not loyal enough to put aside your pride and just explain. What a joke! You're both a joke! And you're sitting here seeing who can be more vindictive, not even noticing what the hell is going on with anyone else. God! You saw what just happened with Enrico, my parents are getting divorced, I'm losing my goddamn house, my dad's moving God knows where, and if I go with him, I'll probably never see you guys again. I can't stand either of you!"

As Birdie finished, she swiped at where her hair had pasted into her eyes.

Leeda was driving very slowly and steadily. Murphy was still staring over the seat at her.

"I'm sorry, Birdie," she finally said.

Birdie just peeled the tape off her thigh and looked out the window.

She didn't say another word. She didn't understand herself. She felt like a monster inside.

After that, the car was silent as a grave.

It had started to rain.

By the time they reached Bridgewater, it was pouring. Leeda leaned forward over the steering wheel of Yellowbaby like an old lady, trying to peer through the huge, relentless drops as they smacked the windshield. She didn't want to make a wrong turn and give Murphy a reason to make fun of her, even though Murphy had been quietly staring straight ahead, her bare feet clenched together and resting against the glove compartment.

Birdie was curled into a ball in the backseat, like a heroin addict going through withdrawal. Leeda could see her in the rearview, her big brown eyes staring out the window but not really focusing. They navigated their way to the back side of the orchard, driving slowly along the property line. The potholes in the road were filling and overflowing with rain, and the car shook and bobbed as it dipped into one and then another. Big leaves pasted themselves against the windshield, only to be crushed to either side by the wipers. They had just made it a few hundred yards when the car gave a gasp and then went silent, rolling to a complete stop.

"Crap," Murphy said, not moving, not even shifting her gaze from straight ahead.

Leeda yanked it into park.

They sat for a few seconds, thinking. "Well, maybe we should wait out the storm a little and . . ."

Crack.

Birdie had thrown the car door open. In another moment she was up and out, running into the orchard.

Murphy and Leeda exchanged one dumbfounded look.

"Birdie!" Leeda called, throwing her door open and leaning over the top of the car. She was immediately drenched.

Murphy jumped out of the car too. "Where's she going?" she yelled.

Leeda shook her head. She had a vision of Birdie jumping into the lake and never coming up. She wouldn't do that, would she? She was just at a line of trees now. Leeda could see the back of her sopping T-shirt, and then she disappeared.

"Birdie?!" Murphy called. Then she started after her. "Wait up!"
They ran into the orchard, dodging bushes and trees. "Birdie!"
The wind was so strong it was actually pushing against
them, making it hard to move fast. They came to the rise near
the cider house, where there was a clear view of the farmhouse.
But Birdie wasn't headed in that direction. She had veered left
and was advancing farther out into the trees.

"Birdie!"
Leeda felt a gust of wind so strong that she almost went tumbling backward. "Jesus."

"Oh my God," Murphy said, sending chills up Leeda's spine.
"Look."

A cabana from the Balmeade Country Club was blowing
across the field below, catching itself on a tree and flapping
against it madly.

Murphy had her hands against her chest. "This is not good.
This is a bad storm."

They started running again, splitting apart but going in the
general direction of Birdie. Leeda's heart was in her throat.
She'd never seen anything like it.

The ground was already sloshy and sludgy and she went sliding forward a few times, surfing mud slicks and righting herself.
She couldn't see Murphy anymore either. And then she spotted
a giant lump on the ground up ahead.

"Birdie!" She flew down beside her. "Are you okay? Did you
break something?"

Birdie was curled in a tight ball, crying.
Leeda surveyed her body, wincing because she was expecting to
see something sticking out at a weird angle. Birdie just kept crying.

There was the thud of footsteps and then Murphy appeared at her side.

"Is she hurt? Are you hurt?" Birdie shook her head and Murphy sank down on her knees. "What's wrong?"

Birdie uncurled from the ball and lay flat on her back. "I didn't renew the insurance."

Murphy and Leeda exchanged confused looks. "Birdie, this is a bad storm. We've gotta get inside."

Birdie just kept crying.

Leeda didn't know what else to do. She lay down beside Birdie and put her arm over her. "It's okay. Come on, Bird."

"C'mon."

Birdie wouldn't budge. Her hair was plastered to the sides of her face and her forehead and cheeks were smeared with mud.

Murphy leaned down close to her ear. "Bird, I bet if Enrico could see you right now, he'd dump that girl in a second."

Leeda shot a death glare at her, then looked back at Birdie. She'd stopped crying, snuffling, anything. She was deathly silent. And then she started to laugh. And cry harder. And laugh.

"Nice," Leeda said, rolling her eyes.

Together, she and Murphy hoisted Birdie up by her shoulders. She stood the rest of the way on her own, rubbing her face against her sleeve. They dragged through the grass, barely able to see, and slammed their way into the cider house, having to force the door closed behind them.

The storm sounded different from inside. Echoey.

Murphy peered around. "See, the perfect place to be during a hurricane. In a shoddily built shed full of sharp tools."

Leeda shot another look at Murphy. But she knew she was

right. Only Murphy seemed amused. Maybe that was the only thing to be. About everything.

Birdie slumped against the wall, snuffling. Murphy and Leeda sidled next to her, Leeda holding her hand.

After a long while, when Birdie had quieted, Murphy asked, "Do you think if we stay in here, we'll land in Oz?"

Birdie smiled a little.

Far off, a tree splintered with a loud crash.

"Well, it'll save the Balmeades money on bulldozers," Birdie said, sounding very Murphy. The girls laughed and then fell completely silent. They could hear the sound of metal cracking and more trees, big trees, breaking.

"Do you think we might die?" Leeda asked. Nobody answered. "Because in case we do, I think we should have one of those deep talks where we spill our guts to each other."

Birdie and Murphy looked at her for a second. And then they burst out laughing, sort of desperately.

"You're such a dork," Birdie said.

Leeda felt herself blushing. "Shut up."

They all fell silent again. From then on, they listened to the rain. Leeda knew they were all thinking about their families, their homes. But nobody said it. From time to time the shed shook. Outside, the wind was relentless.

And the rain sounded like it was washing the whole world away.

Twenty-three

When Birdie woke, the first thing she noticed was the tickle of Murphy's hair resting against her leg. Her eyes adjusted to the darkness, and she saw Leeda too, sleeping a few feet away with her arms crossed over her chest like a mummy.

Birdie hadn't forgotten, even while she slept, about the storm. The weight of the world rested wholly at the bottom of her stomach as she extracted herself quietly from Murphy and walked to the door. Gray light was coming through the cracks. She blinked several times and put her hand to the handle. She took a deep shuddering breath, which got caught in her throat. Then she turned and knelt by Murphy.

"Murphy? Murphy?"

Murphy started and looked up, brushing the tiny curls out of her eyes and sitting up. "Yeah." She looked around groggily, trying to orient herself.

"Will you go outside with me?"

Murphy's expression shifted from sleepy to sympathetic instantly, her green eyes widening. "Sure, Bird," she whispered. "Let's go."

Birdie stood back so that Murphy could open the door. When she did, the white-gray light filled the doorway, like something straight out of purgatory. Murphy stepped outside and disappeared. Birdie waited for her to say something, but there was only silence. "Murphy?"

"Oh my God."

Birdie swallowed deeply and followed after her.

Murphy had climbed the hill beyond the cider house and was turning in a 360. Birdie scrabbled up after her, her feet slipping on the rain-soaked grass. Birdie had a view of the road first. The power lines lay all over it like dead snakes. A power *pole* and several trees lay crashed along it like dead bodies.

Then she turned toward the orchard and blinked.

"Oh ..." she gasped.

She and Murphy looked at each other, their eyes huge, and then she peered back down at the view.

The orchard stretched out thick and green, its trees dripping and heavy, the grass churned up and muddy in several places, a few limbs lying here and there. But otherwise it hadn't been touched.

It hadn't been touched.

Birdie immediately burst into tears.

After a few seconds she felt Murphy's arm around her shoulders, which shook with her sobs. She reached out and wrapped her arms around Murphy's waist, leaning her head against her shoulder, her tear-drenched face sticking to her curls. Birdie inhaled a lock of hair and snorted, then pulled back and laughed. Murphy was looking at her and beaming.

"What's going on?"

They both turned to see Leeda standing in the outline of the cider house door, looking pale and dirty and disheveled. "Are you okay?"

Murphy stiffened beside her, but it hardly registered. Birdie grinned from ear to ear.

"Come see."

Leeda climbed to the top of the hill, standing on the other side of Birdie. "I can't believe it."

They stood there for several seconds.

"You wanna go home, Birdie?" Murphy asked.

"Oh yeah," Birdie said. "Definitely."

Poopie was on the front porch when they came straggling in, beside herself with worry and anger. But once she'd yelled at them and scowled at them and pounded her fist on the table a few times, she told them what had happened was a miracle.

On Poopie's orders, Birdie called her mother while everyone gathered around the radio, listening to the reports. Power lines down everywhere. Homes destroyed. All of the pecan and peach orchards within three states had been ripped apart.

"Terrible," Poopie kept saying in Spanish and English, shaking her head and clucking her tongue, her chin resting on her hands. And then, scattered between the *terribles*, every once in a while she'd say something else. "But good for peach prices."

Walter had already called to talk to Birdie, making sure she was all right and saying that he was in town, that nobody had been hurt, but that Bridgewater would have a lot of rebuilding to do. He was so caught up he didn't yell at Birdie for her lies, which Birdie figured had quickly been uncovered once he and

Cynthia had communicated about the storm. The phone rang several other times, but they were all business calls, getting the word out that the Darlington peaches were still all right, that orders were pouring in, and that the grocery chains were practically knocking down doors in panic over the shortage of southern peaches, not only for whatever the Darlingtons had left in stock, but for next summer. Even if the other orchards planted right away, it would take at least two years for their trees to bear fruit.

Murphy had never been so happy for anyone else in her life, but she also felt like she wasn't just happy for Birdie, but for the orchard itself. They were sitting around on the porch, finally exhausted and coming down from the huge high, when the sun peeked through the clouds.

Only Walter looked less than gleeful when he came through the door about half an hour later. But he looked less than miserable too.

Birdie jumped up and hugged him, chattering about how great it was, and wasn't he excited, and could he believe it.

"It's a good turn of luck," Walter said seriously, nodding and rubbing his thumb against his index finger. "We may actually be out of debt when we sell."

Every single person in the room froze. Birdie looked at her dad like he'd punched her in the stomach. Then she turned her eyes to Murphy and Leeda, as if they could do something. Murphy gave her a helpless look back.

"Well, I'd better get home," Leeda said awkwardly, standing up, her body seeming tightly strung together, like it might snap. "My parents think I'm still in Texas."

"You take my car," Poopie said, very low and evenly. "You and Murphy. Bring it back tomorrow."

Murphy didn't think she had much of a choice since her car was still stranded back on the side of the road, so a few minutes later, after they'd each hugged Birdie tightly and wordlessly, she ducked into the passenger seat of Poopie's car and sat tensely on the ride home, directing Leeda to turn this way, turn that. Mentally she dared Leeda to say something about her trailer when they pulled into Anthill Acres so that she could snap back. But Leeda kept her eyes coolly on the road in front of her.

"Well, thanks," Murphy said, letting it come out colder than she'd intended.

"It's no problem." Leeda met her eyes once, briefly, and then Murphy shut the door and she pulled away.

Murphy's mom's car was in the driveway. Murphy climbed the stairs and stepped inside, noticing immediately that the trailer felt as stuffy and closed in as a hothouse.

"Mom?"

She walked through the kitchen into her mom's bedroom and stopped. Jodee was curled up on the bed, used, balled-up tissues lying all around her. She looked tiny and delicate, like a teenager in her Bad Girl shorts and a little red tank top, her copper hair strung out in all directions.

Murphy sat on the bed and gently pushed her hair out of her face.

"Mom, I'm home."

Jodee looked up and sniffled. "Hey, baby."

"Hey," Murphy said, stroking her forehead. "You feeling bad?"

Jodee curled up tighter into her ball. "Feeling stupid." She looked at Murphy. "I'm sorry, honey, I really thought it would work this time with him. I guess I need to grow up."

She reached for Murphy's hand, and Murphy took it, looking down at her fingers. "Mom, what happened to the seagulls?"

"I don't like them anymore."

Somehow this made Murphy sad.

She crawled behind her mom and curled up behind her, fitting against her body and wrapping her arm around her waist. She couldn't bring herself to tell Jodee that she understood or that she empathized, but she hoped showing it was enough.

After a few minutes Jodee's breathing went back to a slow rhythm. Murphy lay thinking about her in wonder. How did she do it? Open her heart up time and time again, when every time she ended up hurt? Murphy's mom really was like a child. She didn't have the fear that Murphy did. It wasn't that she was stupid or blind, as Murphy had thought more than once. She was just hopeful. Naive. How did she manage to hold on to that?

There was something there that Murphy wasn't strong enough to emulate. After all the thinking about other people as foolish, and fearful, and weak, Murphy knew what she had, in fact, always known. That it was she who was the coward.

Twenty-four

A t dusk Birdie took a long walk through the orchard, walking up and down the rows, looking at each peach tree, occasionally running her fingers through the leaves, occasionally rubbing her fingers on the soft fuzz of the peaches. It was truly amazing. Not one of the trees had been hit. Not one. Birdie's wonder grew the longer she walked.

Occasionally her mind turned to Enrico, and even though she was alone, a huge blush unfurled across her face, and then an ache of loss throbbed in her chest.

After covering every row, Birdie went down to the lake and threw rocks in the water, thinking about all the times she'd gone swimming there, and smiling when she thought about being there with Leeda and Murphy.

Birdie had never felt so empty and so full. She guessed it was because there was so much she would be leaving behind and because she knew that she had so much to leave in the first place. It seemed like her world had grown hugely. And there was more to love and more to miss.

As it got a bit darker, her legs carried her back along the

pecan grove and along the property line. There, Birdie came to a halt and stared. On the other side, the Balmeade Country Club had been leveled. The water was in the sand pits and the sand filled up the water holes. Just over the rise she could see that a roof or two had been ripped off the condos. And strewn across the grass were tables, chairs, even doors—all mutilated—and a toilet bowl. It was amazing nobody had been hurt.

There wasn't a sign of life except a duck waddling across the grass, quacking away happily.

Seconds later Birdie found herself standing outside the entrance to Camp B. She pushed through the creaky screen door. She made her way down the hall to Enrico's room.

His room looked extremely empty and barren now that the rest of the house was empty too. Birdie sat on the bed gingerly and then sank onto her back. Her heart ached, but it felt good to be there, remembering her time there and how happy it was.

She closed her eyes, pulled her hands up beside her face, and drifted off to sleep.

When she woke, Birdie noticed two things immediately. It was dark. And there was someone else in the room. Birdie sat up in bed and stared down at the figure lying on the floor.

"Enrico?" She knelt beside him and put her hand gently on the back of his shoulder, shaking him gently. He stirred and rolled onto his back.

"What are you doing here?" Birdie whispered, as if there was anyone else around.

Enrico let out a sleepy sigh and sat up. "She is just a girl. Not my girlfriend."

"What?"

"I'm sorry, Birdie. I am not good at . . . I was not sure. I thought, but then . . ." He paused and smiled shyly. "You are always running away."

Birdie watched his face as he thought through how to say what he wanted to say. Finally his expression settled on a worried but tender look.

"I told her I will not see her again. Am I late?"

Birdie stared at him, unsure, trying to fit the pieces together. But before she could, Enrico put his hands on either side of her face and pressed his warm lips against hers. She responded immediately, kissing him back.

"I am not late?" he asked, grinning, looking at her lips, stroking her cheek. Birdie breathed in the amazing smell of him and feel of him and smiled back.

"You're not late."

She leaned forward and kissed him again.

The next morning, for the last free weekend of the summer, Leeda was going to Tybee Beach with Rex. Tonight she was relaxing on the white leather lounger in the Cawley-Smiths' home theater, running her hands over her soft skin. She'd gone to the hotel spa that afternoon, where they'd scrubbed her and rubbed her and slathered her with all sorts of lotions and muds, getting her back to the old Leeda. The softness of her skin felt foreign to her.

Alicia was sprawled out in the next lounger over.

"What do you wanna watch?" Leeda asked, nodding to the big screen.

"I don't know. What about you?" Alicia had come to get body

wrapped with her and see her off for her trip. Only Leeda wished she hadn't invited her. It just made her feel more alone.

"Why don't you pick something?" she said, standing up irritably and ducking into the minibar for a club soda. The door to the theater cracked open, and Mrs. Cawley-Smith stood in the doorway. "It's Danay, for you."

"Really?" Leeda hadn't expected to hear from her sister for at least another week, which was how long she and Brighton would be in the West Indies. She took the cordless from her mom and walked into the living room, sinking down on the couch.

"Hey."

"Lee," Danay said through static. "What's going on?" She sounded exuberantly happy, giddy.

"Nothing. Just getting ready to leave for Tybee in the morning."

"With Rex?"

"Yeah." She braced herself for a lecture.

"Oh, well, I just wanted to thank you. For your speech. I didn't get a chance to the other night."

Leeda plucked at the beads on her sundress. She was still a little sheepish about her speech. "You're welcome."

"It's funny, you said it was easy to be jealous of a sister like me. I've always felt the same about you."

Leeda let out a half laugh. "Jealous of what?"

"Oh, I don't know. You're just different than me and Mom. I feel like a clone sometimes."

Static cut in again and then out. Leeda didn't respond. She didn't know what to say.

"I talked to Rex at the wedding," Danay said, seeming awkward. "He's actually not such a bad guy."

Leeda breathed into the receiver. "I know."

"Lee, I have to go. Have fun at Tybee, all right?"

"Yeah, okay."

"Byeee." Danay's voice was punctuated with a laugh as she hung up the phone. Leeda held it for a minute, then hung up too.

The next morning, Leeda was sitting on the stairs of the verandah when Rex pulled up. They were going to the beach, but he looked like he was on his way to a funeral. As soon as he saw her face, he lowered his head and walked up to sit beside her.

They sat like that for a long time, Rex finally reaching out and taking her hand.

"Don't say it," she said, pulling her hand away gently and clasping her fingers in front of her. "You don't have to break up with me."

"Leeda, we can't . . ."

"I'm not going with you to Tybee. I don't think it's working out, Rex. I don't think I can be with you anymore."

Rex looked at her, then down at the stairs beneath their feet.

"I don't think you were ever really in love with me. Do you?" Leeda asked.

He let out a long sigh. "I do love you, Leeda."

"I know, but that's different than being in love, isn't it?" She looked up at him. His eyes were wide and sad. "It's a lot different, right?" she pushed.

He nodded very slightly.

"Rex, I'm not in love with you either. And the thing is, I don't think I need you anymore, the way I did. I think I can take my family. Or myself. Or whatever it is I need to take."

Rex looked a little hurt. But she didn't really have much sympathy for him right now.

"The fact is, you're the guy who broke up me and Murphy. And I think that makes me angrier than anything."

Rex clasped his hands in front of his mouth and ran his thumbs along his closed lips thoughtfully.

Leeda kept her eyes steadily on his profile. "I know I'm not perfect. But I deserve better." Rex didn't answer. Looking at him now, she marveled at the idea that she had turned to him so long for some kind of strength, and she was so much stronger than him.

"Look," she said, her voice cracking. "I love her too. But you should have told me. You owed me that."

"I know. I wanted to. I thought maybe it wasn't the right time. And then what happened at the orchard . . ."

Leeda held a hand in the air in a stop motion. "I'm not that evolved. Please don't tell me."

"Sure. Sorry."

She shook her head, her curls wafting around her ears, using her own breath to calm herself down. "You've acted like such a dumbass."

"Yeah," Rex said.

"Say it."

Rex looked at her. "Say what?"

"Say, 'Leeda, I'm a dumbass.'"

Rex raised his eyebrows at her. She couldn't keep a tiny

smile from playing at the corners of her mouth. She shoved her knee into his, forgetting that she might bruise.

"Go on, say it."

Rex rolled his eyes, pulled his hands from his mouth, and spoke flatly. "Leeda, I'm a dumbass."

"And you are a goddess."

He smiled slightly. "And you are a goddess."

"And from now on I'm going to do anything you say."

Rex looked at her like he'd had enough. But she continued. "And I'm going to make it up to you."

Rex shifted uncomfortably, then managed to blurt, "Ditto." It was good enough.

Leeda nodded once decisively. It gave her a sadistic pleasure to see Rex looking so uncomfortable and so desperate. She knew that it wouldn't last—his discomfort and her pleasure in it. She cared about the guy, after all. But she milked it anyway.

"Now," she said, her chest pinching a little at the thought of what she was about to do but pinching in a satisfying way, like she was overcoming a small part of herself and leaving it in the dust. "Are you ready to make it up to me?"

Twenty-five

$\mathcal{B}$irdie couldn't believe that it was light out. She curled instinctively against Enrico, pulling his arm tighter around her. It tightened gently and she felt his warm breath on her neck. "What is it?"

"My dad," she said, sitting up. "He's going to kill me."

They both got up, readjusting their clothes, patting down their hair, staring at each other. Quickly Enrico walked Birdie to the front door, then out onto the porch. She pivoted and kissed him quickly, breathlessly. "Will you be here later?"

Enrico beamed. "Of course, Birdie."

"Kiss me," Birdie said boldly, and he kissed her one more time. Then she hurried up to the house. Walter was sitting on the porch.

"Where were you, Birdie?" His voice was deadly angry.

"Um, I fell asleep in the dorms, Dad. I'm sorry."

"Fell asleep?"

Birdie nodded, her heart racing. "Go on inside and get cleaned up," Walter said. "We've had good news. Balmeade is going to buy."

"No."

Walter snapped his head to look at her. "Birdie, this is a good thing. Now go on and get cleaned up. I want you to be polite to him. He's on his way over with his lawyer. The man has lost a lot this week, so he's not in a great mood."

"But if he's lost so much, why is he buying? I don't . . ."

"Birdie, this is for adults to figure out."

Birdie planted her feet where she stood. "I am an adult."

Walter shook his head. "You don't know what that means." He stood up to walk off the porch. Birdie blocked his way.

"I know it means carrying the load with Mom gone. I know it means all the work I did all summer, doing your office work, directing the harvest, making sure the tractors were running. I know it means picking up the slack and all the things you weren't doing."

Walter shook his head at her. "Birdie, shut your mouth. . . ."

"Does it mean giving up? Because that's what you did, you know." Her voice broke all along the syllables of the words.

Walter's hands shot out and grasped her shoulders. "Go up to your room. I don't want to see you. . . ."

"You don't *see* me anyway. You know, I spent the night with a *guy*, Dad. Is that adult enough for you?"

Walter let go of her shoulders and sank back on his chair, stunned. Birdie knelt beside him and put her hand on his. "And I want to be with him. And I want to stay here. I don't want to leave. I don't want to do just what you and Mom want."

When her dad looked at her, it broke Birdie's heart. He was crestfallen.

"I exist, Dad. It's my life too."

•   •   •

Murphy hated to be interrupted when *Days of Our Lives* was on. With the remote still in her hand, she slunk to the door and peered outside. Rex stared back at her.

Murphy turned the lock and walked back to the couch.

Knock knock knock.

"Murphy, let me in."

Murphy held the remote slackly and raised the volume. Bo was just about to say that the case Hope was on was too dangerous. And Hope was going to assert that he would never let personal feelings get involved with being a good cop. Murphy had the whole formula down.

"Murph, come on."

"It's Murph-y," she muttered, upping the volume another few bars. But not loud enough to drown out Rex's voice when it said Leeda had sent him.

Murphy walked up to the door and peered out at him again.

"I have something from her for you. . . ." Rex was holding a brown paper bag and what looked like a little manila envelope.

"You can slide it through the cat door."

The McGowens hadn't had a cat for many years, but their trailer had always had a cat door. Rex frowned at her, then stooped and disappeared. A second later the package came creaking in.

Murphy sank down beside it on the ground and picked it up. It was a large, square envelope and it was blank on the outside. She ran her index finger into the seal and ripped it open, then turned it over. Out fell a folded piece of paper and a CD.

Murphy examined the CD. In neat purple marker it read THE BLUH MIX. She unfolded the letter.

Murphy,

You may notice I'm sending you a CD of all the crappy music you like. I'm also sending you my ex-boyfriend. I think he belongs to you.

Murphy kept reading.

I hang out with my other friends, and they never screw with me like you do, telling me my faults, making me think about what an anal butt I can be sometimes. They all think I'm perfect, or at least they say they do. It's annoying. But you're annoying too, Murphy. Really annoying. I made a list of the reasons you are annoying.

    I. Show-off
        A. show off boobs
        B. show off things you can do
        C. can't let anybody else get attention
    II. Selfish
        A. about who gets the most attention
        B. about Rex
    III. Evil
        A. no need to elaborate here

But the difference between you and my other friends is that they buy into the crap, but you believe in me in spite of it. My parents don't. And I don't know if I'm willing to go along the rest of my life with people who don't get me. Or try to make people think I'm one way when I'm really another now that I know it can be different. You and Birdie make me make sense. I think I'd rather forgive you.

Murphy sucked in her breath, unsure whether to be offended or not.

I can see you getting pissed off here. The truth is you wanted my guy, and you got him. And that is really hurtful, Murphy. But also, I know it makes sense. When I put aside the stuff I'm insecure about, I see it's not just the way it is. The confident, unafraid part of me knows it's the way it's supposed to be. I can't believe I'm saying that. But truthfully, even though I love the guy, I know he's not for me.

Here is where I get to my apology. I know I let you down. I'm still hurt and jealous, even if I don't need Rex anymore and I want to kick him in the balls. So please don't expect me to say it more than once. But Murphy, I'm really sorry. I was hurt, and I don't believe any of the stuff I said. I'm really sorry. Damn, that's twice.

Murphy took a long deep breath.

It's in your best interest to forgive me, you know. I am a girl people want to be friends with. Ha. And on top of that, I'm a good friend. Because I believe in you too. With you and Birdie, I am the kind of friend I always thought I should be. I didn't think that would ever happen.

Anyway, thanks for the summer. It was the best I ever had.

Love,

Leeda hadn't signed her name. She'd just drawn a little swan at the bottom of the page.

"Murph?"

"I want the bag she sent me too."

"It won't fit through the hole."

Murphy stood up and rubbed away the tears gathering in her eyes so Rex wouldn't see and unlocked the door. He pushed it open and held out the bag. "It's from me anyway."

Murphy took it and looked inside. It was filled with nectarines. Messed up as it was, she was suddenly pissed off at Rex on Leeda's behalf. He looked so vulnerable, though, and so in love with her that the anger evaporated and didn't come back.

"You should have brought peaches. These are only my second favorite."

Rex smiled unsurely. "If I brought you your favorite now, what would you have to look forward to?"

She glowered at him.

"I can't help it, Murphy. You're the coolest girl I've ever met."

Murphy knew that people only recognized parts of each other. But also, she *was* very cool.

Murphy couldn't help smiling. Rex leaned toward her, and she pressed her nose into the softness of his cheek, tilting her head forward so that their faces fit like a puzzle, and her eyelashes fluttered against his skin.

"I gotta go," she whispered, keeping her face there.

"Please don't."

"I'll be back," Murphy said, pulling away. She grabbed her purse and her keys while Rex stood in the doorway, wounded.

She rested a hand gently on his shoulder. "You're gonna be my boyfriend, right?"

He smiled, his body relaxing. "Yeah. That's what I was thinking."

"Great. I've never had one." Murphy pressed her lips against his, softly. And then she turned and walked toward her bike. Yellowbaby had died for good.

Even in cases where she was extremely nervous, Murphy liked the element of surprise. She didn't call Leeda to let her know she was coming. She just showed up at Breezy Buds Plantation, only to be told that Leeda had gone out and that they didn't know where.

Murphy hopped back on her bike. It was over ten miles to the orchard, and there was no guarantee she was there. But Murphy was impatient. She couldn't go home and wait. So she pedaled. Thankfully, the air had started to get cooler.

The orchard already felt different when she pulled onto the drive. Like a person, even a little bit of time had changed it a little. It was the first day of September, and on cue the leaves had started to turn slightly brown; the peaches had all disappeared. It felt like the orchard was curling up on itself to wait for the winter, hoping to keep warm.

Murphy was sweaty and exhausted when she pulled up in

front of the house in a cloud of driveway dust that had been churned up before her arrival. She parked her bike at the foot of the porch and hopped up, rapping on the door. Poopie answered.

"They've gone walking, Murphy," she said, grinning. "Maybe there are still some berries left for pie." Poopie was fondling her necklace and her grin was from ear to ear. "Why don't you sit and wait?"

Murphy shook her head. "Why do you look like you ate the canary, Poopie?"

Poopie squinted at her. "Canary?"

"Why do you look so happy?"

Poopie laughed. "It's a great day," she answered, shaking her head. "You missed it. Balmeade come over and yelled and yelled about how people don't keep their words. And something about squid that made no sense. But Walter kept saying he is keeping the orchard. First time that man ever surprised me in my life." Poopie laughed, and her eyes danced.

"Are you serious?" Murphy grinned. In reply, Poopie hugged her and kissed her on the cheek.

Energy zinged from Murphy's fingertips to her toenails. "Birdie knows?"

Poopie nodded. "She knows."

"I'm gonna go look for them. Thanks." Murphy skipped out onto the porch, and noticed on her way down the stairs that the statue of Saint Jude was gone.

As she walked down the rows of trees toward the lake, her heart thrummed. She couldn't wait to see Birdie now. But she also had the urge to turn and run, like Birdie had run in Texas.

She heard them laughing before she saw them. They were

jumping around playing Frisbee with a guy. For a moment Murphy thought it was Rex, and her breath caught. But then she realized it was someone who looked like Enrico. All three turned toward her at once.

"Hey," she said, walking slow now up to where they were standing, hurting slightly that they were all here without her. And breathing easier because she was here now. She squinted at Enrico, feeling self-conscious. "Enrico?"

"Murphy." Birdie leaned forward and hugged her tightly. "He chased me from Texas. Isn't that sweet? And did you hear about the orchard? Did you hear we're staying?"

Murphy blinked a few times, then smiled. If she hadn't been so nervous, she would have jumped up and down, but she shoved her hands into the pockets of her cutoffs. "I'm so happy for you, Birdie." She looked at Enrico. "Welcome back."

"Thanks." Enrico nodded, looking around like he recognized he was in the middle of a weird moment he didn't belong in. "But actually, I have to go."

After they all exchanged good-byes, Birdie walked him up toward his car, her dogs trailing behind them as Leeda and Murphy stood watching them. They disappeared into the trees, and then Leeda and Murphy had nothing to look at anymore except each other.

"That's great about Birdie, right?" Murphy said awkwardly.

"Yeah." Leeda smiled, but nervously.

They nodded and Murphy shoved her hands deeper into her pockets.

"You wanna go for a swim?"

Leeda looked over her shoulder at the lake, considering. "Yeah."

They both stripped slowly and awkwardly to their undies and waded in, Murphy too unsure to dive. They swam around each other carefully, Murphy watching to make sure she didn't swim too close to Leeda or too far away. Without Birdie, it all felt lopsided, and when Birdie returned, looking slightly crushed, they were still swimming circles around each other.

Birdie looked from one to the other, her brown eyes dancing. "You guys are idiots," she finally said, sounding very much like Murphy. Murphy and Leeda looked at each other. Leeda smiled.

Then she dove under and grabbed Murphy's ankles, yanking her under. When they both spluttered their way up, Leeda was laughing. Murphy dunked her back under the water, Murphy opened her eyes, and a stripe of afternoon sunlight lit up the particles and the tiny water bugs that spun and ducked and dove around them. She heard the splash of Birdie leaping into the water. They were, finally, complete.

On a warm late August evening, after one of the most surprising summers of her life, Poopie Pedraza tucked her statue of Saint Jude into a box. Now that she believed in miracles, she wanted to share them. Poopie sent the box to a children's cancer ward in Atlanta, but the box was taken home by a postal employee who had a number of personal problems, including an addiction to stealing mail.

Twenty-six

*B*irdie had forgotten what it felt like to stand on solid ground. Lying on the grass after they swam, the feeling flooded in on her all at once, and she laid her hands on the softness of her less-soft-than-it-used-to-be belly and felt herself breathe. She listened to the heartbeat of the orchard and felt Leeda's and Murphy's pulses where their ankles touched.

Honey Babe and Majestic had stopped competing for her attention for the moment. And they sat still when Birdie hoisted herself over onto her elbows and pulled out the Swiss army knife she had used to cut tufts of fur for Enrico, and cut some for Leeda and Murphy too. She shoved them into the pockets of their dry clothes, piled nearby. Murphy made a face and complained about the dogs, but Birdie knew Murphy liked them, and she just didn't want to say.

When they all got hungry, they tromped up to the kitchen to munch on the last of the amaretto-peach salsa, which Poopie swore she would show them how to make. Then they sat on the porch, drying themselves in the breeze. Walter came by once, on his way out to his truck, and patted Birdie gently on the head, almost shyly, like she was a stranger, but someone he would be willing to get to know. That's how Birdie saw it anyway. On a day like today, everything seemed goodwilled and perfect and right. Even when her mom called, and she ducked in to talk to her for a few minutes, and Cynthia guilted her again about her decision not to move in, Birdie hardly noticed it. She told her she'd see her tomorrow at Liddie's Tea Room for lunch. Her mom, for the moment, seemed perfect too.

Leeda and Murphy kept saying that they were going to get going, that they had to get ready for school, and that they both had a ton of stuff they had to do. But nobody moved from the porch for an hour, and when they did, it was to walk down to the pecan grove and look for nuts, which they then threw at each other. Murphy and Birdie convinced Leeda to climb one of the trees, but the limb she hoisted herself onto splintered and broke, and Birdie—slapping her hand against her forehead, feeling stupid—suddenly remembered pecan wood was the most brittle wood there was. Leeda said she hated trees. But it was obviously one of those things Leeda said to cover up her embarrassment, even though she didn't really seem all that embarrassed anymore. Birdie was wiser now. About them both.

The day, though days were supposed to be shortening, seemed to stretch longer than any other they'd had that summer. And Birdie kept expecting to see sunset, and then she'd look at Leeda's watch, and it would only be two, or three, or four. She wondered if the day wouldn't end at all because they all, including the orchard, were still holding on to it as tight as they could, unwilling to let it go.

They did headstands against the trees. They carved their initials into the magnolia by the cider house with Birdie's Swiss army knife. They lay on their backs and talked about Enrico, but not Rex. They watched a random duck waddle by on his way to the lake. Birdie had a feeling that they all noticed the chill in the air, that the day seemed to be getting cooler, and that fall was just around the corner. But nobody said anything about it.

They ended up in the lake again in the late afternoon. Their feet took them there without them deciding.

As they swam and talked, dusk finally fell around them, so slowly that they barely realized it. At dark they ended up on the bank on their backs again, dripping onto the grass. The day had turned out like circles—turning back on itself, bringing them to the same spots over and over. And it almost made Birdie's heart ache that time was passing. It was all too good to let go.

A gaggle of lightning bugs popped their lights on just above the grass. They seemed to be blinking in unison, over and over, lighting together on some secret signal that Birdie would never have been able to explain but that she understood.

"Look at those bugs," she whispered, pointing it out to the other girls.

"I don't see anything," Leeda said, tugging at her wet hair.

"You're a nature freak, Bird," Murphy added, not even turning around.

Birdie sighed. She knew it meant something.

The day felt almost like any other day of the summer, like they'd rewound and summer was still ahead of them. But this time, from the start, there would be no question of whether they had each other or not.

This time, they would know.

On September 1, though nobody knew it or ever would, the Darlington Orchard peaked at the most tree carvings per capita anywhere in the United States. As one peach tree unfurled the words MILLER ABBOTT LOVES JODEE MCGOWEN 4EVER *for the thirtieth year in a row, and an oak bearing the names* CYNTHIA AND WALTER *inside a jagged heart went brown at the leaves and began to decay, churning itself back into the Georgia soil one letter at a time, a magnolia next to the cider house came to bear three sets of initials:*

M.M.
L.C.S.
B.D.

For years after, it grew, and the scars of the wood deepened, and stretched out. Until the letters were no longer anything but puckered, jagged lines marking the time the tree had passed. Marking life.

Acknowledgments

This book would not exist without Dan Ehrenhaft, and it would be missing much of its heart had Sara Shandler not been there to provide it every step of the way. I'd like to express my admiration and gratitude to my agent Sarah Burnes, as well as to Les Morgenstein, Josh Bank, Kristin Marang, and Elise Howard. Much thanks to the kind people at Lane Packing Company and Dickey Farms—especially David Lane III, Betty Hotchkiss, Ryan Cleveland, and the Dickey family—for sharing their valuable time and their peaches. Appreciation to Mike Vermillion, and to Alexia James for her nurturing presence. Thanks always to my family.